A
DEADLY
WEB

TITLES BY KAY HOOPER

BISHOP / SPECIAL CRIMES UNIT NOVELS

Haven
Hostage
Haunted

THE BISHOP FILES

The First Prophet
A Deadly Web

A
DEADLY
WEB

KAY HOOPER

JOVE BOOKS, NEW YORK

THE BERKLEY PUBLISHING GROUP
Published by the Penguin Group
Penguin Group (USA) LLC
375 Hudson Street, New York, New York 10014

USA • Canada • UK • Ireland • Australia • New Zealand • India • South Africa • China

A Penguin Random House Company

A DEADLY WEB

A Jove Book / published by arrangement with the author

For information, address: The Berkley Publishing Group,
a division of Penguin Group (USA) LLC,
375 Hudson Street, New York, New York 10014.

ISBN: 978-1-62953-439-8

PRINTED IN THE UNITED STATES OF AMERICA

Cover design by Rita Frangie.
Cover photo © Romany WG / Trevillion Images.
Stepback: Spiderweb © Frank L. Junior / Shutterstock.
Text design by Laura K. Corless.

To Whom It May Concern:

My understanding of the situation involving psychics has increased substantially since my last report, even though I still do not have proof that would stand up in court. As I last reported, I know psychics are being taken, vanishing without witnesses, while others at least appear to have died in accidents that left bodies all but destroyed. I suspect, but cannot prove, that at least some of those "victims" were in fact also abducted rather than murdered, the bodies left behind "identified" by falsified dental records and planted DNA.

"Bodies," of course, implying that other innocent people are being deliberately murdered only to provide cover for what are true abductions. I suspect but cannot prove that these bodies are most often likely transients, people expected by local law enforcement to move on or disappear, with no family to know or care what happens to them, no one to file missing-person

reports. However, I also believe at least some bodies of supposed psychics were not transients; there have been too many "convenient" and unsolved deaths along the way for me to believe anything else.

That alone would most certainly be cause for grave concern, above and beyond the disappearance of psychics. An enemy ruthless enough to murder innocents for no other reason than to have a convenient body is an enemy who will stop at nothing. An enemy who has far too great an access to medical and investigative documents and files—and quite likely has allies or confidential informants inside law enforcement, possibly even inside government.

Aside from that elusive information, what both interests and troubles me is the fact that at least some psychics are simply abducted, vanishing without warning and without a trace. My only explanation for that is a growing understanding that until they are abducted, the psychics who merely disappear live very quiet and normal lives, attracting no attention to themselves, perhaps unwittingly making themselves targets simply because their disappearances raise few if any alarms. When they disappear, it seems to be or is reported by law enforcement to be a local family tragedy: runaway teenagers, unhappy wives, men overwhelmed by family responsibilities. Perhaps inexplicable but attracting little if any attention even from a news-hungry media when so much of seemingly greater importance is happening all over the globe.

Still, though I have learned more, the ultimate answer eludes me. I know some psychics are aware of a faceless enemy, that they fear being taken or killed, but I also know they seldom trust and never trust lightly, which makes it all the more difficult to even locate them, far less protect them effectively. I know that throughout my years-long search for psychics suited for law enforcement work, I have met and spoken to some who have since vanished without a trace.

I know there is some kind of organization or group of people fighting to help and protect psychics. They are nearly as secretive as their enemy, and with good cause. I have learned more about that group, and have managed not only to make contact with at least one "cell" of their organization, but even, I believe, to at least begin to win their trust. I do have some resources they lack, and long experience in locating and contacting psychics. I have value to them.

How much remains to be seen.

In this report, I offer the circumstances and results of my contact and interaction with the group, and of the events taking place at the time, events that for our purposes began in January of this year.

Respectfully submitted,
Noah Bishop, Unit Chief
Special Crimes Unit, FBI

PROLOGUE

The roses will be beautiful this year . . .

. . . and he said to me, he said it was all my fault . . .

That poor child always has bruises, and I know, I just know what's really going on in that house, but should I get involved?

No vacation this year. Lucky we don't have to sell the house . . .

Should I call the cops again when I hear her scream? They didn't do a thing last time, didn't even go inside the house . . .

The carpet in the bedroom really should be replaced.

How will I feel when she turns up dead or disappears?

They're coming.

How was I supposed to know he hated pets? What I get for letting friends fix me up, dammit.

Jesus, why don't people know how to drive . . .

. . . you know how your mother is, and what am I supposed to do?

You put up with her, it's just for two lousy weeks.

Yes, but—

The concert will be fun, you know that.

No, my mom won't let me go—

They're coming.

The club sandwich looks good. Maybe I'll have the club sandwich.

The lawyer said I had a case. I can't just stand by and pretend the bastards aren't walking all over me.

They should serve wine with lunch. I don't have to drive, after all.

I'm so afraid he'll hit me again. I have the gun. But do I have the nerve to use it? I'm so afraid . . . if I miss he'll kill me.

They're coming.

She's cheating on me, goddammit. I know she is.

I don't know why they can't trim their side of the hedge, it looks ridiculous like this . . .

He'll never promote me, the son of a bitch. Millions in sales for his fucking company, and he still believes women should be fetching coffee when they aren't barefoot and pregnant.

Coming . . .

If I'm very, very quiet, if I don't make him mad, then maybe he won't hit me again . . . Maybe I don't need the gun. Maybe . . .

Really gorgeous roses . . .

If her dog shits in my yard one more time . . .

Coming . . .

Painting their house just shows how much mine needs it . . .

If I'm a good girl. I try to be a good girl . . .

There's just no money to buy a new car, we'll have to fix what we've got and live with it for a while.

Here.

What d'you mean I can't play baseball this season? Dad—

He's here.

The blue dress, I think.

You know . . .

I look good in the blue dress.

. . . he's going to . . .

Damned high heels . . .

. . . kill you . . .

Damned . . .

. . . don't you, Tasha?

ONE

Her eyes snapped open, and Tasha Solomon fought to control her breathing. Fought not to betray the dagger of icy fear slicing deeper than her marrow.

The cacophony of voices in her head was instantly muted, shut in a room in her mind, the door slammed closed against them. She could still hear them, but only distant whispers now.

Most were her neighbors or at least from this general area, not all of them here but most nearby or passing by, their homes or jobs all around this small local café, their thoughts the ordinary ones of ordinary lives. Observations, absent thoughts, pain. Irritation, fretting, planning, worry, admiration, jealousy, envy.

Fear.

Worry about some poor little girl being abused.

Tasha wanted to home in on that one, that worry, so she could find out which neighbor was hurting their kid. She'd damned well do something about *that*, and it wouldn't involve cops. And the abused wife, who was that? Living in her secret hell, probably behind a smile of normality, thinking of the gun she had dared to buy but probably lacked the will to use. Alone. So alone.

Tasha wanted to help her too.

But . . . it was that other voice that kept her mental door firmly closed, at least for now. Because she couldn't risk reaching out again, listening again, opening herself up like that again. That other voice, or maybe it was many voices, she could never tell for certain. Many voices speaking as one. That was how it felt, how it sounded in her mind.

Many, many voices. Certain. Implacable.

And when she tried to see them . . .

Shadows.

Tasha always felt more than saw them. Shadows. Watching. Listening. Waiting. All around her, but not close enough to touch.

Not yet, at least. But they had been getting closer, she knew that. Biding their time, but creeping nearer.

So they could watch her, as they had watched her for a time now.

It was difficult to focus in such a public place as the café where she sat, especially filled with a lunchtime crowd, but she closed her eyes and tried. Opened that mental door cautiously just a bit, just far enough, she hoped. Still somewhat protected, but . . . She tried to listen, see, with senses other than her ears and eyes.

Shadows.

Dark, misshapen, slipping away when she tried to see them, vanishing like smoke through her fingers, the shadows were as elusive as they had been for more than a month now.

Elusive—but always near.

Always watching.

Even in broad daylight, they watched her. Followed her. And she couldn't tell from the faces around her, as she moved through her days, whether any belonged to the shadows. She didn't want to believe that anyone or anything watching her was so near, literal shadows on the edges of her life. But she didn't *know*. In a crowd, how could she tell?

She couldn't.

If Tasha had been a nervous sort of woman, she'd be in a straitjacket by now. Or at least heavily medicated.

As she would be if she had told anyone about the shadows.

Because that was crazy, right, being haunted by shadows she could see only in her mind? That was nuts. Virtually always feeling an almost primitive sense of danger, the inner urge to run or hide—

But not alone. Every instinct compelled her to stay visible as much as possible, to avoid dark corners or quiet places where they could . . .

What? Kill her? Hurt her? Take her?

Change her life forever?

"Miss?"

Tasha blinked, brought herself back to the here and

now. She looked up at the waitress, who was displaying slightly uneasy concern.

"Miss, are you okay?"

Forcing a smile, Tasha said, "Yeah, fine, thanks. Meditation. When it's crowded like this, I try to . . . go somewhere else in my mind."

The waitress's young face relaxed and she even popped her gum, cheerful again. "Oh, I see. I wish I could do that. Often." She glanced around, then smiled wryly. "Can I clear this away for you? Would you like coffee?"

Tasha glanced down at the plate before her, at the half of the turkey sandwich still untouched, and knew she wouldn't finish it. "Yeah, thanks. To both."

"Would you like a box for the rest of the sandwich and fries?"

She wouldn't eat it herself, Tasha knew, but there was a big dog in a fenced yard she always passed on her way home, and he always welcomed leftovers. "Please."

The waitress smiled brightly. "Be right back."

Tasha looked at the check lying on the table, grimaced, and dug in her purse for her billfold. She was taking up valuable table space with her lingering, and she could see that there were a few people waiting at the front with varying degrees of patience to be seated. She pulled out cash to cover the bill, plus a generous tip. Generous enough that the waitress would be happy to allow her to sit here a bit longer and enjoy her coffee.

Not that she would enjoy it. There wasn't a lot she enjoyed these days, and that was something she resented.

Something that pissed her off.

Because as much as the weird and mysterious shadows she sensed made her afraid, they also made her angry. She'd lived her whole life with the ability to pick up the thoughts of people around her, most people, and she'd learned to deal with that, privately, without becoming some kind of public freak.

The trick was not talking about it. At all.

To anyone.

She didn't hang out a shingle and tell fortunes or claim to be some kind of mystic, bending over an outstretched palm even as she listened with that odd extra sense to the thoughts of the person across from her.

Well . . . she had once. A charity fund-raiser, and she'd volunteered to be the "psychic." Yards of colorful, silky material draped around herself, and fake gold bracelets jangling on her arms, and a crystal ball lit from below to look properly mysterious.

Tasha had done that only once. It had been unexpectedly exhausting to sift through the chaos of impressions to find mental truths and mine just enough nuggets to impress her "clients" without scaring the shit out of them. And even so, she knew at least a few people had left her tent not a little spooked by her accuracy.

She'd had to consciously dial that back, making use instead of vague "impressions" that led her to predict happy lives and prosperity and correct decisions made.

That had been a year ago, and Tasha had no intention of doing anything like that again. Just that one innocent event had roused the uneasy suspicion of several people she knew, and it had taken all the casual amusement she'd been able to muster to convince them of what they wanted to believe anyway.

That it had all been pretend. Not real.

Because it couldn't be real, of course.

Nobody could do that sort of thing.

———

The man in the black leather jacket stayed close but took care not to allow himself to be seen. There would come a time for that, a moment now and then to be briefly visible, to allow her to catch only a glimpse of him slipping out of sight.

They had learned the effectiveness of such glimpses, and just how to build on them, just how to elicit the fear and even panic that served them so well.

First only a glimpse, barely noticed, easily dismissed. Nothing identifiable except that black leather jacket, a subliminal trigger of uneasiness for so many people in this culture, a hint of danger. Then a glimpse elsewhere, here and there along the regular routine, and so the almost wordless suspicion of being followed.

A glimpse just before darkness. Slipping away, too far to identify except by that jacket. A glimpse in the neighborhood, outside a store, a theater, a church. At the bank, the dry cleaners, the local coffee shop, a favorite restaurant. A lurking presence that could not be innocent and so had to be potentially dangerous.

He was watching. Was he following? What did he want?

A glimpse outside, across the street, the automatic checking that doors and windows were safely locked for the night interrupted by uneasiness. Locks checked again. Security systems tested and set. Because everyone knew stalkers weren't just after celebrities, not anymore.

So . . . possible. Maybe. A faceless enemy.

Somebody watching? Somebody waiting for a chance, the right moment in which to act . . .

Maybe.

Shattering the illusion of safety.

They had learned well how to unsettle, to worry, to panic.

People who panicked made things so much easier.

People who panicked made mistakes.

———————

Grace Seymore woke to darkness, and for a long and panicked minute or two she thought she was blind. But then she realized she could see dim shapes around her. People moving—but with an eerie silence.

She wanted to speak, to call out a question and demand someone tell her what the hell was going on, but for some reason she was unable to make a sound. And her memory was . . . fuzzy. She thought she had been at home, taking advantage of the waning winter sunlight to do a little yard work. Not that she could do much except weed this time of year, but that was enough, that was necessary, and it kept her from thinking very much.

Usually.

Her second marriage had just crumbled around her, and Grace felt nothing but bitterness about that. It wasn't her fault, after all, that she'd been born with the family curse.

She'd been raised to hide it, naturally, since it totally creeped people out if she reached for a phone before it began to ring, or knew things about people she shouldn't have known.

It wasn't her fault her abilities had grown stronger over the years.

That they'd grown more and more difficult to hide.

As for the two men she had loved and married, she honestly couldn't decide if she was a bad judge of character or if both husbands had simply been unable to live with a woman who too often knew *exactly* whom they'd had lunch with that day.

Or that they'd spent that lunch in a motel room.

Grace pushed that out of her mind and tried to remember today. She had been on her knees wrestling with a stubborn weed and then . . . nothing. A moment of icy coldness that had made her wonder idly if a rare winter storm was heading for Charleston—and then blackness.

Now, she was . . . here. Wherever here was. Lying on something hard, in darkness, unable to speak. And— when she tried—unable to move.

She was strapped down.

Hard as she tried, no sound escaped her. Fear became terror, roiling around in her mind and body, leaving her even colder than she had been in this cold place. In desperation, she reached out with that other sense, that curse she'd been born with.

Shadows. Misshapen, distorted, blacker than black. Sliding away when she tried to focus on them, uttering low sounds that made the hair rise on the nape of her neck in a primitive response.

Bad. Very bad. Evil. Not . . . human. And they want . . . they want me . . . they . . . No. Oh, please, no! Don't make me . . .

But she couldn't protest out loud. Couldn't cry out against the prick of a needle that made the fear recede, made her feel as though she were floating on a peaceful sea. For a moment. And then she became aware that they were moving her body, spreading her legs, raising her knees.

Oh, God, no!

Their hands on her were cold, so cold, and she could feel breathing, even colder than the touch, cold and reeking of something that smelled old, older than the earth, older than time. She wanted to cry out, to scream a protest, but she could make no sound.

No sound when she felt them penetrating her body. No sound when she understood what it was they were doing to her.

Grace Seymore could do nothing except lie naked and exposed on a cold table in a cold, dark room, while the monsters changed her life forever.

John Brodie was always cautious; it was his nature as well as his job. But he was more cautious than usual about this particular meeting because even the idea of it made him profoundly uneasy.

There were so few in law enforcement they could trust.

A precious few, as he had been reminded.

"He can help us, John."

"From all accounts, he has his hands full with that unit of his."

"All the better for us. Despite their efforts to remain low-key in the public eye, the truth is that the Special Crimes Unit is the most safely visible group of psychics we know of—and they're within law enforcement. We haven't been able to find a reliable, trustworthy source inside law enforcement; to have someone like Bishop on our side can give us an enormous edge."

"I don't know about that, boss. We don't know who Duran has on his payroll. It seems every time we turn around, we stumble over another dirty cop or fed working for his side." Brodie found that knowledge very grim, and it showed.

"Granted. Which makes it vital for us to have a well-placed source of our own. Someone with high-level access to information and the authority to act with virtual autonomy. Someone who knows the value of discretion. Someone who knows about psychics and psychic abilities, quite likely more than we know. But aside from all that, just to have a unit chief inside the FBI . . . You know what that could be worth, potentially, John."

"He has as many political enemies as he does allies."

"Arguable, I suppose."

"Do we really want to catch the attention of either?"

"I don't believe we will. Not through Bishop. No one else on his team, other than his wife, knows about us. He says he doesn't plan on sharing with his team, unless and until we okay it, and I believe him."

"Yeah, maybe, but isn't his team largely made up of telepaths? I'm guessing it's hard to keep a secret in that group. And even if he manages that, odds are that sooner or later one of his people is going to have a close encounter with either one of our psychics or else with somebody on the other side, and if he or she is as powerful as Bishop's people are supposed to be, then we've got even bigger trouble than we have now."

She was thoughtful. "Maybe not. The one thing most of Bishop's people have that ours tend to lack is consistent experience in using their abilities, and much stronger shielding to close out the minutiae of everyday life, the background chatter that tends to bombard most telepaths and clairvoyants. With only a few exceptions our psychics are rarely able to shield effectively and are understandably wary of exploring the limits of their abilities. And rightly so, since we know it draws all the wrong kind of attention to them. So even those who use their abilities do so defensively, not as weapons or even tools.

"But Bishop's agents use their abilities as investigative tools, often openly and virtually always under the intense pressure of deadly conditions, *and* under law enforcement and media scrutiny."

"Okay, but I don't see how that helps us."

"I don't know that it will, except in the sense of keeping them too well known to be considered viable targets; having a team of powerful psychics beyond the reach of the other side could be an ace in our pocket. And maybe there's a lot we can learn from Bishop in the meantime. As a good-faith gesture, he's provided us with an extensive file containing information on several of their more complex investigations, cases where psychic abilities made the difference between success and failure."

"Names redacted, I assume," Brodie offered dryly.

"Of course. As well as some of the details on nonpsychic aspects of the cases. Which is understandable, given his position. I'd be less trusting if he seemed willing to share everything."

"True enough. Is any of the info helpful?"

"Maybe. Some of his people have displayed some pretty remarkable abilities, which at the very least makes room for possibilities with our own psychics. Those willing might be able to learn how to make better use of their abilities and even shift the balance in this struggle. We have people going through the file."

"Well, let me know what they find if there's anything useful to us. I, for one, really am getting tired of mostly fighting a holding action. In the meantime, what I want to know is how Bishop found out about us. None of us approached him, right?"

"Certainly not officially, though as you said, it was bound to happen that he or one of his team would encounter one of us. That's what happened, and why he asked for a meet."

"Who did he cross paths with?"

She smiled.

Brodie sighed. "And you're not going to tell me."

"It isn't necessary for you to know, not just now. All you need to know is that he was already aware there was a . . . situation. And that his awareness makes sense. He's spent years searching for and tracking psychics, for the SCU and for that civilian investigative organization he co-founded, Haven. He's apparently crossed paths with

a number of us at various times, and even interviewed a
few psychics who weren't suitable for law enforcement
work but who later joined us. Since he's far from being
stupid, he realized—a long time ago, I think—that something was going on. He began to notice patterns, the
same sort of patterns that alerted so many of us. Psychics
he met there one day and gone the next. Too many convenient *accidents* involving psychics to be coincidence.
Too many reported deaths with no bodies recovered, or
bodies too damaged to be identified by more than dental
records or DNA—both of which we know the other side
can and does plant or fake.

"The other side has taken extreme forensic counter-
measures, including spreading out their activities so that
no one law enforcement agency would be able to connect
even two events, given differing jurisdictions and the
reluctance of most agencies to share information. There
was no notice on a national scale or by any federal organization, no awareness that something was happening.
Until Bishop saw it."

"I'm surprised he didn't launch an investigation," Brodie said.

"I'm not. He was building his unit and forging as many
potentially useful connections as he could find, both inside
the FBI, other areas of law enforcement, and in the private
sector, all the while working to make sure psychic abilities
as investigative tools would be taken seriously *within* the
FBI and other law enforcement. Everything grounded and
reasonable, not fanciful or outlandish. Abilities based at
least on scientific possibilities, nothing mystical or magical,

no mystery about it, nothing that isn't entirely human and even remarkably commonplace. If he had gone out publicly or even within the FBI and declared there was a conspiracy to abduct or kill psychics, reasons unknown but mysterious, how long do you think he would have lasted, let alone his unit?"

"True," Brodie admitted grudgingly. "He wouldn't have been taken seriously at all, and that had to be the last thing he wanted. Bad for his purposes and work, but best for ours. It's what's kept our problems on a par with Bigfoot and alien abductions as far as the media is concerned. On the rare occasions when something is noticed, at best we're conspiracy nuts and at worst deluded people imagining some faceless enemy around every corner. Not fun to be considered crazy, but we'd never be able to operate as quietly as we do otherwise."

"Well, I give Bishop credit for not only noticing, but finding the time and energy to put enough disparate pieces together to realize something was going on. Not his line, not serial killers or other murderous psychopaths, not crimes the FBI could or would legitimately investigate. But something involving psychics, and if there's one thing I'm certain of, it's that he knows and values psychics."

"True he's one himself?"

"A touch-telepath, very powerful. He also has an ability to focus his normal senses in a hyperacute way his team informally refers to as spider senses."

"Comic book terms?"

"Well, informally. But it's something that allows him—

and some members of his team—to see and hear things normally beyond the limits of those senses."

Brodie eyed her. "He's seen them?"

"I'm not sure it's that definite. All I can tell you is that he knows about the shadows. Calls them that, a term he was not given by any of us. And says they're something he's never sensed even in the worst cases the SCU has investigated."

"Comforting," Brodie said sardonically. "I'm assuming he'd have to touch one to know for sure?"

"I assume the same thing. Though even if he did touch one of them, there's at least a twenty-five to thirty percent chance he wouldn't read anything from them, assuming they *can* be read. Bishop says his solid range tends to be about seventy-five percent of the people he meets; those he can read. Others are apparently not on his . . . frequency."

"What happens if he touches somebody like me, somebody on our side without much of a shield who knows maybe too many of our secrets? Do I shake hands with the man and give up more information than I want?"

"Brodie, he's perfectly aware of his own abilities, and despite having his shields raised—which he promised to do—I'm betting he'll take care not to touch you at all. He wants to help and protect psychics, and that means he wants our trust. Being suddenly in possession of too many of our secrets without our permission wouldn't exactly be a good first step."

"Okay. But, so far, I'm not seeing much benefit for us in taking him into our confidence."

"John, he can get us access to the kind of information we could never get on our own even with all the sources we do have, and he can do it quickly."

"Without attracting official notice?"

"If anyone can, it's Bishop. Plus, I'm betting he knows the whereabouts of a lot more psychics than we do, and the word I got was that he monitors those he's met—and a few he hasn't. He keeps eyes on them, or has a different way to monitor them, but however he does it, he knows what's going on with them. Maybe even in time to save some of them. And from a purely practical point of view, just because he knows they aren't suitable for the FBI or investigative work when he encounters them doesn't mean he believes that's always going to be true, or isn't aware they might someday need his help or protection."

After a moment, Brodie shook his head. "Mine not to reason why, I guess."

"You know better than that. And you also know that if you aren't convinced Bishop can be trusted and can help us once you've met him, that's it. He won't be brought into any of the cells or used as a resource."

"But he'll still be aware of us, boss."

"We can't stop that. Also can't stop him trying to put the puzzle pieces together on his own, something I doubt very much we want to happen." She paused, then added, "He kept an eye on the situation with Sarah and Tucker. In fact, I'm reasonably sure he was present more than once while they were trying to get to safety, remaining in the background observing unobtrusively."

Brodie opened his mouth and then closed it, frowning.

She nodded. "Yeah, there was no way he could step in to help, not when he wasn't sure what was going on. He likely would have made bad worse, and I give him credit for recognizing that."

"Okay, that makes a certain amount of sense. Anything else I should know about him?"

"He shares his wife's precognitive abilities. Extremely powerful precognitive abilities."

Brodie frowned. "Have they seen a future in this?"

"If so, Bishop didn't say. Why don't you ask him?"

"Maybe I will. Because if he has that answer . . ."

"Then he could be a lot more to us than merely another useful resource, another ace in the hole. He could be a game changer."

TWO

Moving had seemed like a very good idea.

Tasha Solomon had, around six months before, sold the Atlanta house her parents had left her and bought a condo in the downtown area of Charleston. It had cost her a pang to give up the house, but since her parents had shared a nomadic nature as well as jobs that allowed them to settle in different parts of the country for a few years at a time, they had lived in the house for less than a decade before their deaths in a car accident.

And since Tasha had been in college for part of that time, she really didn't have all that many family memories associated with the house. But it was the last place she had shared with her parents, and clearing it out to put it on the market, boxing up memories to put into storage, had been unexpectedly painful.

She might have kept the house, except that the vague uneasiness that had plagued her since shortly after her parents' death had grown stronger in the year afterward.

She did not like being alone.

There was something . . . vulnerable about it.

It hadn't helped that the house was a solid one with good locks on the doors and windows and a dandy security system she'd updated herself. It hadn't helped that neighbors were friendly and helpful, and that the house was, really, in a very good, historically safe neighborhood where little was really required for security except a deadbolt.

It hadn't even helped that she was well trained in self-defense and perfectly capable of taking care of herself.

She had still felt too . . . isolated. Too vulnerable. Not safe even behind locked doors.

And she had been aware of the strong urge to leave Atlanta, perhaps having inherited more of her parents' nomadic natures than she had realized before then.

Perhaps.

Besides, change was inevitable, wasn't it? And she had options. As painful as it had been, the deaths of her parents had provided her with not only life insurance bequests, but also a healthy investment portfolio and a very nice house that had sold at well above market value even in a depressed economy.

The third-floor corner condo she had found and purchased was small by comparison but very nice and more than adequate for her needs and comfort, the complex very secure even to the point of having manned twenty-four-hour security/concierge desks in the lobby, monitored cameras on all the entrances and exits *and* the hallways, and individual security in each unit, and it was virtually new.

The view she saw out her windows was hardly desolate or lonely; her main windows looked out on the bustling area of Charleston filled with galleries, stores, markets, and restaurants, everything conveniently within walking distance and well lit all night long. The area had a relaxed vibe despite the usual crowds, an area filled with art and music and wonderful cuisine.

There were virtually always people near, people around her, and from her first night in the condo, that had given her comfort.

There was alone—and then there was *alone*.

The inheritance had also allowed Tasha to quit her unsatisfying job as a paralegal and take some time to decide what she really wanted to do with her life. She had rather idly attended a few classes on various subjects and attended the occasional interesting-sounding seminar, but so far nothing had really drawn her toward a particular field.

She had found a great deal of satisfaction in volunteering with the Charleston Animal Society two or three days each week, and had made friends in the world of animal rescue as well as among some of her neighbors, but . . .

She was still alone, reluctant to get too close to anyone for reasons she couldn't always explain even to herself. And still hesitant about plotting some specific direction for her life. Not so much because she felt a tendency to drift with the tide, so to speak, or even because she lacked interests to choose among from which to plan a future.

No, it was . . .

It was the wrong time. The wrong time to plan a future. There were things she had to do first. Things that needed to happen first. She didn't know what those things were, but every instinct told her that until she found her way through this very odd and unsettled part of her life, the future wasn't something she should be thinking very much about.

Something wasn't . . . right. Something around her, close to her, was . . . unnatural somehow.

And a threat.

Even here, even feeling safer and less alone in the condo, in Charleston, she was still aware of a niggling unease, a sense that she needed to look over her shoulder.

Often.

Most of the time.

A sense that, sometimes, she was being watched.

Most of the time. Now.

And that whoever or whatever was watching her wasn't friendly.

Whatever?

Now why had that very unsettling word entered her mind? How could a *thing* be watching her? A camera, maybe? Was somebody taking pictures of her, even filming her, for reasons unknown?

A stalker?

Oddly enough, that was almost reassuring. Not that she wanted a stalker, of course, but at least that was something . . . normal. Well, not normal, but at least not . . .

She didn't finish that. Even in her head.

Tasha left the café and headed home, stopping at the fenced yard of one of her neighbors, to the delight of the big mixed-breed dog who came bounding over to greet her with a bark and then sit politely, waiting for the treat he knew was coming.

"You're spoiling him," her elderly neighbor called from the other side of the yard, where he was pulling summer weeds from his flower beds—a leisurely task that seemed to occupy him for most of what passed for winter in Charleston.

And gave him an excuse to spend time in his small, neat front yard and interact with his friendly neighbors.

"As long as you don't mind," Tasha called back cheerfully.

"Nah, he's a good boy. Besides, you never give him junk that could make him sick."

Tasha wasn't at all sure Max the dog was even capable of eating anything that disagreed with him as far as people food went, but since she had fed him this exact food before, she didn't worry about it. Instead, she leaned over the fairly low wrought-iron fence Max could have jumped any time he felt like it and fed him the leftovers from her lunch. As always, he took the food gently and politely, and when the last French fry was consumed, he offered a paw in thanks.

"Tell me you taught him that, Mr. Arnold," Tasha asked with a laugh as she shook the offered paw.

"Nope, all his own idea." The elderly Arnold was clearly proud of his dog, the only family Tasha had ever seen about the place.

"Then he's a very good boy indeed." She straightened back up, waved a casual good-bye, and continued on toward her condo, dropping the take-out box into a trash container as she passed.

Very clean place, this part of Charleston.

The pause to feed the dog and chat briefly with her neighbor had occupied her attention, but now that that was past, Tasha found the almost-constant uneasiness returning. She really wanted to look back over her shoulder—but when she did, nothing unusual was there.

She felt a bit better as she neared her condo complex and the sidewalk strollers and shoppers became more of a crowd. She felt . . . safer.

Still, even with the relaxed crowd all around her, the uneasiness never entirely left her. And she was bothered by the fact that even after she greeted the pleasant security guard in her very safe building and headed up to her very safe condo, she was still tense.

Even inside, door locked and security system activated, she was tense. Hell, she even checked out her closets and under her bed, peering into corners, looking behind draperies.

Nothing.

She was alone.

So why didn't it feel that way?

———————

"She's getting jumpy, boss," Murphy reported, using a disposable cell as was her habit.

"How do you know?"

"Usual. Glancing back over her shoulder, tense, preoccupied. In that state, I get the sense of all defenses up and ready. I also get the sense that sometimes, very cautiously, she reaches out, or at least opens herself up. Seemed to almost go into a trance in the café, but passed it off to the waitress as meditation."

"Maybe she's picking up on you."

"I'm closed up tight as a drum. If she can feel me around her she's more than psychic." Murphy was one of the very few psychics on their side who could shield, could hide her abilities from every other psychic they knew she had encountered. And one of even fewer trusted to be actively involved in virtually every aspect of their struggle, out and about most of the time on her own, gathering information as well as serving other functions.

"Do you think she senses them?"

"Could be. Do we have anyone close enough to scan her?"

"On the way. But if she knows how to block, you know we won't get much. And since she's lived with this all her life, it's a safe bet she knows how to block."

"Ah, shit," Murphy muttered. "It means I get to play conduit, right?"

"Well, it increases the chance of successful contact, using two psychics when one of them has your unique ability to link with a third. Besides, the psychic capable of scanning her can't get too close or take the chance of being seen by any of Duran's goons."

Murphy knew exactly whom they were talking about then, but all she said was, "Tell her to take it easy, will you? Last time I thought my head was going to explode."

"Copy that."

"And make sure somebody tells me if we find out Solomon can identify any of these bastards. I mean before they arrange a neat little *accident* and disappear her."

"You think they may be planning one?"

"Hard to say. I've spotted a couple of their watchers in the last week or so, but they're hanging back pretty far, not *quite* being their usual creepy hovering selves."

"Any idea why?"

"Maybe because she caught them off guard when she moved here and began taking care never to be alone except in her condo. Her very secure condo. I'd think twice about trying to get in there myself. She's on the third floor, and on the corner, with main windows very visible, and in an area of the city that really doesn't sleep."

"So any move they made against her there would have to be a very public one."

"Yeah, unless they managed to pay off the security and concierge staff. I did some checking, and my bet is that isn't likely. They're well paid with great benefits, plenty of manpower, and many in security are ex-cops or retired military with very good records who got in their twenty and retired to a nice city and a very good job to supplement the pension and other benefits. A job they appear to enjoy, with no signs of restlessness or boredom. Not the sort of people Duran could hope to bribe unless he can offer something one or more of them *really* wants. Not the sort to have dirt in their pasts to invite blackmail—and I looked. Very clean records, and not the sort to bow to pressure. Just not in their natures, at least as far as I can tell."

"And the concierge staff?"

"Pretty much the same. Well paid with outstanding benefits, highly trained, more than enough manpower so nobody's overworked and the job gives them good time off in a wonderful city." Murphy paused, then added, "The people who built Solomon's condo complex knew what they were doing. It ain't cheap, but most working professionals could easily afford to live there. They provided a safe, service-oriented set of homes for busy people living in a lively city, and they didn't cut corners doing it. They even built well above code for hurricane safety."

"You think she was consciously looking for safety?"

"I think she had a lot of choices, especially given her sizable inheritance, and chose a place where security, especially for singles, was at the top of the list of selling points."

"Has she made friends?"

"Selectively. Through volunteer work with an organization here helping animals, a neighbor or three outside the complex but nearby, a few casual acquaintances met through school, a couple of other single women in the complex she occasionally meets for dinner, maybe one or two in the gym she goes to. She doesn't lack for acquaintances, just doesn't seem especially close to anyone. I get that's an intentional choice, not a cold nature."

"She's a beautiful woman. Dates?"

"Not that I've seen. She's worked with a few men in the volunteer organization, and of course some attended the same classes she was taking or auditing, but when I audited some of the classes myself, it looked to me like she rebuffed a few tentative passes. Politely and pleasantly, but not really leaving any room for a second try. If I had to guess, I'd say she was a bit wary of men, though I'm not sure if it's because of what she senses or some past experience."

"Nothing stands out in her past, certainly no trouble with men or any man, at least that anyone noticed. Good family, no abuse suspected or reported, she did well in school, even kept her nose clean in college, as far as we can tell. Not known for partying and got top grades in every class. Casual dates, more often with groups, but she did see a few men during her college years and nothing unusual was noticed or reported."

"Well, then, my bet is that whatever she's sensing, it feels male to her whether she's conscious of that or not, and threatening, and she's leery of taking chances. In this age of stalkers, and given the stats surrounding women who get murdered, I can't say that I blame her much. If she does have shields, she's probably keeping them up and especially solid around men."

"Brodie's going to love that."

Murphy smiled. "Yeah."

"And so will you. Because it'll cause Brodie problems."

"I take my fun where I can get it, boss." Murphy's tone was unapologetic, and brisk when she continued. "Solomon strikes me as a very strong woman with nothing fragile about her, emotionally or physically. She believes she can take care of herself, and in just about any situation she's probably right; she's had self-defense courses on top of martial arts training from childhood right up through the present. Even if all the training is an enjoyable activity to her, something to help her keep in shape, merely precautionary or something she followed through on after childhood due to simple interest or habit, the fact is that she's been taught to be aware of her surroundings and alert to any possible danger. She listens to her instincts, and her instincts are naturally suspicious. She's going to mistrust a hand of friendship, at least initially."

"So if she can't read Brodie, she won't trust him."

"Not as far as she can throw him."

"What do you know about her psychic abilities?"

"Being buttoned up myself, no more than what you told me. She's telepathic, open rather than touch, and possibly clairvoyant. Born active, or became active as a teenager the way so many do. Learned how to hide it, and fast. Maybe even did her best to deny it. Plenty do."

"Maybe why it took this long for her to show up on our radar."

"Could be. Far as I can tell, she's taken care not to draw attention to herself and hasn't done anything that could even hint she might possess psychic abilities. If we hadn't stumbled on them keeping an eye on her only because we were keeping an eye on some of *them*, we might never have known about her."

"Any idea why Duran is suddenly interested?"

"No—unless it's because she's become aware of them. Maybe that makes her dangerous to them. Or maybe it makes her more valuable. One of those things we don't understand yet, right?"

"Unfortunately."

"Okay, well, I'll keep on lurking and see if anything changes before Brodie shows up. Where is he, by the way?"

"Making contact with a new ally."

"Hope he or she is a good one," Murphy said matter-of-factly. "We've lost too many soldiers as it is. We're in this thing up to our necks and still don't know enough of what it's all about."

"Yes. Report in if anything does change, Murphy."

"Copy that."

"Base out."

Murphy turned off the phone, automatically pulled the battery out, and unobtrusively tossed phone and battery into separate trash containers as she moved casually past them.

I should have bought stock in disposable cell phones.

There were half a dozen others, as usual, in her roomy shoulder bag.

The Charleston street was busy but not especially crowded. Murphy blended in. It was one of her things, blending in.

When she wanted to.

She wandered with the crowd a bit, finally winding up near but not too near to Tasha Solomon's condo complex. A sidewalk café provided a secluded corner and a dandy view of Solomon's condo.

Murphy ordered a latte, one of her few weaknesses, and a muffin she didn't really want.

Then she settled back to lurk.

———

Tasha couldn't have said what woke her somewhere around three o'clock in the morning. One moment she was dead asleep, the next wide awake and straining to listen.

She had spent so much time over the years practicing raising and lowering her mental walls that she was usually able to keep them up while asleep—at least she thought she could—so those senses were registering nothing.

Neither were the normal five.

But something was wrong, and she knew it. Instincts deeper than any senses told her so.

She slipped out of bed, hesitated for an instant, then quickly straightened the sheets and duvet and put smooth pillows in place so that the bed looked as if no one had slept there during the night.

If I were them, I'd check underneath the duvet for warmth, though.

They? Who on earth *were* "they"?

All her instincts were screaming at her to leave now and think about the why and who later. But she still paused an instant in the doorway of her bedroom, looking back to make sure it appeared undisturbed.

It did.

The pajamas she wore were of the boxer shorts and tank top variety, so she was decently covered, and she didn't stop to grab a robe or take the time to change or even find her shoes. Instead, she moved quickly through the apartment, grabbing her purse and keys from the entry hall table, to the door.

She looked through the spyhole, not surprised to see an empty hallway.

But they're close. They're nearly here.

She slipped out of the condo quietly, making sure the door locked behind her, hesitated for only an instant in the hallway, then headed for one of the two stairwells each floor allowed access to.

They're coming up in the other stairwell.

Tasha had no idea how she knew that, but what she felt was certain. As was the absolute certainty that even though hallways and stairwells were covered with security cameras, somehow they had been tampered with or interfered with. And that access codes to all the security doors had also somehow been breached.

Security is an illusion. You know that.

For the first time, Tasha wasn't entirely certain that voice in her head belonged to her own mind.

Chilled, she used the security keypad beside the stairwell door and punched in the code, then opened the stairwell door as quietly as possible and passed through, closing it just as quietly behind her. There was a small, high window, heavy-gauge wire between two pieces of shatterproof glass discouraging anyone who might have made it this far from an attempt to reach through, even if they could pop the glass out, and open the door from the hallway; it was high enough that Tasha, a tall woman, had to stand on tiptoe in order to see through it.

The stairwell was well lit, but the lights dimmed at night; the computer controlling security for the building controlled that and would, in an emergency situation, turn all the lighting up to full wattage and, in case of a fire or other official need to evacuate the building, disarm all the security doors so that residents and staff could exit quickly and safely without having to remember security cards or codes.

It was one reason the system had to be monitored 24/7

by experienced security personnel, and one of the major reasons Tasha had chosen the building. Because it was the most up-to-date and security-conscious of any she'd looked at.

And security is an illusion. Got it.

She kept back at an angle, making herself as unseeable as possible as she fixed her eyes on the far end of the hallway and that other stairwell.

In less than a minute, three men entered from that stairwell.

Tasha was somehow surprised that they seemed . . . ordinary. Like anyone she might pass on the street without a glance. They wore casual clothing rather than being in all-black as she imagined an ordinary burglar would wear.

Then again . . . these men were not burglars. She didn't know much, but she knew that, *felt* that. Not burglars. And stalkers, as far as she knew, were always singular, one person stalking another.

Kidnappers?

Assassins?

Neither possibility made sense, but Tasha pushed that aside to be considered later. She studied them, baffled. They moved with evident quiet, yet didn't seem to worry about cameras or being observed any other way. They were all curiously interchangeable, nothing about any of their faces especially memorable.

Just ordinary men, perhaps in their thirties, well built but not imposing, all with brown hair and regular features.

Expressionless.

That last gave her another chill, for though they moved

with ease and without, seemingly, undue care, there was something . . . implacable about them. Something cold and relentless and remorseless.

They didn't speak to each other.

Apparently, they didn't have to.

They didn't hesitate at any point in the hallway but went straight to her door. Standing rather close together, they blocked her view of the door handle, but whether it was with a key or some other means, the door was open within seconds, and the three men slipped inside the condo.

She hadn't seen any sign of weapons, but Tasha was nevertheless very glad she had fled the apartment. She could imagine, with total clarity as though she watched from inside, them moving with that same relentless determination through to her bedroom, knowing exactly where it was, because they would and because it was a small condo with the two bedrooms in a fairly obvious location.

Would they search the condo when they found her not there?

If so, they were incredibly fast, because in less than three minutes by Tasha's internal clock they were back at the door, moving out into the hallway, still expressionless.

If her absence either surprised or disappointed them, they gave absolutely no indication.

Tasha hesitated, then slid back along the wall and, very swiftly and silently on bare feet, climbed the stairwell up to the fourth floor. She pressed herself against the wall beside the door in case she might need to escape the stairwell that way.

She'd pull a fire alarm if she did. Yell. Pound on doors as she passed them.

They want this to be quiet. They need it to be quiet.

She heard the very slight sound of the third-floor door to the stairwell opening. Straining her ears, but keeping every other sense as quiet and still as possible, she heard the click of it closing.

She counted to ten, then moved just far enough forward so she could see the stairwell below.

They had already reached the ground floor and moved to exit the building, leaving as silently as they had come.

THREE

It was probably a good ten minutes before Tasha could persuade herself to return to her apartment, and even then she argued with herself for at least half that time.

Notify security.

No, don't.

Why? They should damned well have been watching. Why weren't they watching?

They were. They thought they were. It's a computerized system; anybody could have hacked in and put the camera video on a loop or something. This late, there wouldn't be much if any movement in the hall except for the guards, and even if they do *vary their patrol patterns like I was told, there has to be plenty of time they wouldn't be visible on any one floor. The guard downstairs at the desk probably saw . . . just what they wanted him to see.*

Sure, because that's *a common skill, computer hacking.*

Not all that uncommon these days, especially with so much Wi-Fi.

The building has a closed system, apart from the Wi-Fi residents can use. Remember? You have to use a special code to access it, and that code is a lot more elaborate than the usual Wi-Fi system. One of the reasons it seemed like such a safe system. Unhackable.

No system is unhackable. It could have been hacked. Had to be. Unless I find sleeping or missing security guards downstairs, what else could it be? Those men damned well weren't invisible.

Maybe to cameras they were.

And to guards?

Maybe. Sleight of hand. Misdirection.

How?

I don't know how. But they got through the doors easily enough. Even the ones requiring cards and codes. Did they get cards somehow? Did they know the codes? Or did they have a way to bypass those locks?

You don't know much, do you?

No. I don't.

And during all that, tumbling through her mind below the surface thoughts was the cold realization that even though they hadn't found her there, the men could have left something behind in her condo. Something bad.

Something to finish the job they hadn't been able to finish.

You think they want to kill you.

What else could it be?

Kidnap you?

And ask ransom of who? My financial manager?

Maybe.

No. It can't be that. Not . . . not, at least, for money. I'm not worth that much, not worth enough for the trouble. Investments and other assets would have to be liquidated, which takes time. And, anyway, kidnappings for ransom have gone way down. I read about it. Easier ways to make money, even illegally. Because of all the cameras everywhere, on the streets, in stores, at ATMs, never mind nosy people with cell phone cameras, it's harder to grab someone, harder to get to a cash drop unseen, and electronic money transfers are traceable.

No one would have seen you being grabbed tonight. Apparently.

There was that.

Tasha finally persuaded herself to return to her condo, to unlock the door and reenter warily. She paused right there, touched the small LCD screen/keypad by the door, and called up the lobby security camera, the one camera all residents could access. For peace of mind, the real estate agent had told Tasha when she'd been condo shopping. So she could always be reassured that the security staff were doing their jobs. And so the security staff were aware that anyone could check on them at any time.

Extra motivation to be alert on the job.

The security desk was manned—and nobody was asleep.

She could just barely see the bank of monitors where one guard sat; from all appearances, he was alertly scanning the different feeds of all the cameras on his monitors. Each camera in its own square, what looked like nine per

large-screen monitor. There were no dark squares, nothing to indicate that any of the cameras had for any reason
malfunctioned. Just clear images of doorways and hallways and the parking spaces out behind the building.

No movement anywhere, as far as Tasha could tell.

Two other security guards stood talking a couple of
feet from the desk, then separated, one going outside to
presumably do his perimeter check, while the other
headed for the elevators to, presumably, begin the hourly
check of each floor.

Twenty-four hours a day, seven days a week, every floor
was patrolled at least once each hour by a security guard.
And they varied their patrols, since burglars liked nothing
better than routine.

As Tasha watched the security monitors in the lobby,
the guard who had gone outside appeared on the front
door monitor as the other became visible on a different
monitor getting into the elevator.

At the concierge desk, the night clerk was also awake
and clearly aware, doing something on his computer that
might have been work and could have been solitaire or a
role-playing game, or some online social networking site.
Or just e-mail.

*How the hell did those men get past everyone? How did they
even get in? You can see the front and rear entrances from the
lobby, see the stairwell doors, see the elevators. Both exterior
doors are security doors that require an ID card swiped and
a code punched in; if you've forgotten your card or the code,
you can call the desk from the system's intercom right there at
the door. But they never just let you in without checking. Never.*

A guard comes to meet you, and if you're a visitor, they call the resident you're visiting before you can come in.

Almost all the windows on the ground floor were in front, the lobby. Not many other windows, and those covered by "decorative" security bars. Outside lighting around the doors, plus landscape lighting all around the rest of the building meant no blind spots, no dark places in which to hide. No residents on the ground floor, either, just office services, that small gym, maintenance rooms and closets.

Those men should have been seen. Why weren't they?

More disturbed with every moment and every increasingly baffled inner question, Tasha remained wary as she left her purse and keys on the entry hall table and began a methodical search. Room by room, closet by closet, even checking the kitchen cabinets. And underneath her bed. Making sure all the windows were secure. Turning on lamps and other lights as she went.

Nothing.

Not a single sign that anyone but she had been here.

She stood in her bedroom for several minutes, looking around. Nothing disturbed. The bed as she'd left it, duvet smooth, pillows neatly decorative. The book she'd been reading earlier in the evening on one nightstand, along with the usual nightstand clutter.

Lamp. A bottle of water. A clock radio that also served as a sound machine providing assorted soothing noises. A box of tissues. And on the other nightstand, another lamp, a stack of books she wanted to read, her cell phone plugged into its charger.

Her cell phone.

Tasha walked around the bed, eyeing the phone. She had to charge the thing every single night, all night, and even then it virtually always went dead at some point during the day. It didn't matter what kind of cell phone, what brand, what service provider, how much or how little she used it. They all died on her within a matter of hours.

The fact that it was here, in this day and age when so many people were practically attached by umbilical cords to their cell phones, would be evidence to some that she had not just gone out somewhere, but had fled the condo in haste.

To some. Maybe to those men who had come for her?

She hesitated a moment, then leaned down and rather gingerly touched the screen so it would light up. Then she pressed her thumb to the screen, using yet another layer of the security that had become such a big part of her life. Anyone who had her very unlisted number could call the phone, leave a message or text, but once there it was locked in her phone until she unlocked it. Without her thumbprint, the phone offered only a lighted screen with a box in the center, a box blank until it read her thumbprint. Then only she could access information contained in the elegant little device, numbers, contacts, even the number of the phone itself and the apps she used.

The home screen came up, just as it always did. Showing her the time, the date. Call and text icons. Message icon. Menu and browser icons. Icons for the apps she used most often.

Tasha checked to make sure that the last call made was

the one she had made. Checked to make sure there weren't voice mail or text messages waiting for her.

There was one text message, chillingly simple.

Dead.

———————

"He did what?" Duran looked up from the file he'd been studying, his coldly handsome face not showing nearly the displeasure his normally calm voice betrayed.

"Left a text on her phone." Alastair kept his own voice calm, his own face expressionless. It hadn't, after all, been his fuck-up.

"A text."

"Yes. Just one word. *Dead.*"

"She has a secure phone."

"Yes, sir. Fingerprint activated. Her print, of course."

"Which Graves bypassed."

"Yes, sir."

"And did he say what possessed him to do something so idiotic?"

"He said he thought the idea of tonight's mission was to rattle her. You had told them she wouldn't be in the condo, that you were sure she'd sense they were coming and would get out before they could get in. So the idea, or part of it, was to let her see the team getting in and out so easily, see them apparently bypass all the expensive security of her building, her condo, even her cell phone, let her be rattled by them. Threaten her sense of being safe. Graves thought the text would help accomplish that objective."

Gently, Duran responded, "And did he explain why he felt the need to think for himself?"

"No, sir."

Duran leaned back in his chair. "When we're done here, send him to me."

"Yes, sir." Alastair was very glad it hadn't been his fuck-up.

"She was gone, as expected." It wasn't really a question.

"Yes. We had the real-time security video, of course; she slipped out of the condo and waited in the stairwell, hardly more than a minute before the team arrived on the third floor. The stairwell the team wasn't using, obviously."

"Even though that stairwell was farther from her apartment."

"Yes. Didn't take the time to dress, even put on shoes, but had her purse and keys. And she had made the bed look as though no one had been sleeping there only minutes before."

Duran considered briefly. "But she left her cell phone behind."

"Yes, sir. That's what gave Graves the idea. It was on the nightstand, charging. He used one of the disposable cells to leave her the text."

"Not a complete idiot, then."

Alastair thought it prudent to remain silent.

"Did she notify building security afterward?"

"No, sir. According to the security computer, she did access the lobby security camera as soon as she returned to her condo."

"Checking to see if the guards were where they were supposed to be."

"I assume so."

"And, of course, they were."

"Of course, sir."

"So now she has reason to doubt or even mistrust the security personnel, the security system—any illusion of safety, in fact."

"Yes, sir."

"And now we know for certain she has some awareness of us. Or at least some awareness of danger."

"Yes, sir. But she didn't run away; the stairwell cameras show that she stood at the door and watched as the team came and went. Climbed up to the fourth floor before they entered the stairwell to exit the building."

"So alert and careful, but also curious."

"Apparently."

"And confident of her ability to escape."

"I suppose so, sir, yes."

"When she returned to her condo, did she find them?"

"No, sir."

Duran's smile wasn't at all a humorous thing. "Good. That's good." He returned his gaze to the file before him on his desk, adding almost indifferently, "Send Graves up here."

"Yes, sir." Alastair didn't waste any time leaving the office, and he didn't waste much sympathy on Graves.

Stupid bastard. They all knew it wasn't wise to cross Duran, and in his eyes any deviation—*any* deviation— from his orders was considered by him a betrayal.

Everybody knew that.

Alastair did wonder, briefly, what fate lay in store for Graves, but his mind skittered away from the question before he could really begin to ponder it.

There were some things it really was best not to know.

———

Miranda Bishop watched as her husband cradled the phone in their hotel room. Cell phones were convenient—unless one was a psychic and routinely drained their power. Bishop seldom carried one these days, at least not on or near his body, despite the fact that their bright boys and girls on the technical side of things had designed protective cases that allowed most psychics to at least drain their cell batteries at a slower rate.

Not that it mattered at the moment.

"Still no luck?" she asked.

"No. Katie Swan isn't answering." Bishop was frowning, which was rare.

Normally Miranda would have known every thought and emotion her husband was experiencing because they had a unique and rather remarkable psychic/emotional connection. But that connection had been shut down as much as possible by both of them, because in this particular place and time it could prove a definite and deadly danger.

"The list is getting longer," she noted quietly.

Bishop nodded.

"And," she added, "you aren't content to just report it to your new contact and walk away."

"Brodie told me himself that once a psychic goes

missing, they've never been able to recover him or her. They become notes in a *Lost* column. Some supposedly turn up as bodies destroyed beyond recognition; some are reported as runaways; some have a backstory in place before they supposedly jaunt off to another country somewhere. And some just vanish."

"Never to be heard from again?"

"The suspicion seems to be that at least some psychics are taken to be used as soldiers in this secretive war. To gather information, to monitor psychics on this side, to look for weaknesses, to . . . label all the players."

"You have a problem accepting that?" she suggested.

"Not exactly. I think some abducted psychics *are* being used as tools. But there has to be more at play here, there just has to be. Something this big and . . . sprawling . . . has to have more structure than we're seeing. I believe Brodie's side is organized just as we thought, composed of smaller cells around a central base only a handful of their people know anything about. But the other side, the ones they've been fighting so long . . . There has to be an ultimate goal, and that can't just be . . . inexplicably collecting psychics."

"Some have said that's what you do," she ventured.

"Sure. Collect them, train them, and give them badges or private investigators' licenses, for the SCU or for Haven. But what I do, what *we* do, is very much out in the open. We may keep things quiet, but even the most suspicious cop hasn't called us secretive. We use our psychic abilities as tools, as quietly—or as openly—as necessary to do the job."

Miranda nodded. "And this group, this faceless enemy, has to be doing some kind of job or have some kind of goal. Otherwise none of it makes sense. They can't just be about trying to beat Brodie's group to psychics."

"Exactly. Brodie and his people believe that this other group has been taking psychics for decades, at least. But they must have been a lot more careful and quieter until fairly recently, if that's true. Because I never got a hint about them during the early years when I was searching out psychics for the SCU." He shook his head slightly. "Granted, I wasn't nearly as powerful then as now, and I wasn't looking for patterns, but I interviewed a *lot* of psychics, Miranda. All over the country and even a few overseas."

"And there were no fearful psychics?"

He leaned back against the desk behind him, frowning. "Plenty of fearful psychics. But naturally fearful, of their own abilities and the way other people in their lives reacted to them. Wary, suspicious, a lot of them in denial. But none I talked to was frightened by a secret conspiracy of stolen psychics and shadows."

Thoughtful, Miranda suggested, "Maybe there's a difference now. Maybe they're running out of time for some reason, feeling pushed to accomplish whatever it is they set out to do. Maybe Brodie and his group have had more of an effect on this enemy than they realize."

"Could be."

Eyeing him, Miranda said, "You promised not to interfere."

"I did, didn't I?"

"But?"

He smiled slightly, a smile few but his beloved wife ever saw. It made the scar on his left cheek all but disappear, and warmed his cool silvery-gray eyes by a good twenty degrees. "But Katie and Henry aren't psychics Brodie and his people have been aware of. At least, I'm fairly certain they haven't."

"So you wouldn't *really* be interfering if you did a little quiet detective work of your own."

"As long as your shield holds out, love, they'll never know we haven't gone obediently back to Quantico. Not, at least, unless or until we want them to know."

―――――

Not surprisingly, Tasha didn't sleep much the rest of the night. She went over and over in her mind every thought, every question—and every action of those men.

Who they were was such a giant question mark that she didn't spend too much time considering that for now.

They were men who intended something bad for her. That much she was certain of.

Why, she didn't know; another giant question mark.

How they got into the building . . . that was the most immediate worry. Because if she wasn't safe here, in a building like this, if men could slip in past all the security both technological and human and get to her here, then safety really was an illusion. And then there was her cell phone. They shouldn't have been able to leave that text without the number, and she could count on the fingers of one hand how many people had that number. With fingers left over. So how had they managed that? How had they managed to so easily just walk through all the security barriers she had wrapped around herself?

What was she supposed to do, lock herself into a bank vault?

I think they'd get to me even there.

Don't let fear rule you.

How about panic? I think panic is good.

Not panic either. Don't let others dictate your responses.

My responses?

They act. You react.

They who?

We aren't thinking about that right now.

For several long minutes, Tasha stopped thinking about anything but the growing certainty that she really *wasn't* arguing with herself. Because that other "voice" in her mind seemed way too calm, and way too knowing about what might have happened tonight—and why.

Tasha.

Go away. Whoever you are.

I can help you. We can help you.

Well, that was sure as hell unnerving.

We? There's a we? A we and a them?

Two sides. They want to hurt you. We want to help you.

Oh, yeah? And why is that?

Which? A twinge of humor there.

Oddly reassuring.

Both. Who are they? Who are we?

We don't know who they are. A group. Motives unknown, but actions definitely deadly. We believe they've been . . .

active . . . a long time. A large group. Organized. Secretive. Incredibly skilled at . . . disappearing people.

Disappearing people? Why?

Tasha, their interest is in psychics.

Another unnerving moment. Tasha wished the sun would come up. She wished daytime would come. Because everything was normal in the day. Normal, and ordinary, and not scary.

The other voice in her head *was* hers, that was it.

Anything else was her imagination.

You know better. You know yourself. You know this voice isn't yours, isn't you.

Sure. Sure.

All right. Think that way if you wish. For now.

Enough. I'm over this. I don't know what happened tonight or why, but tomorrow I'm going to the building super and—

And what? Tell him someone broke into your condo in the night, you watched them do it, the security cameras didn't *and the security guards* didn't, *but you did? You watched from the stairwell and alerted no one? You don't know who they are or why they were here. You can't explain how they got past security. You have nothing missing, no damage. No witnesses. And the building's security system won't show any signs of tampering.*

How do you know that?

Because they're good, Tasha. Very, very good. They don't leave evidence behind. They don't leave witnesses.

I'm still here.

Yes. You sensed them coming.

Tasha hesitated, but . . . *Yes.*

Maybe that's what they wanted to accomplish. To find out if you'd sense them coming.

That doesn't make sense.

Be rational. Think about it reasonably.

There's no reason to this.

There's reason to everything, even if it's only their *reason.*

Which is exactly zero help to me, because I don't have a clue what their reason could be.

You're psychic, Tasha. They value psychics.

Why?

We don't know.

Then why the hell should I believe you?

Think about it. Reason it out. There were three of them. Professionals. They weren't here to kill you; it only takes one to kill someone sleeping in bed, as any normal killer would have expected you to be.

Normal killer. Nice world you live in.

You live in it too, Tasha.

Tasha threw back the covers and slipped from bed. She went to the window and stood to one side looking through the blinds out on the quiet Charleston streets below. Even this late, this early, there were a few people about. Early-morning joggers. People who went to work very early or came home very late. A street-cleaning crew. A couple of yawning people who looked as if they had dressed in the dark walking their dogs; there was a small park half a block west, and most dog owners in the area clearly took advantage of it.

A normal morning. Normal people doing normal things, things they did even before the sun came up.

Tasha.

Go away. I don't believe in you.

I want you to think about tonight. I want you to come up with a reason why those men would have come to your apartment.

I already said. There's no reason.

They didn't steal anything.

No.

They didn't lie in wait for you to return.

Another unsettling possibility Tasha hadn't considered.

Tasha?

No. No, they came and went quickly. Very quickly. Maybe five minutes on this floor. Seven minutes at the outside.

Also not here with rape on their minds. A gang rape is a brutal assault triggered by surroundings, by actions, by a situation. Almost never something cold-bloodedly planned beforehand.

It made her feel queasy, but . . . *Yes. I know. That's not what they wanted.*

And yet they did want you.

I can't know that.

Yes. You can. That's why you sensed them. That's why you were able to escape them tonight.

Tonight. Escape them . . . tonight.

Do you really believe it's over, Tasha? Believe they won't try again?

"No," Tasha heard herself whisper aloud. "I don't believe that. I believe they *will* try again."

Yes. They will. And next time, you may not sense them coming.

FOUR

Tasha wasn't sure whether she was able to erect her walls and so finally block that other voice in her mind or whether it simply went away; all she knew was that the inner conversation ceased.

At least for a while.

Not that she was able to sleep. In the end, by the time morning sunlight began to brighten her windows, she was up, showered, dressed, and very restless.

That other voice had made a lot of sense about the uselessness of Tasha going to the building's superintendent to report the break-in, seeing as how she had no evidence it had happened. And hadn't reported at the time or afterward anything she had seen. Of course, she could always at least ask to see the security videos from the previous night, but . . .

What would that accomplish?

Nothing.

Electing to have her morning coffee and some kind of muffin or pastry out of the apartment that no longer felt at all safe to her, Tasha went downstairs and through the lobby, casually greeting the security guard at the main desk and the concierge at hers as she passed.

She knew both of them by name, just as she had known the guards she had seen working the previous night. She had made it her business to know who guarded her building, her condo.

For all the good that had done.

Security is an illusion.

Definitely her own voice in her mind now, nothing else.

Tasha went out into the mild January morning, joining the other early risers on the sidewalk. It was a Saturday, so the people moving about were mostly casual and unhurried, enjoying the sunshine and fresh air.

At least, that was how they appeared.

But Tasha had the notion that at least some of them were not what or who they appeared to be. She wanted to chalk that up to paranoia, but it was less a thought than a . . . an odd, inner chill breeze causing the hair on the nape of her neck to stand out.

Instinct.

She felt surrounded somehow, and not at all in the sense of being part of a crowd. Not because she was on a city street. Not because people were all around her, most clearly preoccupied by their own thoughts and concerns.

What Tasha felt was something a lot more primitive, even primal.

There was a threat.

Someone was watching her.

Right now.

She hesitated for only a few moments near the doorway into her building, then ignored her own uneasiness and headed for the crosswalk, her ultimate destination the coffee shop on the corner diagonally across from her condo.

It wasn't part of a chain, the coffee shop, but a local business that had been here for a long time. There were little tables both inside the shop and outside on the wide sidewalk. Tasha as usual chose a table outside, sitting with her back to a little corner niche that was brick rather than glass window. Something solid at her back, positioned so that no one could approach her unseen.

She'd begun to think of it as "her" seat, and had been amused to find herself feeling offended the previous week to find it occupied one morning. She thought she might have even glared at the woman who had sat there totally focused on her cell phone.

Tweeting. E-mailing. Sending someone a text or replying to one. Playing a game.

Who knew?

Just a few moments after Tasha settled into her corner, someone came to take her order. As jittery as she felt, she still needed her morning caffeine, and so she ordered a double-shot latte and a muffin.

Waiting for her order to come, Tasha wished she could pull out her cell phone and occupy herself with it. But there were two reasons why she couldn't do that. One, the more she used the phone, the quicker it died on her, and she was wary of not being able to use it if she really needed to at some point.

And, two, there was no way she could focus on anything as innocuous as e-mail or a game.

Not when she felt so edgy.

Not after last night.

And there was a third reason she really didn't want to think much about. That text. She didn't want to look at her phone and find another text like that one waiting for her.

Dead.

A threat?

A promise?

Or just a taunt?

Tasha didn't know, but as she looked out on the people moving casually along the sidewalks, the Saturday traffic passing her little corner of the world, she admitted to herself that it was something she couldn't avoid thinking about.

And yet . . .

It was, if anything, less unnerving than watching three men silently enter her apartment in the middle of the night. The text was . . . like a flourish somehow. Done for show rather than purpose.

It had certainly given her a chill, if that had been the objective. But the eerily silent visit from those men had been more than enough to do that much.

She was still chilled, if the truth be told. And she found

her gaze roving all around, not really looking at any one person, yet watching all of them.

Wondering who was watching her.

———

"That's a lot of aspirin," Brodie noted as he watched Murphy swallow half a dozen pills with a drink of her coffee.

"I have a lot of headache." Murphy grimaced and shifted her chair a bit back under the shade of the awning. "Jesus, it's bright out here."

"The sunny South."

She grunted.

"Not a morning person, are you?"

Murphy didn't waste a glare. "No. Not when I've been up all night."

"You couldn't take a break?"

"She was awake, so I was awake."

"And you didn't see how they got into the building."

"I did not." There was something in her grim tone that said she took that failing personally.

"And they were able to hack into the security system. Without raising any red flags."

"Apparently. Building security looks calm today and I doubt they would if they were aware of what happened last night. No technical people in the building to check out, service, or fix anything. The other residents I've seen leave the building so far also looked as though they had no worries at all. She's the only one, and you have to look close to realize just how jumpy she is."

"She knows she's the one they came for."

"She watched them come for her. From the stairwell."

Brodie looked thoughtful. "So alert but curious. I'm not sure that's such a good thing."

"She's known for a while she was being watched. Last night, she saw men come for her. Three men. So she knows, if she had any doubt, that it isn't a stalker kind of problem. It's worse than that. A lot more inexplicable than that. A lot more deadly."

"She didn't call the police?"

"She didn't even call the building super or the security desk in the lobby. She's not a stupid woman, Brodie, and she doesn't know who to trust. All she knows is that danger is all around her. That she's safer with people all around her. And she's not sure if it's instinct or something else urging her to stay put rather than run."

"How long were you in her head?"

"It's not quite like that, and you know it."

"How long?"

"Off and on all night."

"That part of the reason for your headache?"

"Oh, yeah. Sleepless nights I can handle. It's no sleep on top of being a psychic conduit that's causing the jackhammers pounding inside my head."

"You need to get some sleep."

"No shit."

Brodie sighed. "Look, I'm sorry I was delayed. It couldn't be helped."

"Meeting a possible new ally. I heard. Good one?"

"Very, I think. Offers us a pretty long reach inside law enforcement. But his position is . . . a little tricky. A lot of people are close to him, maybe too close. Maybe close enough to know too much about us before we're ready for them to know. If we ever are. And I'd feel better if I knew how he found out about us. He was very elusive about that without raising red flags in my head. Neat trick, that."

Murphy eyed the big man across the table from her. He was a physically powerful man, enough so as to give anyone pause even slouched down in the chair as he was. And he was very good-looking in a dark, brooding way. But his eyes, those very, very sharp eyes, sentry eyes, gave the lie to his seemingly relaxed body.

He was a born guardian.

A born Guardian.

Murphy wondered, actually for the first time, if that was the way of things in their very unusual world. Had they all been born to do this, after all? Was it as random as it appeared, or was it fate? She had often felt that she herself had been born for this work.

"You're frowning at me," Brodie told her.

"My headache is giving me ideas I don't like."

His brows lifted in question.

"Never mind." Murphy glanced around them, more by habit than anything else, to reassure herself they couldn't be overheard. Yet she still lowered her voice when she said, "You were meeting Bishop."

Brodie's sentry eyes became even sharper. Sharp enough, Murphy thought idly, to slice through something.

Or someone.

"Want to tell me how you know that?"

"Just trying to ease your mind. He knows about us because he made contact with me a few months back."

Brodie didn't look as if his mind had been eased. At all.

She shook her head slightly. "I move around more than most, you know that. I've crossed his path a few times, his and some of his team members."

Grim, Brodie said, "Please don't tell me any of his team know about us. He said not."

"He was telling the truth. Just him and his wife. Miranda. A unique connection between those two, and it has nothing to do with marriage vows or wedding rings."

Brodie refused to be sidetracked. "From what he told me, nearly every member of his team is psychic, and a fair number of them are telepaths. You really think something like this can be kept secret inside a group like that? Doing the sort of work they do?"

"It's *because* they do the sort of work they do that they aren't likely to even notice us. Bishop trains his people to shield whenever possible, and to focus—very narrowly. Their focus is killers, mostly of the serial variety, and they have plenty to occupy their minds. Which is sad when you think about it. On the other hand, they go up against murderers they can actually chase and catch and cage—or kill. And we have on *our* hands virtually invisible enemies and a mysterious conspiracy. Or several of them. I've never been quite sure."

"Murphy."

She frowned at him. "Look, Bishop put that unit of his together in the teeth of official opposition and scorn within the law enforcement community. It's been an uphill battle for him all the way, still is in some situations. But the thing he's held to with teeth and claws is that there's nothing at all unnatural or inhuman about psychic abilities; they're just other senses not everybody happens to have."

Brodie waited.

"He and his people have worked their asses off for years tracking and caging or destroying human monsters, and they've done it using a combination of law enforcement and investigative training *and* their psychic abilities. Which they bend over backward to keep matter-of-fact and firmly grounded in scientific possibility. Just other tools in the toolbox, like their guns and expertise with computers or martial arts or profiling, or whatever else each agent specializes in.

"Bishop and his people can't do their jobs if other law enforcement officials can't take them seriously. Any *hint* of some vast, mysterious conspiracy linking abducted psychics, and his unit would be laughed out of the Bureau. It's in his best interests to keep our secrets to himself, and nobody knows that better than he does."

After a moment, Brodie said, "I don't doubt his intent. Much. But in a unit full of telepaths—"

"Listen, you know that old saying about how two people can keep a secret only if one of them is dead?"

"Yeah."

"Well, we both know people *can* keep a secret. People can keep a lot of secrets, for a long time. If the stakes are high enough. If the secrets are important enough. If it matters enough." She paused. "It matters to Bishop. What's happening to psychics, the threat against them. It matters to him. If we need him to, he'll take our secrets to his grave."

———————

Henry McCord had a lifetime of practice in hiding what he could do. Thirty-six years, more or less. He could actually remember the first time he had seen a spirit.

At his grandfather's funeral. The old man had stood on the other side of the casket and winked at him.

Henry had been six.

So, thirty years of learning to cope in whatever way he could. Realizing early on that grown-ups didn't want him to talk about the dead people, that it made them really uncomfortable. Which had puzzled a childish Henry, since it seemed they would have liked to know that something of themselves survived death. It had reassured Henry, at least then.

Now . . . he didn't even know if he still believed that. And despite his several conversations with Bishop, he was still unconvinced that he could ever learn to control his abilities well enough to make some use of them. He had tried to open a connection, a "door," Bishop had called it, without success. He had tried meditation and biofeedback, which had left him feeling calm but still unable to see spirits when he wanted to.

There had even been a few dark times when he'd tried both alcohol and various drugs, also to no effect. Except to leave him grateful that he didn't have an addictive personality.

So Henry went on with his pseudo-normal life, as an architect who specialized in restoring historic old buildings, and never told anyone—except Bishop—that his seemingly uncanny knack for finding valuable original doors and windows and other fixtures for old houses was simply the fact that most original owners showed him where to look.

He never asked. They just appeared and showed him.

Unlike what he'd seen in various movies and TV shows about ghosts and hauntings, Henry had never had to face a negative experience. No angry or malevolent spirits, no spirits that looked disfigured or deformed or even showed the causes of their deaths.

Just helpful spirits dressed in period costume who led the way through basements and attics and storage buildings to things that belonged in whatever building he was restoring.

His own theory was that because he was restoring old buildings to their former glory, there was no reason why any spirit should have negative feelings toward him. Bishop had said it wasn't that simple, but Henry hadn't been interested in learning more and it had showed.

Just because he had to live with this didn't mean he especially wanted to understand how it worked.

So Henry went about his life as though everything were normal. He did his work, talked to investors and clients and landlords, and of course an endless parade of inspectors whose job it was to make sure he was doing *his* job correctly. And followed a seemingly endless succession of spirits to odd storage areas where he recovered original fixtures and fittings and even furniture designed and built—probably on-site—for the project he was working on.

Long and erratic hours had prevented him from having much of a social life, or at least that was what he told himself. It was okay with him, because he was a solitary soul at heart, and perfectly comfortable with his own company.

But then, while working just after the New Year on the restoration of a plantation house outside Charleston, he gradually realized that spirits had stopped showing up. Common sense told him there should be a *lot* of spirits at a place like this one, because it sure as hell had a lot of history.

But no spirits showed up.

He hadn't tried reaching out for them in a pretty long time, and didn't consciously do so then. But, entirely without thinking about it, he opened a door.

Almost at once, he was aware of spirits all around him. But . . . hiding somehow. Drawing back away from him, as if in fear.

Henry barely had time to register the absurdity of that when he became aware of something else. It was getting dark.

In the middle of the chilly January day, inside a huge house whose many windows let in lots of light, it was getting dark.

He thought maybe a rare winter thunderstorm was brewing up at first, but when he turned to look at one of the windows, he saw that it was very bright outside, the sunlight glinting off the windshield of his car. And the glimpse he could catch of the sky showed it clear and blue.

But it was getting darker all the same.

Close the door!

Close the door, hurry!

Henry, you have to close the door!

"What the hell?" he muttered. Because the spirits had never talked to him. They led, they pointed, they smiled. Silently. Even inside his own head, only silence.

Until now.

The urgency was unmistakable, and Henry tried to close a door he wasn't even sure how he'd been able to open.

He tried.

And then he felt as well as saw the shadows closing around him; not spirits, something else. Something that made his very soul quiver in absolute terror. He kept trying to shut the door but felt some kind of force he didn't recognize holding the door open so they could get to him. Inky black, icy cold, sliding and blending and slithering all around him, touching him. Taking him.

The blackness swept over Henry McCord, and the last thing he remembered was suddenly wishing he hadn't lived his life quite so alone.

———

It was one of her volunteer days at the shelter, and Tasha was grateful to be busy and occupied, even above the satisfaction she always felt in doing the work of helping abandoned dogs and cats. And there were people around all day, people she knew, people she had never once felt threatened by in any way, so that helped too.

For a while she was almost able to forget a threat existed.

Almost.

At the end of the day she went along with a few others to a casual restaurant near the shelter, because they were all tired and the only decision they wanted to make about dinner was to point at something that looked good on a menu.

So it was a bit later than usual when she pulled her car into her space outside the condo, well after the winter night darkness descended. Her space was as close as possible to the building, another of her attempts at safety and security. And the entire parking area was, actually, designed with safety in mind. It was well lit and surrounded by wrought-iron fencing that was attractive but would also be difficult to scale; residents gained access to the small courtyard via a gate that, as part of the entire security system, was manned around the clock.

The guard manning the gatehouse tonight had been cheerful and calm, nothing at all in his bearing indicating he felt at all uneasy about the security of the parking lot that was his area of responsibility.

And still, with all that, Tasha found herself hurrying to the building's door, hurrying to swipe her card and punch in the code, hurrying to close the door behind her.

She didn't realize she'd been holding her breath, and for way too long, until she leaned against the wall by the door and heard it escape her tense body in a rush.

Dammit.

Tasha hated to feel so . . . out of control.

Someone was watching her. She *knew* someone was watching her. But she couldn't see them, didn't know where they were or who they were—or why the hell they were watching her at all. She wasn't being paranoid, she *knew* that. She was being watched.

Because she was psychic, that other voice in her head had told her the previous night. The voice that, all day today and even now, even when she let herself think about it, was absent.

"Everything all right, Ms. Solomon?"

She started and looked at the security guard. "Yes. Yes, of course, everything's fine, Hawes."

His last name, no title; it was the compromise the security staff and residents had reached after some debate when the building had been completed and waiting residents moved in. No one liked the formality of honorifics or titles for the security staff or the *in*formality of first names on either side, so they were left with this.

So far, it worked.

"I'm heading back toward the elevator," Hawes said.

Tasha managed a brief laugh. "Do I look . . ." She didn't quite know how to finish that.

"It's an odd night," Hawes said, matter-of-factly. "Most everybody who's been out tonight has come home jumpy. I expect it's the full moon. Affects people even when they don't realize."

Tasha hadn't even realized the moon was full.

She headed for the elevator, Hawes walking more or less beside her. He was a former cop, she knew that much, a Chicago street cop who had chosen to semi-retire in a warm southern city.

Most of the security staff had the same sort of

background, former cops or retired military, if anything overtrained for security jobs in a residential condo. They were all very calm and seemingly unflappable, the women as well as the men; the security staff was roughly one-third female, while the concierge staff was about two-thirds female.

Every single one of them a trained professional who at least appeared to take this job as seriously as they had taken their previous ones.

So how had those men gotten past them the night before?

Tasha almost asked Hawes about it. Almost.

Instead, keeping questions and doubts to herself, she stepped into the elevator when the doors opened and lifted a hand in farewell as they began to close. "Good night."

"Good night, Ms. Solomon."

The ride to the third floor was brief and uneventful. The hallway was empty of any threat. The apartments she passed on the way to hers were quiet no matter what activities might have been going on inside, thanks to excellent soundproofing.

For the first time, Tasha thought that maybe the soundproofing shouldn't be quite so good.

Because if anyone inside were to cry out for help . . .

Refusing to finish that thought, she let herself into her apartment. The lights she always turned on before leaving were still burning; she hated walking into a dark room, always had.

Even before all this, before she'd been conscious of any threat against her, she had hated walking into darkness.

I wonder why. Did I always know there was a threat out there somewhere, sometime? No. No, that's stupid.

No inner but alien voice offered a response.

She didn't put her purse down as usual but first methodically searched the apartment. Just as she had after those men had left. Every room, every closet, every cabinet; she opened everything that was closed and checked thoroughly inside.

She found nothing, which should have made her feel at least a bit better.

It really didn't.

Tasha turned on the TV in the living room more for background noise than anything else, and chose a channel that tended to run science documentaries. The one airing at that time appeared to be something about how life in the universe had begun.

She went into her lamplit bedroom, hesitated for a moment, then gathered up her pajamas and went into the bathroom, pushing the door to behind her. Living alone, it really wasn't her habit to close doors between rooms, but her edginess also made her feel oddly exposed.

It made sense, she thought. When you knew someone was watching you, you felt watched all the time, even safely alone behind walls and draperies and locked doors.

Security is an illusion.

Her own inner voice, reminding herself of something she had no need to be reminded of. She *wasn't* safe here, and it was both useless and stupid to pretend otherwise.

She stripped, put her clothing into the hamper, and then took a long, hot shower. The water felt good, breathing in the steam felt good, and Tasha felt considerably better and more relaxed when she finally stepped out of the shower. She wrapped her hair in one towel and dried off with another, rubbed a lavender-scented body lotion into muscles that had worked hard that day, and then pulled on her pajamas.

It wasn't until she was loosening the towel covering her hair that she turned toward the mirror. It was steamed over, not surprisingly. But Tasha realized she could see bits of herself.

A pale green eye that was oddly wide. Strands of dark auburn hair. Her fingers near her temple as the towel fell to the floor behind her.

She could see bits of herself, she realized, because letters were written on the steamy mirror. Words that made her go cold to the bone.

YOU CAN'T HIDE, TASHA.

FIVE

"I thought you would have made contact today," Murphy said.

"No good opportunity." Brodie shook his head. "I'm glad she's cautious, but it isn't making it easy to approach her. She's never really alone."

"Not necessarily a bad thing."

"True. And I'll probably have to make contact with her in some public place just so she'll feel relatively safe. Besides, since Duran has already made one move, he's more likely than not to move against her again sooner rather than later."

"I'd still like to know how she showed up on his radar." Duran was one of the few enemies, a leader on the "other" side, that they could put a face to, yet their best investigators had been able to find out nothing more about him than a name that led nowhere. He was a cipher.

A deadly cipher.

"Yeah, you and me both. Look, go ahead and take off, get some rest."

They had been splitting the watcher duties.

Murphy said, "Okay, but I'm coming back to relieve you around four. You'll need to rest yourself if you mean to approach her tomorrow."

"No argument." Brodie settled down where they had decided was the best position to watch Tasha Solomon's condo during the night, the corner of a rooftop on a three-story building that housed on its ground floor her favorite coffee shop. From their position they could see both entrances to her building and had a good view of her corner apartment.

Both the blinds and the curtains were drawn.

"Think she's in for the night?"

"Yeah, pretty sure. Honestly, I don't think she'd risk going out at night right now. She's even more jumpy than before. The only time today she seemed able to put any worries or uneasiness out of her mind was when she was working at the shelter."

Brodie eyed Murphy. "You think or you know?"

"Think. Her walls are up and we haven't tried getting through."

"It might make my job easier if you do."

"Or the opposite. An alien voice in her mind spooked her. Duran's goons spooked her. If we push, she could get spooked enough to haul ass away from here. And I have a hunch she wouldn't be easy to track. At least not for us. The last thing we need is her in the wind."

"True enough. Get some rest, Murphy."

"See you around four." She lifted a hand in a brief salute, then left the roof and made her way down to the street. She was somewhat preoccupied, tired but not enough to stop her mind from considering various possibilities and probabilities, weighing her own options, still walking the fine line she had been walking for some time now.

They had so few answers. So damned many questions.

And too many psychics like Tasha Solomon in danger and yet also in a position to possibly give them more information, more answers.

What she knew.

And what Duran might reveal in trying to get to her.

Murphy had been involved in this secretive group they had never really named for several years now, and in her time the only certainty she felt able to count on was that there were two sides to this . . . conflict.

Not a war. Exactly.

Maybe a struggle. A struggle to find and protect psychics from some mysterious "other" that wanted them.

Reasons unknown.

They did know of a few of the . . . soldiers . . . on the other side, the way they *knew* Duran. Not where he was born, or when, or where he'd gone to school or, really, anything about his background. Duran headed up their field operations, most of them, they knew that, but who or what he reported to was a mystery.

Still, after years, a mystery.

So there was also a struggle to gather information.

A struggle to understand. To learn who was behind this and why. To have it make sense somehow. To be able to look back and reaffirm that those who had fallen, to the other side or because of them, had given their freedom or their lives in a good and just cause.

Melodramatic.

Yes. But also true.

There was just so damned much they didn't *know*.

They hadn't even found a single way to protect psychics; each one was a unique situation and called for unique measures to make them safe. Some were in hiding, not really living any kind of a normal life and yet the only sort in which they felt even marginally safe.

A few had taken the opposite tactic, going public in a major way, drawing media and other attention to themselves. Sarah Mackenzie came to Murphy's mind, at least in part because Sarah's was both the most recent and the most successful case she knew of.

With Tucker Mackenzie's celebrity status as a very famous best-selling author, and the publication of his book about his wife's rather astonishing abilities garnering them both a lot of media attention, it at least appeared that Duran had backed off. They couldn't even find evidence that he had the couple under surveillance where they lived in Richmond.

But they weren't *sure*, of course.

They were never sure.

And just when they thought they were sure of something, just when they thought there was a fact they could stand on, it was neatly pulled out from under them.

Usually by Duran.

Don't think about Leigh. Don't think about the others lost along the way. But good people, dammit. Good people.

Murphy slipped away from the downtown area where Tasha Solomon's condo was situated, but she didn't return to the small apartment several blocks away, rented for the duration.

Instead, after hesitating only briefly, she stood in the shadows of a darkened doorway on a quiet, peaceful street, and pulled one of the burner cell phones from her bag.

Dead. The next two were dead as well, their batteries drained even though they had not yet been turned on.

Murphy cursed under her breath, making a mental note to charge all of them later tonight.

The fifth one she tried still had some power. Maybe enough. She punched in a number. Always the same one. He never worried they could trace the call, even ping the cell he always used.

Because they had never been able to.

Dammit.

"Yes?"

Murphy recited the address of a bar a couple of blocks from her location. A dark place, open late. Quieter than most bars, its patrons mostly intent on drowning their sorrows and not interested in what was going on around them while they did so.

"Fifteen minutes," she said.

"I can make it in ten," he responded, calm as ever.

It was a little game they played. Murphy tried to gauge how close by he was at any given time, and he consistently surprised her.

"So you are in Charleston," she said.

"Didn't you expect me to be?"

Murphy didn't want to talk about what she expected, not during a cell call. So all she said was, "See you there."

She didn't wait for a response, just ended the call, turned off the phone, and removed its battery. She then went on her way, tossing the phone and battery into different trash receptacles.

He's here himself. Which means Tasha Solomon is more important than we knew. Maybe more powerful. More . . . useful somehow? Or . . . is it just one more game of his, to keep us guessing?

To keep me guessing?

Murphy headed toward the bar, wondering vaguely if the high wire she walked was actually visible beneath her.

And wondering how long she could continue to walk it before she lost her balance and fell.

Undoubtedly into a very unpleasant pit.

————

Jeffrey Bell hadn't asked to become psychic. And since the car accident that had resulted in a head injury hadn't been his fault, he felt a bitter sense of resentment toward the universe that he hadn't just ended up with a totaled car, but pretty much a wrecked life as well.

"Please." Her voice even over the phone was desperate. "You have to help me, Mr. Bell. You don't know me, but—"

He didn't want to listen to another of the stories that had begun to haunt every day of his life.

"Listen," he said to her, keeping his voice even and calm even as he made a mental note to himself to change his home number yet again. And to fucking screen his calls with voice mail. "I can't help you, lady. Really. I can't just flip a switch and predict something for you or anyone else."

"But I just need to know if he'll come back!"

"And that's something I can't tell you. I'm sorry."

"If we met in person—"

"Nothing would change." Somewhat grudgingly, he added, "If I'm going to see anything at all, your voice would have been enough of a trigger. At least that's the way it's been so far. Look, I'm sorry, but I just can't help you."

"But—"

"Sorry," he repeated, then hung up the phone. And immediately unplugged it.

So far nobody had gotten his cell number, but he figured it was only a matter of time. He could give up the landline. Change cell numbers. Move again as he had moved here to Atlanta only a month previously.

It wouldn't help.

Sooner rather than later, they would begin to find him again. The desperate. The lost. The greedy. Needing something from him, urgent and pleading. Sometimes demanding.

As if he owed them.

In Jeffrey's mind, he didn't owe anybody a damned thing. Except maybe a kick in the balls to the universe, if he could have done that. Because his life had been fun before the accident. A job he found satisfying, an apartment perfect for his needs. Friends and family around.

Normal.

But nothing had been normal since the accident. Family and friends, if they believed him at all, were wary of him. Avoided him. Clearly uneasy about what he might tell them.

And it looked spooky, he'd been told, whenever a new face or voice or place triggered one of his visions. His girlfriend told him he went white, his eyes went dark, and his stillness, for minutes at a time, was truly creepy to see.

She told him that just before she dumped him.

As for his job, they hadn't *said* he was being laid off because of what he was suddenly able to do. The economy, they said.

"I'm sorry, Jeff, but you know how it is." His supervisor sounded calm in the way that someone very nervous forced himself to be calm. "But there's always a demand for IT people, so I'm sure you won't have trouble finding another job. You'll have an excellent recommendation from us, I can assure you of that."

"Except," Jeffrey had responded evenly, "there's this lousy economy. That might factor into my ability to get another job."

"Yes. Well, maybe a different city . . ." He didn't quite say the more distance Jeffrey put between them, the better.

Except that was what he was saying.

Jeffrey had risen to his feet and headed for the door, almost wishing he knew something he could have tossed over his shoulder, something seriously spooky. But he had discovered that his "abilities" were beyond his control, grabbing him unexpectedly in damned inconvenient moments, and virtually never something he could trigger at will.

So he cleaned out his cubicle, and he left.

He left, moving temporarily to New York, where he could feel anonymous, sending out résumés all over the country. And the job offer from a company in Atlanta had been reassuringly prompt.

A better job, actually. And he had tried to avoid betraying this "gift" he had been cursed with. Had tried to limit his contact with other people, avoiding crowds whenever possible, remaining detached from others emotionally. Doing his best to isolate himself.

And it worked. For about two pretty lonely weeks. And then somebody Googled him *because* he was so quiet and kept to himself, and the gossip started. The questions asked jokingly became patently uneasy. Somebody blogged about him, there was an anonymous tip or two to the newspapers—and word got out.

Word got out, and people began contacting him.

The desperate. The lost. The greedy. Believing he could help them find something, someone. Pick a winning lottery number. Believing he was the answer to all their problems. Believing he could make their lives better, or at least reassure them that their lives would have meaning.

And then there were the disbelievers, the ones who wanted to challenge him, test him, prove he was a fraud.

So here he was. Packing a bag to go stay in a hotel, because his address had been posted by some nitwit on Twitter *and* Facebook who had thoughtfully tagged a whole bunch of the Roswell, Area 51, ghost hunting, paranormal believers—and he knew all too well what that would mean.

People turning up at his door.

A lot of people.

Jeffrey was nearly packed when a vision slammed into him as they sometimes did, without warning.

Darkness. Then the overwhelming, unsettling sounds of whispering, as though from a thousand voices, ten thousand, all saying things he couldn't quite hear. And the darkness lifted just enough for him to have a sense of vast space all around him, space filled with . . .

Shadows. Misshapen, sliding away when he tried to focus on them. Somehow alien, unknowable. Moving all around him, the faint rustling sounds they made closer than the whispers.

Unthreatening at first. He had the odd idea that they were talking among themselves, discussing . . . him.

Weighing him somehow.

Was he valuable enough?

Was he ready?

Whatever their conclusions, Jeffrey felt, sensed, them coming closer. Closer. Reaching out for him.

Almost touching him.

He had no idea what it meant, but an almost primal fear sliced through him suddenly, as sharp and cold as a knife, and he fought to escape the shadows, the vision.

Don't let them touch you.

Don't let them have you.

He fought as hard as he could, and . . .

He almost got away.

Almost.

He could feel it, like surfacing in a pool and sensing the warmth of sunlight on his face, beginning to open his eyes to brightness. But then, beneath the surface, something caught at him. Tugged. Dragged him back down into the dark water.

Nobody heard his scream.

Nobody that mattered.

Days later, when his concerned boss asked the building super to check on him, his apartment was deserted. His clothing and personal belongings gone, including the boxes he hadn't even had time to unpack. The apartment keys left on the kitchen counter.

Nobody was really surprised that he had left. Nobody in Atlanta had known him very well, but the rumors had circulated, and it seemed reasonable to believe he had just moved again, to escape the people who had left desperate notes and pleas stuck to his door in a multicolored sea of Post-its.

To escape his creepy abilities, maybe.

In any case, Jeffrey Bell was gone.

And no one ever saw him again.

————

Tasha spent another mostly sleepless night after the incident with the mirror. She had wiped the words away with a towel, convincing herself that the men who had been there the previous night had somehow left the message for her, a message that would only appear later, when she showered and steamed up the room.

It didn't help.

Who were they? Why were they after her?

Was it because she was psychic? And, if so, why?

That alien voice in her head had said "we" had more questions than answers about "them."

But how could that be? Tasha had never believed in conspiracies, firmly of the opinion that it just wasn't human nature to keep any secret for long. By her reckoning, only some military or intelligence agency secrets were kept quiet for years, decades.

Except . . . Now that she was thinking about it, she supposed she couldn't say with certainty that no people, no organization, could keep a secret indefinitely.

No way to prove a negative.

So maybe there *were* secrets out there. Maybe there were a lot of them. But a secret organization kidnapping or killing psychics for no discernible reason?

And whose activities most of the people around them never even noticed?

That didn't just seem unlikely; it seemed absurd.

Today's mainstream media was an around-the-clock business hungry for headlines on dozens if not hundreds of channels and newspapers and magazines. And when you added to that all the Internet and social media, the websites, the blogs, the tweets and Facebook pages, *and* the fact that virtually nothing could happen without someone capturing it on a video camera or cell camera and posting it on YouTube or Instagram . . .

Well, nothing could happen unseen in the United States, at least.

Still, she couldn't help wondering if that was why, although she felt watched almost all the time now, she only really felt *threatened* once it got dark. Did "they" move at night, in the middle of the night, largely to avoid attention?

Made sense—if anything in all this made sense.

Though that didn't, of course, explain how they were able to gain access to her building, her apartment, when it was so well guarded.

Not that Tasha had asked building security any questions or asked to see the security footage from that night. She hadn't asked them, and didn't know *why* she hadn't asked them, except . . .

She really didn't know who to trust.

So Tasha tossed and turned most of the night, napping more than sleeping, and felt both unrested and on edge when she pulled herself from bed around eight that Sunday morning.

On past lazy Sundays, she had often taken a book to the park, but she wasn't sure if she could even concentrate long enough to sit down and read. She did, however, want her usual morning coffee, so as soon as she was up and dressed, she made her way out and through the typical Sunday traffic and foot traffic, which was a bit thin as usual this early but would pick up later in the day, after church.

She went to her usual place at the coffee shop and placed her usual order. The Sunday morning customers sitting outside were reading newspapers or talking on their cell phones, or texting, or whatever. Preoccupied with their own lives.

Normal.

Tasha wished that reassured her.

It didn't.

Her order came. She sipped coffee, picked at a very large muffin, and wished she'd thought to get a newspaper or bring one of her books to at least pretend to read. She'd fit in better with the others.

A folded newspaper landed on the table near her elbow and a man sat down across from her.

Oddly enough, though he was big and dark and a total stranger, Tasha felt no threat from him.

"What—"

"Sorry this is so sudden." His voice was deep, calm, pleasant. "We've never really figured out the best way to make contact. You all tend to be wary at least, sometimes scared. So all we really know for sure is never to come to you in the night, the darkness. Because that's when the goon squad usually shows up."

Tasha sat very still, watching him as he sipped a large coffee she was willing to bet was just black, nothing fancy.

He had the sharpest eyes she'd ever seen, eyes that seemed to see her with uncomfortable clarity. And as lazily comfortable as he looked slumped down in his seat, as unthreatening, she could also see that he had to be physically powerful. Very powerful.

"Your name is Tasha Solomon. My name is John Brodie. And I've been sent to help you. To protect you."

"I can take care of myself," she said slowly.

Are you the voice I've had in my head?

No answer to that.

"Yes, you can," he said matter-of-factly. "Training, good instincts, the ability to think on your feet and make good choices. You've chosen a building with outstanding security, and you take care never to be alone unless you're securely locked inside your condo."

"Have you been watching me?" she demanded.

He answered readily, if inexplicably. "Yes, for the last couple of days, but I'm not the one you felt watching you."

"Why not?"

"Because I'm not psychic. And because psychics generally don't pick up on me unless I let them. And because you know very well I'm no threat to you."

"How would I know that?"

"You feel it. You always feel when you're being watched, when there's a threat nearby. And sometimes, I'm guessing, there's an . . . alien voice in your mind that scares you. Something you know doesn't belong to you. Something that isn't natural."

"So that's common among the psychics you've found?" Tasha said, admitting nothing.

"Not all, but some."

"Who does that voice belong to?"

"We aren't sure. About that inner voice that feels unnatural to you psychics. Though sometimes we try to make contact telepathically, and I'm told that inner voice feels entirely different to you. I'm not sure just how."

"You aren't sure of much, are you?"

Brodie didn't take offense. "Unfortunately, no."

"So why do I need you?" She was still speaking slowly, studying him, still conscious of no threat from him. And still feeling relatively safe with people all around them.

"Because the other side wants you. Badly. And unless you have a better idea of just what's going on and what you're up against, the best training and instincts in the world can't keep you safe." He paused, then added deliberately, "Just like the arguably best security in your building couldn't keep them out when they wanted in."

———

Bishop emerged from the bedroom of the small apartment and offered a grim shake of his head when Miranda lifted her brows questioningly.

"No sign of Katie at all," he said. "No sign anyone's lived here. No books on the shelves, nothing personal on the walls, all the closets and drawers empty. It's clear the apartment super has this place ready for a new tenant but hasn't rented it yet."

"It's been recently cleaned," Miranda offered. It was her turn to frown. "Odd, though."

"What?"

"Well, cleaning services usually leave a place smelling of lemon or pine or something to signal to anyone coming in that it's been recently cleaned. I don't smell that. I *feel* the place is clean, but it isn't because of a scent. Not, at least, a scent I recognize."

With a sigh, Bishop said, "Right now, I'm wishing one of us were either clairvoyant or had some psychometric ability."

"Spider senses?"

"You know as well as I do they're difficult to use at full strength when we have our connection closed down. And I've never been especially good at picking up an energy signature except from a person. I even tried touching Katie's bed, but I'm almost positive the bed in that room is brand-new. Or at least the mattress is."

"They think of everything."

"Apparently. Her boss says she resigned by letter, this apartment is empty of any sign she ever lived here; the keys were left on the kitchen counter, all utilities paid up—and she didn't ask for her security deposit. Even her car has vanished. Probably to a chop shop, its parts being shipped all over the country by now."

"You think they work that fast?"

"I think . . . by now they're a well-oiled machine when it comes to disappearing people. And all without making the authorities the least bit suspicious."

Miranda brooded for a moment, her electric blue eyes tracking slowly around the living room of the small apartment. "Always psychics, and almost all of them living alone. They really don't take people with family, do they?"

"Usually, no. There are a few cases I turned up where an entire family died in a house fire or car accident— including a psychic. Or a body made to resemble that psychic well enough to raise no question of identity."

"But cases like that are rare."

"Extremely rare. I don't know what Brodie and his people have turned up, but I've been tracking psychics long enough to feel pretty sure that most of those who disappear have no family or significant other to worry and pester the police. Though there often is a recent or fairly recent breakup of a marriage, engagement, or romantic relationship."

"Being psychic can be hard on relationships," Miranda noted wryly. "We've seen that play out more than once. Especially if only one of a couple has abilities."

"That's certainly true. And in most of the breakups where I could find a cause, it was easily traced back to a freaked-out significant other. Some were recent enough that they noticed someone they'd once loved had gone missing, but others just seemed to accept whatever the official determination ended up being. Assuming a report was even filed, there are virtually no investigations into the disappearances."

"Didn't you say Katie had recently broken up with a fiancé?"

"Yeah. She's not a born psychic; her telekinetic abilities were apparently triggered when she was thrown from a horse and suffered a head injury just about two years ago. She struggled to control what she could do, and it was a real struggle for her. I gather the fiancé more or less freaked out during an episode in which Katie lost her temper and most of the pictures in the room went flying off the walls. The fiancé left half his stuff behind when he packed up and left, she told me, he was in such a hurry to just get away from her."

Miranda shook her head. "That poor girl. We could have helped her."

"I tried to convince her of that. But it was still too new to her, something she had to deny existed."

"And that made her vulnerable to them."

"If they've found as few telekinetics as we have, a couple of bitter entries about psycho *supposedly* psychic girlfriends on Facebook would have alerted them to what she could do."

"The fiancé, I gather?"

"Trying to hide the fact that anything paranormal had actually happened. Claimed she rigged the room just to scare the shit out of him so he'd leave."

Dryly, Miranda said, "There are easier ways to break up."

"Oh, yeah. But everything has to be dramatic these days, especially on social media and among certain age groups. And way too many people, especially young people, share way too much personal information online with strangers." Bishop shook his head. "Although it does help us. We have programs running to flag certain words and phrases used in social media, and people to monitor and check them out; this enemy Brodie has described has to have the same kind of arrangement or something very like it, especially to be able to move this fast."

"I wonder if they meet as many kooks as we do," Miranda murmured.

"Probably. Maybe why they hang back and watch for a while. The six-month window Brodie mentioned for new psychics is probably just allowing them the time to watch and find out if the psychic is genuine and what he or she can do. I'm betting Katie wasn't on their radar until that Facebook post got shared by a few thousand *friends*—and it was just about six months ago."

"After you'd already talked to her."

"Which makes me wonder if my . . . spy network . . . is actually better than theirs."

"You spent years building it. And you have an awful lot of people from all walks of life on the lookout for potential psychics. People who really know what to look for and who report to you pronto."

Bishop frowned again. "Brodie seemed convinced that the enemy in all this makes use of at least some psychics to search for others."

"Well, we have psychics who serve the same function. Even if that wasn't how we found Katie, we do find psychics that way. Which is why we have our connection shut down *and* are both behind the shield."

She always referred to it that way, as *the* shield rather than hers, even though it was one she had built to safeguard herself and her sister years before, after a serial killer had destroyed the rest of her family and left her and Bonnie in hiding.

In hiding in more ways than one.

It was a remarkable thing, her shield, and unique; Bishop completely trusted the protection it afforded them. But it did have its drawbacks, and one of them was leaving both of them with diminished senses.

Including their extra ones.

"We'll find her," Miranda said quietly, able to read her husband accurately despite that.

"Brodie said they'd never been able to recover a psychic once he or she was taken."

Miranda Bishop smiled. "That was before we joined up."

SIX

"Sir, Brodie has made contact with Tasha Solomon." Alastair knew better than to sugarcoat it. Or add any unnecessary details.

There was a long, silent moment, and then Duran turned away from the window, with its view of downtown Charleston, and went to sit behind the big desk.

"When?"

"Just now. At the coffee shop."

"She was receptive?"

"Seemed to be. Guarded, tense, but listening."

Duran didn't check his watch, but said, "It's early."

"Yes, sir. And the location is very public. So unless they move, we'll have no chance of getting close for the duration." He paused, then added, "Best-case scenario for us is, of course, if they go to Solomon's apartment. But she may be too wary for that."

Duran was silent for a minute or so, the long fingers of one hand drumming almost silently on the surface of the desk. Then he said, "She sensed a threat and took action. She's been cautious since then. But she hasn't used her abilities under pressure."

"Not so far as we know," Alastair agreed.

"Maybe," Duran said, "it's time we all found out just what Tasha Solomon can do."

———

"Why should I trust you?" Tasha asked Brodie.

"No reason I can think of," he replied wryly. "Except that I've been in this a long time, I know a lot of the players, and my job as Guardian is to make sure you stay alive and out of their hands."

"What would they do with me if they got me?"

"We don't know. But the psychics who have . . . caught glimpses into their operation say it's not something pleasant. At all. At best, you'd be their prisoner, possibly for the rest of your life, theirs to use."

"What makes you believe that?"

"Because psychics have been disappearing for years, decades if our research is accurate, and so far none we're reasonably sure were captured by them have ever turned up again. Alive."

She blinked, the only outward sign of disturbance. "Have any turned up not alive?"

"It's debatable. Bodies have been found, the apparent

victims of accidents, fires, drownings. Shallow graves far
off the beaten path. Bodies too . . . damaged or decom-
posed to positively identify."

"DNA," she offered.

"Now, yes, we have that tool. But we seldom have
access to bodies found, and they clearly do. DNA can be
planted, records altered. They seem to be good at that."

"And what is your . . . side . . . good at?"

"Protecting those psychics we manage to locate before
the other side gets to them. There's nothing official about
us, Tasha. Nothing public. We don't have badges or any
kind of law enforcement credentials. We do have a few
allies inside various law enforcement agencies, and sometimes they're able to get valuable information for us. But
we still work . . . out of view, behind the scenes. Trying
our best not to draw attention to ourselves. That limits
what we can find out."

Tasha wondered if he had carefully avoided saying that
they worked in darkness and secrecy, avoided using those
words, because it sounded far too like how the others,
the "them," worked.

"So you have no idea what they would do with me if
they ever got their hands on me. What about you? Your
side? What are your plans for me?"

"I told you. I'm here to keep you safe."

"For how long? Does whatever your side offers also
mean the rest of my life?"

"That depends on you."

"In what way?"

"I won't lie to you, Tasha; there are no guarantees. In

the past, there have been psychics we believed were safe who were taken virtually under our noses. There have also been . . . psychic deaths."

Tasha had a strong feeling he wasn't repeating himself. "Psychic deaths. You mean deaths of the mind?"

His brows lifted slightly, as if in surprise, but he answered readily. "One thing we've learned is that if psychics push their abilities past their limits, past what they can control, especially if they're panicked or afraid, the effort sometimes damages their abilities. And in a few rare cases we know about, psychics have been destroyed. Physically alive, but the mind, the personality, is gone. The body usually doesn't survive long after that, even with medical intervention."

Tasha heard something in his voice and tilted her head a bit unconsciously. "You've had personal experience with a situation like that, haven't you?"

"Yes." A muscle tightened in his jaw. "A young psychic in my care died that way. We were cornered by soldiers from the other side, but in a safe place, and help was on the way. She panicked. She was one of the ones who said she knew, felt, what they would do to her if they got her. And it terrified her in a way I can't even describe. Before I could stop her, she . . . unleashed her abilities."

"And it killed her?"

"Her particular ability, a very rare one, involved channeling energy. Electrical, magnetic, whatever. I'm not psychic, so I can't be sure exactly what she did, but whatever it was, it killed one of the other side's soldiers and seriously damaged the eardrums of at least one more.

They were wearing headsets, presumably to communicate with each other as they were moving to surround us."

"So she used her abilities as a weapon."

"She tried. She was even effective. But it cost her her life, Tasha. It destroyed her mind, and a few weeks later her body succumbed." For the first time, he leaned forward, toward her, and rested his forearms on the table. "That's not what we want, Tasha. We aren't trying to assemble weapons, build an army, even a defensive one. There may come a time when the psychics we help are able to fight that way, but so far attempts have been mostly unsuccessful and sometimes fatal."

"So how do you fight them?"

"Since we don't know what their ultimate goal is, why psychics are so important to them, even who they really are and who's behind them, all we can do is search for information and keep as many psychics as possible protected from them."

"That doesn't sound like much of a strategy."

"Some of us would like to do more," he admitted frankly. "It's a war, and we'd like to fight it like one. Openly. And there have been a few battles between our side and theirs."

"Gun battles?"

Brodie nodded. "But only when it was absolutely necessary and we had at least a decent chance at controlling the fallout. Because until we have a better idea of their resources, their power, we have to be careful. Going public could do nothing except destroy our organization."

"It's an organization?"

"More or less. No name, not even an acronym. Formed around cells, a bit like the French Resistance during World War Two. The cells, made up of differing numbers of people, work independently, gathering intelligence in specific areas, sheltering and protecting psychics, recruiting allies. Reporting information to only one contact outside their cell and without any knowledge of who he or she reports to or who makes up other cells."

"So if one cell is . . . compromised . . ."

He nodded. "We don't all come crashing down. Very few in our organization know the whole setup."

"How many are you?"

Brodie shrugged. "I actually don't know, not for certain. Hundreds, at least. Maybe more."

"Psychics and nonpsychics?"

"We've discovered that having nonpsychics in the cells makes us less vulnerable in some ways."

She was quick to add, "And more vulnerable in others."

"Well, most nonpsychics never learn to shield our minds, so if the other side uses any of their psychics against us—"

"You mean people they've captured? Psychics working for them?"

"Not sure about the former, but definitely the latter. He controls at least some psychics, and he uses them. Why they allow it, whether out of desire, belief in whatever their cause is, or fear, we don't know. Duran is careful to keep their psychics under wraps, protected even when he sends one out to use them against us, so we haven't been able to . . . debrief . . . any of them."

"Duran?"

"Far as we can tell, he heads up their field operations. He's smart, he's ruthless, and he commands a great deal of power. We don't know who he reports to."

"But you're sure he isn't the one calling the shots."

"In the field, I believe he is. Doing whatever he needs to do in order to further their goals. But we—I—have always believed it is bigger than that, more complex. Many more players involved, and higher up the food chain than he is."

"And it's all about psychics."

"Yes."

"But you don't know why? Why the other side wants them?"

"We know they want to use them in some way, that they have a definite plan in mind. Just not sure *how* they want to use them. Other than to find more psychics, I mean."

"Just psychics?"

"We don't know. Maybe there's a larger plan involving others. But we do know that for years, decades, their energies have been concentrated on finding and taking psychics. That's what they do, and what we stop them from doing whenever possible."

"Which brings me back to my earlier question," Tasha said. "If I don't decide to go it alone, if I accept protection from your side of this . . . war . . . is it for life? Will my life ever be normal again?"

"No," Brodie replied bluntly. "No matter which choices you make, once they found out about you, once they noticed you, your life changed forever."

———————

Astrid opened her eyes and shook her head. "Sorry. She's got good shields, and they're up. Typical for born psychics, you know, especially when they've been approached by a stranger and told an insane conspiracy theory."

"I know," Duran said, without turning from the window. His gaze was focused on the corner of a coffee shop he could—just—see in the distance. "Keep trying. She'll let those shields down any minute."

"I thought she was cautious," Astrid said.

"That's why she'll let the shields down."

Astrid eyed him, too accustomed to his habits to take offense at having to address his back. "You sure?"

"Positive. Try again, Astrid. And keep trying."

"Until what? Until I have a migraine or a nosebleed?"

"If that's what it takes."

"You're a bastard, Duran, you know that, right?" Her voice was on the edge of mocking.

"Of course. Keep trying."

"Yes, sir." Astrid relaxed in her chair, closed her eyes, and concentrated.

———————

"So far," Tasha said slowly, "you've talked about a mysterious conspiracy to abduct psychics and possibly use them in some way, but you can't tell me who they are or what they want with the psychics. You can't tell me who's in charge. You can't tell me the endgame. You can't even tell me much about this organization you're supposed to be part of, a group fighting the supposed bad guys."

"It does sound unlikely," Brodie admitted.

"It sounds insane. No offense."

"None taken. What can I do to convince you?"

Caught a bit off guard, she replied, "I . . . have no idea."

"You're a telepath," he said. "So read my thoughts."

"I thought you said most psychics couldn't read you."

"Unless I let them. I'm letting you. Once I let *my* guard down, most telepaths can read me."

Tasha frowned, then shook her head. "Just because you honestly believe something doesn't make it true."

"Look deeper," he invited calmly. "Look as deep as you need to."

"It's not fun, dropping my walls all the way," she told him. "There aren't a lot of people around, but there are some. And I'd have to sift through all their thoughts in order to find yours."

His brows rose slightly. "You can read everyone around us?"

"Probably. Why does that surprise you?" She was still frowning at him.

He didn't answer right away, and when he did, it was slowly. "It's . . . unusual. Most telepaths have limits. The thoughts of each individual, the electromagnetic energy in the brain, produces a unique . . . signature. Think about radio frequencies; not every receiver can pick up every frequency. To my knowledge, it's the same with telepaths. You have a finite range of frequencies you're sensitive to, therefore you can only read people whose unique electromagnetic energy signatures fall into your range."

"I guess I've been meeting all those people, then."

"Your whole life?"

A little impatient, Tasha said, "I tend to go to a lot of trouble to *avoid* trying to read people, especially in crowds. All I can tell you is that I've never not been able to read someone when I tried. Sometimes the thoughts are only surface, bits and pieces, phrases, and sometimes it's hard to understand them because they're jumbled or confused. But I've always been able to pick up something."

If anything, Brodie just looked grim. "I see."

She stared at him. "Did I say something wrong?"

"No. It's just that you may have just answered a question I've had since we stumbled on Duran's goons watching you."

Distracted, she said, "That's how you found me? By finding them?"

"That's how. Not so unusual. He has better resources, or at least knows how to best use them. You weren't exactly hiding, but you weren't using your abilities in any way as to attract attention."

"So how did they find me?"

"I have no idea," Brodie confessed. "But the strength of your abilities may have something to do with it."

"You aren't filling me with a lot of confidence here, Guardian," Tasha told him.

"Just because I don't have all the answers doesn't mean I don't know how to keep you safe. Now, are you going to read me, or not? Because this won't work unless you at least believe I'm trying to help you."

Tasha hesitated for another moment but finally closed her eyes and very carefully lowered her walls. But as careful as she was, she was immediately slammed by the thoughts of those all around her, thoughts and fragments of thoughts she had to pick her way around and through.

They so need a new cook in this place, this muffin sucks.

. . . really don't know why I should listen to his mother . . .

. . . and if I'm really convincing, he's probably good for another thousand at least . . .

. . . thinks she can take my kids . . .

. . . should have spoken up at the meeting, dammit, they'll never notice me at this rate . . .

I can trade my car in for something cheaper, and that'll help.

. . . poor little thing . . .

Christ, you've never heard of tipping the waitstaff?

. . . how anyone could be so cruel to something so helpless . . .

Why do they keep sending me so damned many catalogs?

. . . why he thinks I have to go to church . . . sitting in church doesn't make me a Christian any more than sitting in a garage makes me a car, and it doesn't make him one either.

First thing tomorrow I'll just ask for the raise, they can only say no, right?

. . . something back on my taxes this year, so . . .

I really should just kill the bitch.

———————

"Wow," Astrid said softly, her eyes still closed.

Duran remained at the window, but his head turned toward her.

"Now I know why you want her so badly."

"Are you in?" he asked.

"Almost. Give me a sec."

———————

. . . *shouldn't blame me* . . .

. . . *and one more bet won't break the bank* . . .

. . . *judge'll give me custody, I'm sure* . . .

Tasha?

She went very still and focused on that voice, not at all surprised that it "sounded" to her like his speaking voice, because that was usual, she had discovered. She methodically closed out the other voices, the other thoughts, until only that quiet question sat in her mind.

Tasha?

"Yes." She spoke aloud because it was less confusing to her.

So you can read me?

"Yes."

Okay. Look deeper.

Tasha hesitated, because she had looked beneath the level of surface thoughts only a few times in her life, and it had never been a pleasant experience.

Look deeper. You have to know. Have to understand. You have to trust me.

She drew a breath and braced herself, making what she knew would be a futile attempt to protect herself from what he had felt.

Everything he had felt.

That was something she hadn't told him. That it wasn't just thoughts she picked up from others.

It was emotions too.

There were jagged pictures, like pieces cut from a movie, a scene here, an action there. Calm moments. Desperate moments. Flashing past her, faster and faster, years of moments. Some in color, some in black and white. And with them came the pain and the loss, the anger and frustration, the brief triumphs and more lasting grief.

There was violence in his past, and danger, and a black rage and sorrow so deep and overwhelming she knew he had not yet dealt with it consciously.

So deep . . .

She was too deep.

It was dangerous to be so—

Tasha.

Something tugged at her.

Something pulled her even deeper, deeper than emotion and into a raw, primal place that was dark and terrifying.

You aren't Brodie. What're you doing in his mind?

At the extreme edge of her awareness, she thought Brodie became aware that something was wrong, became alarmed, but then she was pulled deeper still, and she no longer heard or felt him at all.

How are you doing this? It's his mind, I'm still there—

Are you? Are you really, Tasha?

She opened her eyes with a start. And she was no longer sitting in a chair outside the coffee shop. Instead, she found herself in what looked like a maze, with hedges towering much taller than she was, their branches reaching inward above her head, blocking out the light.

If there was light.

She stood at a junction, with mossy paths leading ahead of her, to the right of her, and to the left. And even from where she stood, she could see other junctions, paths leading off in many directions. Dim green tunnels that led to places she instinctively knew were very, very bad.

Oh, how do you know until you try, Tasha? Don't you want to explore what's possible? I know you're curious.

I want out of here.

Then find your way. Mocking. Careless.

Cruel.

She was being tugged toward the left and wanted to resist the guidance, but something told her that fighting this—whatever *this* was—would make it far harder on her.

Smart girl.

Who the hell are you?

Don't you mean what *am I?*

You're another telepath, you think I don't know that?

If you know that, then you must know who I am.

Tasha turned to the left and began walking, feeling colder with every step, aware that there was less and less light. And when she concentrated, probed, when she tried to find identity in that strange voice, all she found were . . .

Shadows. Shadows all around you. I can't see you. But you're there, aren't you? Hidden by the shadows. Protected by them.

Well, I wouldn't go that far. Hidden, yes.

But not protected?

Hidden because it suits them. Can't you feel them, Tasha? Don't you know what they are?

No. No, just . . . shadows. Sliding away whenever I try to get closer to them.

Just as well, I suppose.

Why? Why is it just as well?

Because they're killing you, Tasha. Right now, this very minute, they're killing you.

SEVEN

Without opening her eyes, Astrid asked, "How far . . . do you want me to take this?"

"As far as she'll let you."

"She's strong."

"Be stronger."

———

Tasha ignored the growing chill and kept walking.

Nobody's killing me. I'm inside a mind.

You're open. Vulnerable. You dropped your shields and let us in. Don't you know about pathways, Tasha? You touch another mind, and the contact forms a path between you. Like the one you're walking now.

I'm in a maze. A huge maze.

Well, you've touched a lot of minds in your life. Apparently. Every mind you touched formed a pathway. For some reason, this deeply a psychic's mind almost always visualizes that as a maze.

Tasha reached a crosspath and turned right this time.

You're moving away from the center.

I know. I want the exit. I don't need to see what's at the center.

Don't you?

No.

Even if that's where I want you to be?

Especially if that's where you want me to be.

So distrustful.

You told me I was being killed. I'm supposed to trust you?

Look at your hands, Tasha. At your wrists.

She looked. And saw slashes across both wrists, with bright red blood flowing from the wounds. But there was no pain at all.

It's not real. I'm in Brodie's mind.

You're getting weaker. Can't you feel it?

No.

What she felt, what she saw, was green tendrils reaching out from the hedges on either side of her, wrapping her wrists and then slipping free of the bushes. They were warm in this cold place.

They gave her strength somehow. She could feel it.

Every step is harder than the one before. Your feet seem to weigh twenty pounds each. Thirty. Fifty.

Her feet did feel heavier, but the bands on her wrists

had stopped the flow of blood, stopped her, somehow, from being so easily controlled by that other presence. Tasha wondered, but only briefly.

She was pretty sure she knew what the tendrils were. What they represented.

It was a surprise—and yet it wasn't. It felt right. It made sense.

Though she didn't know if Brodie was going to agree.

Feeling stronger, Tasha followed the path, refusing to stop.

I want out of here. I'll get out of here.

Will you?

Brodie doesn't know, does he? she asked that inner voice suddenly. And in response she was certain of surprise, of hesitation.

I don't know what you mean.

Of course you do. Or maybe only Duran knows. Maybe you should ask him what I mean.

It was getting even easier to walk, step by step, and Tasha realized the voice in her mind, its force and control, could be . . . distracted. Maybe even blocked, its hold on her weakened. Perhaps even broken. She had a feeling Duran didn't know that.

She wondered if he'd be told.

What are you trying to do, Tasha? Do you think I'd let someone like you, someone who doesn't even know how to use her abilities, try to control what's happening here?

I think you don't want me to dwell on what I've just realized.

And what is that, pray tell?

This struggle, this war, it isn't only a thing of the physical world, a visible thing. It isn't even that. This is where the real battles are taking place, isn't it?

Tasha slipped around another corner, certain now of where she was heading, of how to get out of the maze.

Out of Brodie's mind.

I don't know what you mean.

Sure you do. We have all the power here. Psychics. But we tend to be loners, and that makes us vulnerable. To people like Duran, people who would use us. Duran has harnessed your power to do his bidding. He wants mine too. He's testing me, isn't he?

Definite surprise that time.

I don't—

Oh, don't waste my time as well as yours denying it. He sent you to test me. He wants to know how strong I am. And . . . he isn't psychic, is he? He isn't . . . And, somehow, that's what all this is about.

Tasha looked at her wrists again, at the warm leafy tendrils wrapping them. No blood, no slashes. Her step was lighter, faster, with nothing weighing her down or holding her back. She turned another corner, and could see a break in the hedge not far ahead of her.

The exit.

Tasha—

Are you going to tell him how powerful I really am?

Why wouldn't I?

Because you're still psychic. Still one of us.

No. I'm not. Not anymore. Not for a long time now.

Did you go willingly . . . Astrid? Did you join them of your own free will?

Of my own free will. More or less. Grim now.

Did you sell your soul to them, Astrid?

You're out of your depth, Tasha. You may think you can win this, but you can't. None of you can. None of us. There's less . . . damage done if you just give in.

You keep telling yourself that, Astrid. Maybe one day you'll actually believe it.

Abruptly, the air changed, cold washing over Tasha again, and she realized that Astrid wasn't distracted anymore, that she was reaching out with ferocity. With anger.

No. Wait. You—

Tasha felt a sudden tug, so powerful it nearly stopped her in her tracks, but then the tendrils around her wrists shot out, one end still holding her and the other finding the exit.

And pulling her toward it.

Tasha—

See you next time, Astrid.

Before that other presence could even gather itself to respond, Tasha was whisked around the corner.

And everything went dark and still.

Tasha?

Tasha?

"Tasha?"

She opened her eyes slowly, the effort demanding total concentration. Her body felt heavy, impossibly tired, and the brightness of the sunlight hurt her eyes. For a moment, she couldn't really focus. But, finally, she did.

A sidewalk table at the coffee shop. Brodie sitting across from her, leaning toward her, his face intent.

She looked at her wrists, at his fingers wrapping them warmly.

"Yeah," she said, her voice husky. "Yeah, that's what I thought they were. Your hands. Thank you, Brodie."

"For what?" His expression remained intent, and he didn't release her wrists.

"For saving my life, I think. At least the part of my life that really matters to me."

———

Astrid accepted the handkerchief Duran gave her and held it to her nose. Her still-bleeding nose.

"Well?"

Her head was pounding in a way she knew was going to linger, possibly for days. For a moment, she wasn't sure how to answer his demand, but Duran wasn't a man to whom silence was an acceptable answer, so she finally said, "Remember that thing that happened with Sarah Gallagher and Tucker Mackenzie?"

"Of course I do."

"I think you may have the same sort of problem with Tasha Solomon. And Brodie."

"They haven't mated."

"No. Still."

"That's impossible. He isn't psychic."

"No. He isn't, is he? Or, at least . . . he wasn't." Astrid held the cloth to her nose and looked at Duran, feeling despite everything a flicker of real enjoyment. "That's what makes it all so very interesting."

Tasha was somewhat surprised that no one around them seemed to have noticed anything out of the ordinary going on.

"You didn't make a sound," Brodie said, finally releasing her wrists. "Just turned about five different shades of pale and almost stopped breathing. That's when I grabbed your wrists."

She looked at him, still feeling impossibly tired. "Did you just read my mind?"

He looked surprised. "Did I?"

"You know, I think you did. Pathways. Maybe they don't just form between psychics. Maybe that's it. Or maybe because I was so deep. I bet they didn't count on that. I bet Duran is not going to be at all pleased. Even if it was his idea."

She wondered why everything around her, including Brodie, seemed to be just slightly . . . out of focus, somehow. Was this something the other psychic had thrown at her in those final seconds? Was it because she had been so deep in Brodie's mind? Or because she had actually been somewhere else, some place out of time and space where a psychic would always, instinctively, go to forge pathways? Or look for them?

"We need to leave," Brodie said. "Right now. Your apartment is closest."

"Okay."

Except there was no way she was going to be able to get up under her own steam. Because she didn't have any steam. She wanted to sleep for about a week. And then take a nap.

Brodie left a few bills on the table, setting his coffee cup on top of them, then came around and more or less lifted her out of her chair.

"Better?" he asked after a moment.

"I think so." The dizziness had passed. Mostly. She thought she could walk. As long as he didn't let go of her, at any rate.

He kept an arm around her as they walked across the streets to her building.

"You are definitely reading my mind," she told him.

"Let's not discuss this until we're in your condo, okay?"

"Right. Right. Civilians." She fished in the shoulder bag that had somehow ended up hanging from her shoulder and produced her keycard. "Gotta swipe this. And then the code."

"Yeah, I know." He continued to hold her upright as they reached the front entrance of her building. "I just hope security doesn't think I slipped you a mickey."

"Slipped me a mickey. That's an old phrase. You like old movies, don't you?"

"I rarely have a chance to watch the newer stuff. Tasha, it'll look better on the security monitors if you swipe the card and enter the code yourself. Can you do that?"

"Of course I can." She managed, though didn't doubt that she might easily appear to be . . . impaired.

Brodie got them through the door when it buzzed. And as soon as they were in the lobby, the one security guard manning the front desk was on his feet, eyeing them.

"Hey, Ms. Solomon," he said. "Are you okay?"

She peered at him. "Stewart. Hey, Stewart. Yeah, I'm okay. I mean, I got dizzy. So it's a good thing my friend John was with me."

"Yes, ma'am. Sir, if you wouldn't mind—"

"Not at all." Brodie produced an ID card.

His driver's license, Tasha thought. She watched the guard study the card carefully.

"I really am all right," she told him. "Not drunk or drugged or anything like that. Just really tired. I didn't sleep well last night."

Stewart handed the card back to Brodie, still clearly undecided for a moment, then said, "I hope you can get some rest, then, Ms. Solomon."

"That is a very good idea. I will do that." Even to herself, Tasha thought she sounded out of it, to say the least, and added what she hoped was a reassuring parting comment. "John is going to stay with me, so everything will be just fine."

"Yes, ma'am."

In the elevator, Brodie said dryly, "Bet he's either on the phone or on the computer checking me out as we speak. Former cops are always the most suspicious. Not that I blame him. I'm not entirely sure what happened at the coffee shop, but you really are out of it. He has every reason to worry about you and to make sure I'm not on the books as a serial killer or rapist or something."

"Then I hope your record is clean," she told him seriously.

"It is."

"Good. But they often aren't, you know. On the books. Serial killers and rapists. I mean, lots are caught, but lots more fly below the radar until somebody finally realizes what they are. And by then the body count can be . . . really high." She blinked up at him. "I used to work for a lawyer."

"It shows," Brodie told her, polite.

"And you'd know," she heard herself saying. "You used to be a lawyer, didn't you?"

He nodded slowly. "You get that out of my mind?"

"I guess." She thought about it. "I guess I had to."

The elevator doors opened on the third floor, and Brodie kept his arm around her all the way down the hallway to her apartment. She managed to unlock her door without his help, which she supposed was a good thing given that Stewart was probably still watching them.

"So how did they miss the goon squad the other night?" Brodie mused. "We've never been sure how they get into secure buildings, but they have it down to an art."

"Magic," she offered.

"Smoke and mirrors? Maybe so." He opened the door and continued to partially support her as they went inside. Brodie paused just a moment in the entrance hall, his free hand slipping into the pocket of his jacket.

Tasha felt something. She wasn't sure what it was, but something told her some kind of device had been activated.

"What did you just do?" she asked, dropping her bag and keys on the table.

"I just jammed the signal," he said.

"Signal? What signal?"

"The one coming from the cameras the goon squad planted in your apartment before they left."

Tasha stepped away from him, suddenly more alert. "What? They left cameras?"

"I'll have to check to be sure, but probably. They usually do if one of their visits doesn't net them the psychic they're after."

"But I never saw—"

"They're very small, Tasha. They can be stuck on a wall at the edge of a picture frame or mirror, under a bookshelf. You have to know what to look for."

"They've been watching me. They've been watching me? All the time since then?"

He eyed her. "They aren't watching you anymore, I can promise you that. Look, I think you really do need to rest. Why don't you take a nap?"

"It's not even noon. I think."

"I'm betting you really haven't been sleeping well, not since their visit, at least. And after what happened at the coffee shop, you definitely need to rest."

"I don't think I can. Cameras . . ."

"I'll check the bedroom for cameras, and you'll see me get rid of them. Then you can rest. I'll stay here, watch TV or something. And reassure the security guard when he shows up in a few minutes to check on you."

"You think he'll do that?"

"I'd be disappointed if he didn't."

Tasha didn't wait to find out. She was able to stay awake long enough to examine the elegant cameras, no larger than the little chalk boxes used on pool sticks; Brodie found two in her bedroom, one hidden on a picture frame and one under a bookshelf. But none in the bathroom.

"Why?" she asked him. "I mean—I'm glad, but why?"

"No idea. Maybe the sight of naked people offends them." Under her stare, he relented. "We think it has to do with all the tile in most bathrooms, and the plumbing. Not sure just how; you can get cameras similar to these in electronics stores and they work most anywhere, but these are a lot more sophisticated than what the average consumer finds. Sometimes being more sophisticated is a weakness, not a strength."

Tasha handed the camera back to him. "Were they listening?"

"We think so. But everything's been deactivated now, I swear."

"In that case, I think I'll take a nap. Help yourself to whatever's in the fridge. There are a few take-out menus in the drawer by the stove, most from places open on Sundays. Just buzz the security desk if you're expecting a delivery."

"Got it." He eased out of the bedroom. "Rest as long as you need to. I'll be here when you wake up."

"Thanks." Tasha thought it was rather remarkable that she felt comfortable enough to go to sleep with a relative stranger in the apartment. Then again, she was pretty sure she knew John Brodie a lot better than she would ever know most anyone else in her life.

Deciding to think about that later, she pushed the door to but didn't close it completely, shed her clothes and pulled on a comfortable sleep shirt, and crawled into bed.

There were naps . . . and then there were *naps*.

––––––

"So you're in?" Murphy asked when she checked in with Brodie a bit after noon.

"I'm in."

It was difficult to read nuances over cell phones sometimes, but . . . "That was brief even for you," she observed.

"Nothing else to say. Yet, at any rate. They had planted cameras in the apartment. I disabled them."

"And Solomon's asleep?"

"Yeah. Hasn't been sleeping much, I gather."

"Not a surprise."

"No."

She had worked with Brodie for years, and aside from her extra senses Murphy was also highly intuitive when it came to people. So she knew he was bothered by something. And in their world, being bothered by something was seldom a matter best kept to oneself.

"What happened?" she asked bluntly. "Something out of the ordinary, I'm guessing?"

He was silent just long enough to make it obvious, then said slowly, "She needed to read me to know she could trust me."

"Yeah, we both knew she would. And?"

"She's . . . powerful. Read deep, and I mean deep. Quick. Thorough. Even touched a few places I don't believe any of our psychics have touched before." He didn't explain that intriguing bit, just continued in a voice just this side of grim. "But then something else happened."

"What?"

"I'm not quite sure. It was almost like . . . she was in my mind, but somewhere else as well, almost like she went through a doorway and into a dark place where I couldn't see or sense her. That's never happened before when I'm being read or scanned."

"She wasn't still there, in your mind?"

"I honestly don't know. For a while, I couldn't sense anything. Then I got the strong feeling she was in trouble. And somehow, I was able to find her, reach her. Hold on to her."

After a moment, Murphy said slowly, "A few psychics have reported that when they dropped their shields and read one of our Guardians initially, they were pulled deeper, seemingly by a third party. Into some kind of dark maze."

"That's the first I've heard of it."

"Well, it's never happened with you before, right? So there was no reason for you to know. Especially since we don't know what it means. The few psychics reporting that said it wasn't really a big maze, but a dark one, and that they felt compelled to follow a voice urging them toward the center of the maze."

"One of Duran's psychics?"

"That seems to be the consensus. One of his testing

one of the psychics we find, early on before our psychics know they can trust us. Almost like they were . . . given a choice. Trust us—or go over to the dark side."

Brodie didn't appear to find that melodramatic. In fact, he sounded grim when he said, "Not being psychic has its disadvantages. Still, I can sense a psychic when I'm being read or scanned—at least as far as I know—so why didn't I know someone else was there?"

"Not sure. Does Tasha know?"

"I think she knows something, but there hasn't been a chance to discuss it."

"She came out of it trusting you?"

"Yeah, I'm sure of that. But it drained her, and she was pretty out of it. She did say something about pathways, and Duran not being pleased."

"Nobody's ever been able to read Duran."

"I know that."

"Think she did?"

"No, I think it was something else. Something to do with the other psychic apparently communicating with her. I'm hoping Tasha will be a lot clearer-minded when she wakes up."

"If she knows something helpful, I hope she is too."

"I'll let you know."

A little amused despite everything, Murphy said, "Well, since you're there, I think I'll take a nap myself. And I'll keep watch over the exterior of her building tonight while you do your Guardian thing."

"I didn't say I'd be here tonight."

"No. You didn't. Then again, you didn't have to."

EIGHT

"The cameras have been disabled, sir," Alastair reported.

"Of course they have. No doubt the first thing Brodie did when he entered her apartment."

"Yes, sir." Alastair waited patiently, without fidgeting; like certain sentries in very visible posts around the world, he was capable of standing still as a statue for a long time.

Which, working for Duran, was something that came in handy more often than not.

Several minutes passed.

Finally, Duran said, "The watchers around her building. Pull them back another two blocks."

"They won't be able to see the building at all. Sir."

Duran lifted his gaze from the papers before him, those odd green eyes of his unreadable. "Do you think I'm not aware of that information, Alastair?"

"I'm sure you are, sir. Apologies. I'll send the order to the watchers immediately."

"Yes. Do that."

Alastair slipped from the office, without visible haste but without wasting a moment. All the while reminding himself yet again that it just wasn't wise to question an order from Duran.

Ever.

Alone in the very nice suite on the top floor of the hotel his team had rented for the duration, Duran sat at his desk frowning in thought. It wasn't an expression he usually allowed his team to see—and most certainly not one he allowed his superiors to see—but he was alone for the moment, and for the first time in a long while, he was more than a little disturbed.

He had grown accustomed to the fact that their psychics often had problems reading new psychics, especially in the early days before their resistance was broken down. But he was looking down at two names of new psychics one of his telepaths had been able, to a degree, to read. And both had thoughts of the same person in their minds. The same man. A man both had been convinced could help them, if they could only reach him. With their minds, their abilities.

Bishop.

Duran wasn't at all sure they were wrong about that. It was something he had considered a possible danger for some years now, though he had hoped Bishop would be too busy with his own team and the considerable dangers they faced on a daily basis to even be aware anything else was going on among the rest of the psychic population.

He should have known better.

And now he was left with the worry that Bishop knew at least something about them, about what was going on, that he was likely to make contact with at least one of those opposing them, and . . .

And what? That was the problem. Duran wasn't at all sure what Bishop would do if he knew what was going on. What he could do. And whether he was powerful enough to discover a truth they had managed to hide for decades.

All Duran really knew was that two psychics taken very recently had recent thoughts of Bishop on their minds.

And no matter which way he looked at it, that was not good.

————

Tasha was reasonably sure she had been asleep a long time, because night had fallen and her bedroom was lamplit. She could hear, dimly, the TV in the living room, too low to bother her. She felt rested and very relaxed.

Very, very relaxed.

And too comfortable to even stir when a lovely woman with long, dark hair emerged from the shadows near the closet and settled into the chair near the foot of Tasha's bed.

"Hello," Tasha murmured.

"I need you to listen to me, Tasha," the woman said, her voice quiet and serene. "It's very important."

"It must be," Tasha responded, her own voice soft. "Because you're here. You came a long way, didn't you?"

"Yes. And I can't stay long. So you have to listen, and remember. I can help you understand."

"Understand?"

"Understand them. Understand what you're up against. And understand him."

"Okay. I'm listening."

The woman nodded. "I was born Elizabeth Lyon, only child of Roger and Patricia Lyon, in Seattle. My parents were very wealthy, and they loved me very much.

"But I was different. I sometimes heard things I soon learned no one else heard, whispers in my head that told me what other people were thinking or feeling."

"Me, too," Tasha said.

"I know. But I didn't learn to hide it as you did, Tasha. My parents were often baffled by me, and worried that my abilities would set me apart from others all my life. Being wealthy, they explored what options were open to them and me at the time, meeting with avowed psychics and with researchers studying what was then most commonly called ESP.

"It was shortly after this period, just a few days before my tenth birthday, that I was kidnapped. I never saw my captors and was kept unconscious for several days, drugged so deeply that even my psychic abilities slept and told me nothing. When I awakened, it was in a hospital with both my parents leaning over my bed. I remembered nothing of what had happened to me. If anything had. I had no injuries.

"Though I didn't know it at the time, to get me back my parents had made a bargain with my captors. They might as well have made a bargain with the devil.

"For several years, my life seemed little changed, except that my parents seemed to worry more about my safety. And something else. I was visited once or twice each month by a *friend* of my parents, a very handsome young man named Eliot Wolfe. He, too, was psychic, and he wanted to guide me, to teach me how to use my abilities. It was what my parents wanted and I was entirely willing."

"Did he help you?" Tasha was listening intently.

"Perhaps. He was the only person in my life who understood my abilities, understood what I was going through in learning to master them. And—I thought I was in love with him."

"How old were you?"

"When he first began visiting, I was seventeen."

"Crush?" Tasha guessed.

"Looking back, yes, of course. Though you couldn't have convinced me of that then. All I can tell you for certain is that my feelings for him blinded me all through the remainder of my teen years.

"But as I matured, both my instincts and my strengthening psychic abilities told me there was something wrong, something hidden from me in my life."

"You sensed it?"

"I sensed something wrong. And there were snatches of conversations I overheard, discussions interrupted when I entered a room. Gradually, I came to believe that my parents and Eliot were hiding things from me. I tried more than once to focus my abilities on that suspicion, but it wasn't until just after my graduation from high school that I was able to break through the walls they had built around me.

"What I discovered on that horrible night was so unbelievable, so shocking, that I could only run, try to escape. What else could I do? The man I had believed I loved was a soulless monster, intended to become my mate so that we might breed and produce psychic offspring.

"It was what my parents had agreed to in order to save my life. The deal they had made."

———————

Murphy was not Alastair, and there was a distinct snap to her voice when she told Duran, "This was not part of the plan. You weren't supposed to test her so soon."

"Not part of my plan," he agreed. "I do wonder about yours, though."

She ignored that. "I told you there was something different about contacting Solomon telepathically. Something unpredictable, maybe even unstable, but she has a lot of power."

"Uncontrolled?"

"Not exactly. She has a lot of control too, it's just that she isn't entirely aware of just how powerful she really is. And that's a dangerous thing."

"Yes. You also told me Brodie wasn't psychic."

"He isn't."

"Perhaps he wasn't, but something has changed. With Tasha Solomon, at any rate."

"That's what Astrid says?"

"She says the telepathic contact was unusually deep. And that Brodie responded. That he helped Solomon. Kept her from losing strength and helped her escape the maze."

"Before she got to the center?"

"Yes."

Murphy wasn't often disconcerted. "I didn't know anybody could do that. Huh. No wonder he didn't have much to say later on."

"I imagine he's . . . learning to cope."

She frowned. "I don't like it. You shouldn't have pushed her, not like that, not this soon. John's been in this a long time, and we both know what's been driving him. If Tasha Solomon becomes more than just another wounded psychic he needs to protect, if she becomes more than that to him . . . He could take her and go to ground. After ten years in this, he may be more than ready to do just that. And if he wants to disappear, wants both of them to disappear, especially to protect her, nobody on either side is ever going to find them."

"You seem very sure of that."

"I am. Unless you're holding one hell of an ace up your sleeve, Brodie alone would be more dangerous than you can imagine if he chose to, if he stopped being a Guardian and chose to fight. Really fight. Or disappear. Either way, we both know I can't afford to lose Brodie or Solomon. And neither can you."

"Solomon's abilities are that formidable?"

"Astrid didn't tell you?"

"She told me there was a lot of power, and that some kind of connection had been made with Brodie."

Murphy wondered just how much of the contact Astrid had kept to herself. And why. She also wondered if Duran was being straight with her; that was *always* a question mark.

"Solomon can do things, Duran, things she isn't even aware she can do. If you push her, if *anyone* pushes her too hard . . . she could destroy herself and anyone near her. We've both seen that happen before."

He heard something in her voice. "Or?"

"Or . . . she could be the supreme you've been searching for. The psychic able to tip the balance in your favor."

It wasn't often Duran's calm face showed expression, but he was very clearly surprised by that. "Astrid didn't feel it in her."

I wonder. "She wouldn't have. I know how much you use and value your favorite psychic, but news for you: Astrid has her limits, just like everybody else. And her blind spots."

"But you were able to feel . . . possibilities . . . in Solomon."

"I got physically closer. Maybe that made the difference."

He frowned. "You aren't connected with Brodie?"

"Are you kidding? Nobody's ever been able to connect with Brodie, not like that. Read him, yes, when he allows it. But not connect to him. Unless Astrid's right and Tasha Solomon has."

"Brodie has experience with psychics."

"Not like this, he doesn't. If she did connect with him, then he'll be feeling something different, and given time he could figure out what it is. Maybe even figure a way to use it against you. But I doubt he has a clue right now. I doubt Solomon does either. I'm betting they're both . . . overwhelmed."

"His wife was psychic."

"I know that. And I know she connected with him on a deep level, but I have no idea if that connection formed a pathway."

"I know. It didn't."

She wondered how he knew, but didn't ask.

A question for later.

"Well, if Solomon went that deep, we can both bet something changed in Brodie. In both of them. How that change will manifest is . . . anybody's guess. Especially if some kind of a pathway was forged between them."

"That was Astrid's take. She's not entirely sure just how, but is certain a pathway was created."

"One way?"

"She says not."

Murphy's brows rose. "If that's the case, we have more than one problem. Solomon's abilities, at least when I touched them, were powerful but not being used for anything except defense. No deep emotion has ever pushed her to explore her own limits. But Brodie . . . there is a lot of rage in him, and he's lost too much already. As calm as he usually appears, he *is* driven by emotion; it's at the core of everything he does. A mental or emotional pathway between him and Solomon, especially if she's as powerful as we believe she is, could supply the strong emotional drive she's never really had. His. It'll likely give her even more power, and much more incentive to test her own limits. And it would mean something else as well. It would mean that all Brodie's experiences in this to date will be viewed through an entirely new set of eyes. He'll have a better idea just what's at stake. And *that* means he is not going to let anyone he cares about be harmed or taken away again."

"The thought had occurred."

"Which means you'll never bring Solomon over. Whether she's strong enough to resist, or could even be safely brought over given the power she possesses, may well be a moot point. *Is* a moot point if she really connected with him. Brodie won't let it happen."

Duran said, "I don't give up easily, Murphy."

"Neither does Brodie. In fact, he doesn't give up at all. That isn't in him, to give up. Not when he really cares. He's stronger than you, Duran."

"You think so?" Duran seemed mildly curious.

"I know so. He was before he met Solomon. And now, if he can tap her abilities in any way . . . if he's connected to her . . . Well, we both know that's an edge you just don't have."

"Perhaps," Duran said. "We'll see, won't we?"

———

Tasha felt deeply disturbed, and on a skin-crawling level she had never felt before. "They . . . sold you? They planned to just hand you over to . . . to breed more psychics?"

"They didn't understand." Elizabeth Lyon's voice was

quiet. "And they didn't understand the worst of what they had done. They had also pledged themselves to aiding the ruthless, secretive organization Eliot belonged to, even though they knew their help would result in the death or destruction of other psychics."

"That's . . . horrible."

"Yes. I couldn't hate them for choosing to save my life whatever the cost, but I could no longer love them for it. I chose to begin a new life, alone, that very night. I had a little money left to me by my grandmother, enough to get by, if I was careful. And I had learned a few things by watching my father get what he wanted; I knew how to find resources. It was a simple matter to get forged identification in a new name.

"I became Elizabeth Storm. It seemed apt."

"And you disappeared?"

"As far as my family and Eliot knew, yes. I gained admission to a small college in the midwest, and there my new life settled into a kind of peace. I had a part-time job and made new friends. I was never quite able to stop looking over my shoulder, and I had to guard myself every minute in order not to reveal my abilities, but I knew that I was as safe as I could possibly be. At least . . . I thought so."

"But you weren't." It wasn't a guess.

"No. I began to feel . . . watched. But before I could really focus on that and try to determine if it was really true, at the beginning of my senior year in college, I met John Brodie."

Tasha blinked. "Oh. Brodie is the *him* you mentioned. One of the reasons why I need to know all this."

"Yes."

"It feels . . . He should tell me himself. Shouldn't he?"

"He won't. Not, at least, for a long time. And you need to know this now. But you mustn't tell him you know, at least not yet."

"When?"

"You'll know when the time is right."

Tasha was still reluctant, but nodded slowly.

Elizabeth went on with her story.

"John was . . . amazing. He was a law student. Brilliant, handsome, and stronger than any man I had ever known. He won my heart so quickly it was almost terrifying. And it was the same way with him, I knew that. We had a connection, a bond, from the very first time we touched, and it only grew stronger as the days passed."

"A psychic bond?" For some reason, Tasha really wanted to know that.

"No. We never connected in that way. But I had to be honest with him, at least as honest as I could be given the facts, so I told him two of the secrets of my life. That I was a psychic, and that I had broken with my family and changed my name. He loved me and asked no questions beyond what I was willing to talk about. I loved him, but . . . I had lived with the secrets for so long that it was difficult to confide in, even trust, just because I loved."

"That must have been tough," Tasha said.

"Yes. But we both thought we had plenty of time. Plenty of time for confidences, for secrets. John wanted me to tell him only what I was ready to tell him."

"You didn't tell him about Eliot?"

"No. Not about Eliot, and not about his organization. Not about what they had planned for me. It all sounded so . . . unbelievable. And even though I knew John loved me, I didn't think he would believe me. That's what I told myself, at least, though I know now that at least part of my reluctance was a bone-deep certainty that the knowledge would put him in danger."

"It probably would have." Tasha tried to console, even knowing she couldn't. Knowing it was too late for that.

"Maybe. Anyway, I was able to put it out of my mind. There was so much else to think about. We married just after I graduated college. I got a job teaching while John finished law school. It was a good life. A happy life." She drew a breath. "I can pinpoint the day things began to change. The day I made another choice I was to bitterly regret."

Tasha didn't ask, just waited silently.

"It seemed a simple thing at first. Another psychic recognized me as a kindred spirit, something psychics can often do. She asked me for help. Pleaded, really. She was young, frightened. She hardly understood her abilities, or knew what to do with them, and was having trouble hiding them. I had to help her."

"Of course you did."

"That was how it began. They came to me quietly, one or two at a time, asking for my help. A surprising number of them, as the months went by. That seemed odd, but I didn't question it at the time. They needed help, and I had learned a lot in my life about my abilities.

"There was no place else for them to go, no one else they could turn to who understood what they were going through. As a cover, I formed a 'study group,' and we met two or three times a week after regular classes. John patiently accepted my absences and secretiveness; I don't think he understood, not completely, but he loved me and respected my need to be independent."

"That's what he thought was going on?"

"From things he said now and then, I think so."

"And he was busy too."

"Oh, very. We didn't have a lot of time together, but we made it count. Those are some of my best memories."

"But then something else happened?" Tasha guessed.

"Yes. I had made many good and lasting friends through my 'study' group. One in particular, a girl in her first year of college, became an especially good friend. And she was an unusually powerful psychic, with great potential. It was out of concern for her that I told her what had happened to me, the fate that had been planned for me, something I had never told anyone else, not even John."

"How did she react?"

"She was shocked. Frightened. And, I felt sure, just a bit disbelieving. Because it all sounded so incredible. I couldn't blame her for that. Someone was . . . breeding psychics? What kind of sense did that make? What kind of reasoning could be behind it? But I had told her, and there was no taking that information back. So I swore her to secrecy, and life went on.

"I suppose it was inevitable that, as our secretive circle grew wider and wider, it would come to include someone connected to the vast organization to which Eliot belonged.

But when the betrayal came, it was so sudden and unexpected that it caught me completely off guard."

Tasha was almost afraid to ask. "What happened?"

"Two people dropped suddenly out of our group and vanished. One of them was someone I'd been feeling uneasy about for reasons I couldn't even explain to myself. The other was the girl in whom I'd confided my story. A few days passed, and I became more and more concerned. And then . . .

"I was supposed to meet John for lunch that day. He was late, which wasn't unusual, so I waited. It was at a sidewalk café in Boston, one of our favorite spots. I was enjoying the fall day, the cool breeze. Fretting about my missing friends, but kids drop out of college all the time, so I couldn't assume they hadn't done just that. And then . . .

"And then Eliot suddenly sat down across the table."

———

Bishop leaned back in his chair, staring grimly at the laptop open on the desk before him. "Goddammit," he said quietly.

Miranda had seen her husband's computer skills many times, but both the speed and complexity of his work over the last couple of hours had impressed her—and momentarily pushed aside the question of what had disturbed him. "Tell me you didn't just hack into the DOD," she said.

He turned his head and looked at her, a faint smile lightening his expression. "The Department of Defense has some of the best and strongest firewalls in the entire cyberworld. Sensible, given the sort of information they routinely handle."

"Noah."

"No, I didn't just hack into the DOD." He paused, adding, "I have clearance, actually. But that wasn't where I was."

"It looked like it."

"Supposed to. A number of the psychics I've kept in touch with over the years wanted a safe and secure way to contact me if they had to. If they were in trouble, or otherwise needed my help. It would have been easy enough to create a private e-mail account a lot more secure than the average person feels the need for, but . . ."

"You wanted real security."

Bishop nodded. "So . . . I piggybacked onto the DOD, in a sense. Created a safe and very, very secure area inside those firewalls, undetectable by the DOD's system, where each of them could leave me messages. None of them could communicate with each other, just me. Individual passwords, codes, all they needed to get through the firewalls and make contact with me without alerting anyone else. And I set it up so that if one of them *did* leave me a message, the program would send an innocent e-mail alert to my FBI account."

"What sort of alert?"

"A note supposedly from a friend in law enforcement here in the South. Very innocent, nothing to send up flags."

"Except to you."

"Yeah. I can't always be close to the laptop all the time,

of course, but I check that account several times every day, and have the laptop set up to alert me with a tone if that note lands in my inbox even when I'm not online or if it's the middle of the night."

Miranda shook her head. "I thought you just plugged in your laptop in the bedroom every night to recharge it. Even with our connection . . . I had no idea what was really going on. It's an automatic thing now, isn't it? Something you don't think about."

"I suppose. It's something I set up a couple of years before I found you again, when I was actively searching for psychics for the unit. And for you."

"I have to say . . . it's not entirely a bad thing to find out we still have our secrets even with the connection. Is it?"

He eyed her. "Trying to tell me something?"

Miranda smiled. "A little mystery is good for a relationship. That's all."

"Uh-huh." He gazed at her a moment longer, then yanked his mind back to far more deadly mysteries. "Anyway, there've been no notes from Katie Swan—or Henry McCord."

"So his client was right in believing Henry has disappeared too?"

"Looks that way. And if the client has his days straight, Henry must have been taken about a week ago."

"They do move fast," Miranda said, sobered. "Henry last week, Katie this week. And there were two other psychics you were concerned about around the end of last year. Two more disappearances."

"Grace Seymore and Jeffrey Bell, clairvoyant and seer respectively. With Jeffrey, all the evidence pointed to him just up and moving, running away. He'd done it before, and the same thing was happening to him again. He tried to disappear into the woodwork, do his job and live quietly, but somebody got curious, looked into his background— and the whole circus started for him again. He couldn't escape the desperate people begging him for whatever it was they needed to know."

"So it looked like he packed up and left."

"Yeah. Grace Seymore, on the other hand, was a more troubling case, at least at the time. She's a born psychic, not triggered like Jeffrey by some kind of trauma. Her abilities had been getting stronger, and her control was erratic, but she was handling it. Mostly. Her second husband, apparently, couldn't. The divorce was barely final when she disappeared. A concerned coworker came to check on her and found everything as it should have been at her house. Nothing disturbed, nothing missing— except Grace. Her car was in the garage, keys in the house, cell phone showing no suspicious calls, house phone the same." He frowned again.

"What?" Miranda asked.

"The only odd thing, at least to me, was that her disappearance *looked* planned. But not obviously, if that makes any sense. She'd just gotten a nice inheritance from her grandmother's estate and used some of that to pay off her house. All of her utility bills were autopays, and there was plenty in the bank account to cover those debits, even for a year or more. Her cleaning service showed up every week to take care of the house; they'd been paid in advance for six months of weekly cleanings."

"The police didn't find *that* suspicious?"

"It wasn't unusual for her, according to the service. She'd been paying them ahead for the last couple of years. Her bank statements confirmed it. Friends said she didn't like dealing with bills and finances, so had streamlined as much as possible. It made sense, given what her friends and neighbors and coworkers said about her. There was absolutely nothing to make the police suspicious."

"Except that she was gone."

Bishop nodded. "I never even found the hint of a trail to follow. Her ex had moved out of the country more than two weeks before she disappeared, had a cast-iron alibi for those weeks. No family to speak of, and a couple of distant cousins we finally located hadn't heard from her in years. She was just gone. Then we got busy on the first of several difficult cases, and before I knew it my list of missing psychics was getting much too long to ignore."

"What happened with Grace's house?"

"Nothing. Her estate is large enough that she has both an attorney and a financial advisor, both honest. And they're just continuing on with the last instructions they were given. The attorney hired a property manager to look after her place and the financial advisor is taking care of investments—conservative—and banking proceeds as instructed. They both act as if she's coming back. And as far as the law is concerned, she could be. At least for the next seven years."

"Until she can be declared legally dead."

"Exactly."

"If Henry disappeared from a job he was working on," Miranda said, "and Grace disappeared from home, then we need to visit both places."

"Yeah. And both are in or near Charleston."

"That's convenient."

"Very," Bishop said. "For someone."

NINE

Brodie was restless. Tasha had slept all day and now into the early evening. Sleeping deeply. She hadn't even stirred when the security guard from downstairs had indeed come to check on her; Brodie had invited the guard in and even encouraged him to peek into the bedroom, which he had done. And since it was obvious Brodie had made himself comfortable in the living room, a sports event on TV and the scent of coffee apparent, the fixings for a sandwich out on the kitchen counter, the guard had relaxed and had left the condo reassured that Tasha was in no danger.

Not something Brodie agreed with, except that she was in no danger from him.

After what had happened at the coffee shop, he wasn't

sure of much else. The connection he apparently had with Tasha after she had looked into his mind had caught him completely off guard. Over the years, he had been "read" or "scanned" by many psychics he was aware of, and quite possibly a few he'd had no awareness of; like most non-psychics, his mind normally provided only minimal shielding against a psychic's probing, and he'd only ever been able to actually *feel* the most powerful psychics when they scanned him.

But today . . . that had been different. At first, no, the same, not really sensing a presence in his mind even though he had known she was there. But then something had changed. His own memories had begun to surface without his volition, passing before his mind's eye in scenes that moved faster and faster until they were only a blur.

Even more, he had begun to feel Tasha's presence, feel her absorbing not only the memories, but his emotions as well. Hell, he'd almost been able to *see* her in his mind, not flinching even though some of his darker emotions had struck her like actual physical blows. She felt what he had felt. All he had felt. That had been a strange, unsettling sensation, and his instinct had been to draw back, to preserve something of himself, retain some sense of personal privacy.

But then something else happened, something he couldn't explain even to himself. Tasha had gone deeper into his mind, below thought, vanishing into some dark place Brodie hadn't recognized as being part of himself.

Really didn't want to recognize if it *was* part of himself.

And if it wasn't . . . then what was it? Where was it?

All he knew was that the experience was a confusing jumble after that. Something about a dark, chilly maze and Tasha being trapped there.

"A few psychics have reported that when they dropped their shields and read one of our Guardians initially, they were pulled deeper, seemingly by a third party. Into some kind of dark maze."

"That's the first I've heard of it."

"Well, it's never happened with you before, right? So there was no reason for you to know. Especially since we don't know what it means. The few psychics reporting that said it wasn't really a big maze, but a dark one, and that they felt compelled to follow a voice urging them toward the center of the maze."

Was that the maze Murphy had spoken of? A maze to test the psychics Duran was interested in?

Inside his mind, and yet not. Tasha drawn deeper and deeper, until he could no longer see her. Another presence shadowing her, challenging her somehow. He had felt more than seen Tasha weakening, because she'd been in that dark place where he couldn't see her, and yet he had somehow felt what was happening to her and instinctively reached out to help her.

When his fingers had wrapped around her wrists, he had been conscious of the strangest feeling. He couldn't really describe it even to himself, except . . . he was connected. They were connected. Somehow a part of each other.

And closer than he had ever been to another human being in his life.

Closer than he had been even to Elizabeth.

————

"He found you," Tasha said.

"Yes. I knew better than to make a scene, but I asked how he had found me. He seemed to take great pleasure in telling me that the student I had been slightly wary of was, in fact, one of theirs. They were everywhere, he said. Sooner or later, one of them had been bound to find me. So he had waited.

"And . . . he thanked me. Because I had, through that agent of theirs, given them a very valuable psychic."

"The young powerful girl," Tasha said slowly.

"Yes. He said they had her."

"Jesus."

"It made me feel sick. Sick and helpless, because he kept talking to me as if what he'd told me didn't even matter. And what he was telling me then, was . . . terrifying. He was so calm, so matter-of-fact and sure of himself as he laid out my future.

"Quietly, reasonably. Implacably. Now that they had found me again, I wouldn't be allowed to go free. My path was with him, and I had to accept that. I was intended for him, he said. We were a genetic match. I could not escape my destiny. John didn't matter. My marriage didn't matter. I was intended for Eliot.

"He was psychic; I couldn't hide from him my revulsion or my soul-deep determination to do whatever was necessary to escape that fate. Even if it meant taking my incredible story public and making sure I could convince everyone it was true. That was in my mind. That was what he saw. That was the threat."

Feeling a bit queasy herself, Tasha said slowly, "I don't think I like where this is going."

Elizabeth sighed. "If I had only guessed . . . But I didn't. Even after what I had felt in Eliot, I didn't know how far they would go to make sure their secrets weren't revealed.

"Eliot got up and walked away. I should have remained where I was and waited for John. I should have stayed around people, because that offered me some protection, a truth you figured out for yourself. But I was frightened. I set out walking, taking a familiar shortcut across a park, meaning to meet John. Instead, I once again met Eliot. But this time, he had a gun."

Tasha couldn't say a word. She just lay there on her bed, on her side, and listened to the dark, lovely woman Brodie had loved.

"I don't remember the shot," Elizabeth said almost conversationally. "Not even the sound of it. I remember a blow to my chest that knocked me backward, and it was dark for a time. Very dark. Then I heard John's voice calling me, and for a moment I could open my eyes, for a moment I could see his face. Just for a moment."

Tasha was silent for several heartbeats, then said slowly, "I guess the rest is obvious."

"I guess it is. My name is Elizabeth Lyon Brodie, and on the twelfth day of September ten years ago, I died."

"And Brodie became a man with a mission."

"Yes. Protecting people like you. Saving people like you. Because he couldn't save me."

Duran didn't follow Murphy when she left him, though he did change his own location, taking the usual precautions. The meeting had given him much food for thought, and though he had not, he trusted, revealed much to Murphy, he'd been left feeling more than a little grim.

Brodie had always been a worthy opponent, and if Duran had privately considered them more equal than many in either his or Brodie's organization, he had told himself it was simply because theirs really *was* a level playing field; between the two of them, it would always come down to a battle of wits, intelligence, strength, and strategy.

And, of course, sheer determination.

But if Brodie could tap into a psychic's abilities . . . especially *this* psychic's, Tasha Solomon's . . .

That changed things.

That changed important things.

And even more so if Bishop had indeed become aware, perhaps even involved. Because he could cause them a great deal of trouble without having to do very much at all, positioned as he was inside the FBI.

Even the possibility caused Duran to rethink what he needed to accomplish at this particular meeting.

He had chosen as this meeting place somewhere a lot more open than a bar, and honestly he wasn't sure if it was his dignity he mocked or that of the man he was meeting.

He was sitting on a park bench beneath a lamppost illuminating the walking path, casually smoking a cigarette.

He felt more than heard the quiet engine of a very expensive car get as close to the path and the bench as was possible, heard a car door open and close with quite excessive noise. Like the footsteps approaching him, too quick and nervous.

Some people just couldn't be quiet about things. And that could be dangerous to more than just their own lives.

"Jesus, Duran—"

"Sit down."

After an instant's hesitation, the other man sat. "I didn't know you smoked," he said.

"I don't," Duran said calmly. "But there are so few acceptable places to smoke nowadays that someone smoking on a park bench at night never causes a second thought in anyone's mind."

"You're always aware of what people might think, aren't you, Duran?"

"I'm still alive, aren't I?"

That silenced the other man, but only for the space of a few heartbeats. When he finally spoke, it was measured rather than hasty or . . . disrespectful. "I had to slip away from the party. I can't stay long, or I'll be missed."

"Since it's a fund-raiser for your campaign, I imagine so."

"The speeches are over and so is dinner, so it's music and half-drunken dancing and a lot of political arguments. Still, I should get back there as soon as I can."

"Generous donors?"

"Very. And a very wealthy political hostess here in

Charleston wants to hold another on Friday. With, she tells me, a whole new crop of very rich people eager to back my campaign."

Duran took a draw from the cigarette and blew the smoke out slowly. "That might not be such a good idea."

"Campaigns cost money, Duran, a hell of a lot of money, you know that. And I can't use any of your funding sources, not without a risk we've both agreed is too great. I have to go the normal, typical, political route—the squeaky-clean version. Fund-raisers and shaking a lot of hands and making a lot of speeches—and staying miles away from any scandal. No backroom deals, no lobbyists, no dirty money. Not a cent. You can spend money on your end, but it can't be traced to me in any way. Not now and not years from now. That was the plan. Has anything happened to change that plan? The one you and your boss have spent decades working toward?" A tinge of mockery had crept into that polished, trained voice.

Duran took a final draw on his cigarette, then leaned forward to drop the butt onto the ground and crush it with his shoe.

Pleasantly, he said, "It might be worth your while to remember that you aren't the only possible candidate we have. It's our habit to have backup plans for our backup plans. So there are others standing in the wings, ready to . . . activate . . . their own political ambitions. Even a few who already have. Starting over at this point would not be so difficult. And we're patient. We're very, very patient." He straightened and turned his head to look at the other man. "You have no idea. You have, in fact, recently become something of a complication. One I haven't—yet—decided how best to deal with. In the meantime, if I were you, I wouldn't value myself so highly that I forgot what my part was in that very careful plan."

"I didn't—"

"There have always been kingmakers. Think of it that way. It's kinder to yourself than realizing you're . . . only a puppet."

The other man stiffened, but nodded. "Yes. Yes, I know."

"Good. Then we understand each other."

"Yes." He drew a breath and let it out. "You don't ask for meetings for no reason, especially when I'm . . . working. What is it I need to know?"

Duran considered, as if making up his mind, then said, "The planned fund-raiser for Friday."

"Yes?"

"If possible, push it back a few days, to the following week. And it would be best if you found a reason not to be in Charleston while your hostess gets ready for your grand fund-raiser."

"Not be here? But—" He caught himself. "Certainly. The campaign has been hectic for weeks now. No one would be very surprised if I flew back home to . . . decompress."

"Leave first thing in the morning." Duran frowned. "We'll plan a few brief and seemingly casual campaign stops coming and going. We wouldn't want anyone to think your campaign was running out of steam."

"That makes sense. Anything else?"

Duran rose to his feet and looked at the other man as he followed suit. "Yes. Have your stylist pick all your ties from now on, and don't argue with her. The one you wore night before last looked ridiculously garish on the news clip. It was almost difficult to take you seriously."

"Right. No problem."

"You'll also be meeting a few more prospective wives, but make certain nothing goes too far. We want the media interested in your love life, but we don't want them hearing wedding bells just yet."

"I understand."

"The women, of course, understand their roles."

"I assumed as much."

"Good. Then you won't make the mistake of taking their smiles and admiration at face value."

"No. No, I won't."

"Enjoy the rest of your . . . event."

Recognizing a dismissal, the man merely nodded, turned, and walked back to his car.

Duran stood where he was, watching the car move away, and then, half under his breath, he muttered, "Maybe not such a problem, Brodie. Unless there's someone on your side now capable of discovering a truth you can never know. Or unless your . . . connection . . . with Tasha Solomon turns out to be something very unexpected indeed."

Or both.

When Tasha opened her eyes, she was half convinced the "conversation" with Elizabeth Brodie had been nothing more than a dream, conjured from a vivid imagination and exhaustion.

Except that she knew better. Even though the room was empty of anyone but herself. Even though no lovely dark-haired woman sat in a chair looking at her with soul-deep sadness in her eyes.

She pulled herself from bed, feeling oddly stiff, probably because she had lain in virtually the same position for too many hours. She found herself very conscious of the low sound of the TV in her living room and of Brodie's presence.

He hadn't left her alone.

Tasha gathered up some clothing and then went into her bathroom, closing the door quietly behind her. She took a long, hot shower, more to ease her stiffness and really wake up than anything else. She thought about the information she had been given, a little surprised that she remembered every detail and yet . . . not surprised at all.

It all seemed so incredible. So unbelievable.

Except that she was right in the middle of it.

She got out and dried off, wiping the fogged mirror that, this time, had no chilling message written on it. Thank God. Just her reflection, still and quiet. Not so weary as it had been lately, but . . . different.

Tasha wasn't sure how and felt too unnerved to probe.

She dried her hair without really looking into the mirror again, then got dressed in a pair of comfortable stretch jeans and an oversized jersey pullover. Dorm socks with kittens on them completed the look. She wasn't going for fashionable or sexy. She wanted casual and warm.

And possibly to hide. Just a bit.

Brodie looked her up and down when she came out of the bedroom but didn't comment on her choice of clothing. He gave the appearance of being relaxed: jacket off, cuffs rolled back.

He was not relaxed.

"I know you'll probably say you're not hungry," he said by way of a greeting, "but you slept hours and you need to eat. So I found the menu for what looks like one of your favorite take-out places and ordered Chinese. They seemed to know what you usually order, so that's what I ordered for you. That okay?"

"It's fine. Did you call down to the desk?"

"I thought maybe you should. The guard seemed reassured hours ago, but it never hurts to . . . reinforce that."

Tasha merely nodded, then went to the LCD screen/intercom by the door—an intercom that was also two-way video when the right button was pushed—and called downstairs, cheerfully telling the security guard on duty that they were expecting a delivery from her favorite Chinese restaurant. She pushed the right button, so he could see her smiling face.

"Got it, Ms. Solomon. You seem much better."

"Sleep. I highly recommend it. Now I highly recommend food. I'm starving." She kept her voice light and casual.

"I'll buzz you when we're on the way up with the food, Ms. Solomon."

"Thanks, Stewart." She released the button and frowned

a little at Brodie as she turned from the door. "He's either working late or pulling a double shift."

"Is that usual?"

"Well, I wouldn't call it usual, but it happens now and then. Security runs four six-hour shifts, and the work isn't exactly hard. Sometimes the guards trade a shift or double up if one has tickets to a concert or something."

Brodie grunted. "I'm betting Stewart is still on because he's concerned about you. He did say he'd buzz you when *we* come with the delivery. Does he usually?"

"No, not with delivery people the security staff here knows. And they know most of them. They certainly know the staff at my favorite Chinese restaurant. It's the same one other residents use because it's closest and the food and service are great."

"Well, it won't hurt to reassure him in person that you're looking as well as sounding better."

Tasha accepted that assessment in the spirit in which she assumed it was intended, and said merely, "Did you get any rest?"

"I dozed now and then. Catnaps. I can get by with them for quite a while."

"I bet," she murmured, moving toward the living area. She eyed a football game muted on her TV. "You're a football fan?"

"Not really." When she looked at him, he added, "Not really a sports fan of any kind. Tasha, I don't usually stay very long in one place, and even though some Guardian assignments are more . . . stationary . . . than others, I still tend to move around a lot. I'd be hard-pressed to tell you which teams are playing right now, and I generally know even less about current TV shows and movies."

I wonder how much of what most of us consider necessary for a full life seems trivial to him.

Tasha went to curl up in the big chair-and-a-half that was her favorite reading chair and frowned at him for a moment before making a determined attempt to wear a more casual face. "You really have given your life over to this." *And I know why. But I can't say I know. Not yet. And I don't think he'll ask if I got information about his wife and marriage out of his mind when I read him. When we connected. I don't think he wants to know whether I can do that.*

He shrugged, keeping it light. "Some people go through their entire lives with boring jobs and nothing that rouses them to fight. Nothing that really matters to them or seems to make a difference in the world. Wondering if they even have a purpose in life that counts for anything. And in case you're wondering, even though this wasn't something I planned, it *is* something I've committed to. Completely."

Because you couldn't save her.

"Yeah, I get that," she murmured. "What I'm wondering about is the endgame."

He sat down on the rounded arm of the sofa, which put him directly across from her. "What do you mean?"

"Well . . . you said it varies from psychic to psychic. The ways they find to protect themselves. That some go into hiding while others go into the spotlight. Right?"

He nodded.

"And I'm sure some join up with you—your side in all this—and find a kind of protection among other psychics and those who understand them, as well as a use for their abilities. Something useful, even important, to devote *their* lives to."

Brodie hesitated, then nodded. "A few have joined up along the way. We're honestly wary of that, especially with telepaths and clairvoyants, because we're fairly certain Duran is using psychics on his side, powerful ones, and quite a few of them. My guess is to gather intelligence as well as locate other psychics for him."

"Which means a psychic on this side, especially a telepath or a clairvoyant, could be an especially good source of information for them. Because one of us could pick up bits and pieces of intelligence we wouldn't ordinarily have access to. Know more about the organization, even outside whatever cell we're a part of."

"It's possible."

Tasha thought about that for a moment. "But we tend to have shields. I don't know about new telepaths, but those of us born with it build our shields early or go nuts. And I'm guessing the born psychics outnumber those . . . created. Yes?"

Brodie nodded slowly. "As far as we've been able to tell, that's true. More psychics are born than created, and those born with abilities tend to have some kind of shield."

"Then it seems more logical that if it's one of his tactics to try to get whatever information he can through psychics, Duran would be using his telepaths to read those of you who don't have abilities and so likely don't have shields, or to read newly created psychics who haven't learned to shield yet."

"That possibility has occurred to us."

"It's happened in the past?"

"Maybe. We aren't completely certain." Brodie shook his head suddenly. "Well, some of us are certain. If you've been in this thing long enough, you see things. Things you really can't explain. You have to theorize, draw inferences, whatever. Newly created psychics seem to be in the most danger from them, and at least some of us have wondered if it's because they simply haven't yet learned to protect their own minds. Duran and his kind have powerful psychics to do their bidding, for whatever reasons, and they want more. They need more."

"And . . . born psychics give them more trouble?"

"I believe they find it more difficult to control born psychics, at least most of them. Those are the ones they have to grab in the dead of night, leaving a burning house or wrecked car or unrecognizable body behind to keep the cops from asking too many questions."

Tasha thought about that, trying not to shiver. "Born psychics. And people working against them who aren't psychic at all. Those are the targets most likely to become the focus of one of his psychics."

"Definitely." He hesitated again, then said, "Over the years, we've evolved our techniques and procedures through experience. We discover something is needed, usually the hard way, and then we have that from then on.

We don't usually discuss it, but Guardians and soldiers—
whoever is out in the field—always have backup nearby.
Gifted psychics, some of the most gifted we have. They
do their job, and it's likely you'll never see them. But what
they do is . . . patrol . . . the general area around us. As
long as we're protecting a psychic. And reach out with
their senses, carefully."

"For the bad guys?"

"More for other psychics working for them. The bad
guys themselves are . . . slippery."

"Because they're shadows?"

TEN

Astrid entered the hotel room, saying airily, "You rang?"

Duran wasn't by the window, which was more customary, but instead was seated in a big chair facing a flatscreen TV he very obviously was not watching. "I have a job for you."

"I'm still dealing with the pounding headache your last job left me with."

"Have one of the healers take care of that."

Astrid almost physically shied away, a betraying gesture that made her grit her teeth and swear inwardly. "I'd rather not," she said, polite.

Equally pleasant, he said, "Did I ask you what your preference was?"

"No."

"Have one of the healers deal with the headache."

She drew a breath and let it out in a short burst. "Look, if whatever this job is involves my abilities, the last thing I need is a visit to one of the healers. They might be able to stop the pain, but it'll leave my abilities . . . muffled. For hours. Is that what you want?"

A rare frown crossed his face. "Can you work through the pain?"

"Probably depends on what the job is," she said honestly.

"I need you to circle the established perimeter around Tasha Solomon's neighborhood."

"And do what?"

"Tell me who their guardian psychic is."

It was her turn to frown. "I thought you knew that."

"I thought I did. Now I'm not so sure."

It was so rare for him to admit to uncertainty that it caught Astrid off guard for a moment. Finally, she asked, "Why not?"

"Because of what happened when you were in Solomon's mind."

"I told you, Brodie—"

"Brodie couldn't have gone into the maze and helped her escape it. Not on his own."

Slowly, Astrid said, "Not many psychics would be capable of helping him like that. Especially without touching him physically, or even being close to him at all."

"I know."

"That's what worries you."

Duran looked at her. "I need to know if this is a new player, or someone we've dealt with before."

"Someone we've dealt with—who didn't come over to this side and didn't die in some kind of accident?"

"Obviously."

"Didn't know there were any of those. Except—you mean the public psychics? The ones who choose to stand out in the open?"

"Maybe we've made too many assumptions about them."

"As in assuming they stepped out into the spotlight to get out of the war as well as make lesser targets of themselves?"

He didn't question her terminology. "It has seemed obvious from those we've observed that once they became public, they had no further contact with the other side."

"That we know of." Hastily, she added, "It makes sense. They're safe in the spotlight, at least from us. I mean, unless you've come up with some nifty way to spirit them away without suspicion. And, no offense, but I doubt you have. Every single psychic I know of who chose to go public isn't alone—and for most of them, it's a whole lot deeper than a partnership. You won't come between them, and if both of them suffer some . . . untimely accident . . . I have a hunch they've left a few letters or packages with friends. Lawyers. In safe-deposit boxes, to be opened in the event of their deaths or disappearances. Letters that could come with proof, or at least enough questions to stir up the authorities."

Duran nodded. "You don't step out into the spotlight without taking precautions first. Yes, I know." He shook his head slightly. "That may be a moot point, at least for now. We have no evidence that any of the public psychics has maintained contact, as I said. This could be someone new. I need to know who he or she is."

"So I circle the perimeter and find out if I can sense anyone."

"Yes."

"Right." But she couldn't help adding, as she turned toward the door, a muttered "My head is gonna be *splitting* in the morning."

Duran looked after her for a moment, then turned his head quickly toward a dim corner by one of the windows. He had thought he'd caught a glimpse of movement from the corner of his eye. But, no.

It was only a shadow.

————

Sarah drew a deep breath and opened her eyes. "Damn, he's quick."

"And you're pushing your luck," Tucker Mackenzie told his wife severely. "It's dangerous enough to listen in on any of their conversations, especially with a psychic in the same room, but to let Duran even suspect he might have seen something—"

"Only a shadow." A bit grimly, she added, "I'd love to give him a taste of what it feels like."

"Maybe he already knows. He is one of them."

Sarah frowned and relaxed against her husband's side. They were in the living room of a hotel suite—more than a mile away from Duran.

"I'm not sure he really does know," she said slowly. "I mean what we sense about them. Easy enough to *say* we sense shadows, but you and I both know the feelings are cold and slimy—beyond creepy."

"You don't think he gets that?"

"On an intellectual level, sure. Emotionally?"

"Does he even have emotions?" Tucker asked, about half seriously.

"I think he has emotions that run a lot deeper than he wants anyone to know. Including himself."

Tucker thought about that for a moment. "Ever since what happened at the church, I've wondered about that guy. Even though he seemed to have won what he wanted, he could have won more. At the very least, he could have caused us a lot of trouble officially. The fire, the dead bodies."[1]

"It would have caused him trouble too. Neither side wants the authorities paying attention. Not, at least, until we can give them something that sounds . . ."

"Rational?"

"Well, something they're more inclined to believe than a vague conspiracy theory involving missing psychics."

Tucker sighed, then asked, "Does Brodie know we're out here?"

Sarah shook her head. "Murphy's his official backup, the psychic monitoring the area to make sure if anybody tries to scan him, they hit a wall. Nobody's going to get past Murphy's guard."

"You mean nobody besides Tasha Solomon?"

With a faint laugh, Sarah said, "She did a lot more than

---

[1] *The First Prophet*

scan Brodie. You know, I was in his mind once. For the same reason, to prove I could trust him. But I didn't go nearly as deep as Tasha did today. I felt his grief and his rage . . . and that was as deep as I wanted to go. As deep as anyone would have *wanted* to go."

"So why did she go deeper?"

"She was pulled."

"Against her will?"

"Arguable, I suppose. Certainly before she could do anything to stop it."

Tucker shook his head. "I only got some of that. Something about a mocking voice and a weird maze."

"I think the maze is something their psychics manifest in the mind of another psychic, a representation of the connections psychics make with other people. Every mind they scan or read. Everyone they touch, psychic or otherwise, forms a pathway between them." She paused. "Tasha Solomon has a *hell* of a big maze. Hard to know this far away, but she may be able to read nearly everyone she tries to read. And probably quite a few that slip in when she isn't trying."

"But she was pulled down into that maze? Why?"

"They were testing her. Duran was testing her."

"And?"

"And," Sarah said with satisfaction, "he got an unpleasant surprise."

"Shadows?" Brodie was frowning slightly. "You see them as . . . *only* shadows? Not human beings?"

Tasha frowned in return. "No, it's not that. I see peo-ple. And most of the time that's all. Just people. But sometimes in my dreams, or when my eyes are closed and I reach out, the people look normal but they have shadows that are . . . wrong. Oddly shaped, or falling in the wrong direction, or just . . . looming behind them."

"When did you first sense someone with a shadow like that?"

Tasha hesitated, then replied, "Before I left Atlanta."

"That's one of the reasons you left?"

"I thought my mind was playing tricks on me, to be honest. But every instinct I could claim told me to leave, to get away. To find a place where I wouldn't be alone. So I came here."

"Have you sensed any of the shadows here?"

Tasha's reply was delayed since the buzzer announced the arrival of their Chinese supper—complete, as Brodie had speculated, with the security guard, Stewart.

Tasha chatted with both him and the delivery man, didn't question when Brodie paid for the meal and added a generous tip, and within a very few minutes they were alone again.

Brodie went behind the kitchen island and began to open bags. "We can talk while we eat."

Tasha sat across from him on one of the bar stools. "Is that one of your duties as Guardian, to make sure I eat?"

He seemed to hesitate, then said matter-of-factly, "My job is to keep you alive and out of their hands. Making sure you eat and rest enough is part of that. Soldiers learn to eat and sleep whenever they have the chance, because

you never know when you might have to move without
warning. And it could be a long time between meals."

She thought about that for a minute or two while he
got plates and glasses from her cabinets and utensils from
a drawer. Clearly, he had familiarized himself with her
kitchen.

Looking in her fridge, he said, "This pitcher of iced
tea might be smarter than wine."

Tasha didn't ask him why; she merely said, "Fine with
me. I don't drink wine very often anyway. And this is the
South. Sweet iced tea is the rule, not the exception."

Despite the utensils, both of them used chopsticks, a
fact Tasha noted with some amusement. But she didn't
comment, because with the first bite she discovered that
she was indeed hungry, and they ate in silence for some
time.

Then she half turned on her bar stool so she could look
at him, and said, "You asked if I had sensed any of the
shadows here."

"Have you?"

"Not exactly. I've caught a few glimpses of someone
from the corner of my eye, slipping away before I could
get a good look at him."

"Let me guess. An otherwise nondescript man in a
black leather jacket."

"Is that one of their . . . tactics?"

"Appears to be. I've heard it from nearly every psychic
I've guarded, and seen a few of them myself. In the distance, of course. I'm guessing they want an . . . identifiable image. So you know you're being watched."

"To keep me spooked? Unsettled?"

"Still guessing, I'd say yes."

"So we don't have much more than guesses to go on?" She didn't say it in a tone of criticism, but rather musing.

Brodie nodded. "That's about the size of it. We extrapolate from their actions, make educated guesses, pool whatever knowledge we have or believe we have. Do our best to make safe contacts who might be able to add to our base of knowledge."

"What about the psychics on this side? Can't they learn more details, maybe a few facts by reading someone on the other side?"

"Not so far."

Tasha looked at him, brows lifting, and waited.

"All I can tell you," he said, "is what our psychics have told me. Whether it's a shield or . . . some kind of mental projection they've somehow built, all our psychics get when they try to read or scan someone from the other side is shadows."

"Astrid had them," Tasha said slowly. "When I tried to sense her, I saw shadows. All around her. I thought maybe they were protecting her, but she said something . . . I don't remember, but it made me think they were more like a . . . cage . . . than a shield."

"Maybe they are. Maybe that's one way they keep their psychics in line. Any of our psychics who get close enough to try to scan or read one of theirs always reports those shadows."

"Misshapen, falling the wrong way, looming sometimes?"

Brodie nodded. "Only not people, just shadows. And they talk about how the shadows . . . feel. Cold, slimy, unnatural. Threatening, and frightening."

Guessing herself, Tasha said, "That's how you've been able to identify some of them. Because despite how they look, your psychics have tried to scan them and saw only the shadows."

"So far, yeah. With one exception. Nobody's been able to scan Duran. No shadows with him. Nothing with him. No sense of personality or thoughts or emotions. It's like he's not even there, according to our psychics."

Tasha thought about that for a while as she finished her wonton soup, then said, "Astrid. Was she ever on this side?"

"No, they got to her early on. Really early, before my time. She's one of their strongest telepaths, and Duran seems to favor her whenever he has a . . . psychic job he wants done."

"You mean like scanning another psychic? Like following another psychic into someone else's mind?"

Brodie just looked at her.

"That's not normal," Tasha told him. "That's not a telepath. Or it's . . . more than a telepath. She was *there*, Brodie. I couldn't see her, but I could hear her and feel her. But not in your conscious mind. Not even in your subconscious mind. It was deeper than that. Deeper than I've ever gone, to a place I didn't recognize."

"That maze."

Tasha nodded. "It was inside your mind, but . . . at the same time it wasn't. Maybe just an image meant to symbolize something to us, but . . . it felt like something real but alien to you, something artificial that had been placed there, in some deep part of your mind."

Brodie grimaced. "Don't much like the idea of artificial things being put inside my mind. How would they even do that?" She was confirming for him what Murphy had suggested earlier, and that made it even more real for Brodie. More real—and more uncomfortable.

But, more than that, it was new information for him, something else to add to the list of things he knew about how the other side operated. And that sort of information was always good to have.

"I have no idea how they'd do it. But they've done it before, to others. I'm sure of that. Some kind of test they've constructed, used. There was something familiar about the way Astrid was there, a . . . comfort she felt in that place." She shook her head. "I'm willing to bet if I read you now, I wouldn't find that maze no matter how deep I went. Because it was only there for a while. Only there while she was there."

"As a test for you."

"Exactly."

"A test you passed or failed?"

"I think . . . it was a result that surprised Duran. I know it surprised Astrid."

"Surprised her how?"

"That you were able to help me. Able to reach into the maze and strengthen me, help guide me out. How did you do that, by the way? Not being psychic, I mean."

"No idea."

"Seriously?"

Brodie shrugged. "I can tell you it's never happened before, not like that. And not just the maze part. I'm usually aware of being scanned, read, but it tends to be a surface thing. Thoughts, strongest memories. With you, it was definitely something different. You weren't just reading thoughts, you were feeling emotions. My emotions."

He didn't, she noted, seem especially disturbed by that.

"So why am I different?" she said slowly.

"It was new for you?"

"Feeling your emotions, no. That happens, but usually only when I'm trying to scan or read only one person. When my focus is narrow. If it isn't narrow, if I'm just . . . looking around in a psychic sense, I usually just get surface thoughts, and bits and pieces of those. I can gauge emotions from the thoughts sometimes, but I don't actually feel the emotions unless it's those of one person. And never before so strongly." If it didn't bother him, why should it bother her?

"Do you think you might have had help?"

Tasha was more than a little startled by that question, and answered honestly. "You made a comment before about me being aware of an alien voice in my head, and I have been, from time to time, a voice that made me uneasy, even frightened me, and I got the sense that was the whole point of it. But the last few days . . . it's been different. It's *felt* different. Almost like a debate or argument going on in my head, me and someone else, someone different, new.

As if that someone else were communicating with me. And I believe someone was, even though it took me a bit to catch on."

"Their side or our side?"

"Well, I was more than a little rattled by it," she admitted, "but I didn't sense anything negative or frightening. In fact, it was more like whoever it was, was trying to help me. Do we have anyone on our side capable of that?"

"I can think of one psychic I know of," he replied slowly. "But that person shouldn't be anywhere near here."

"Where should she be?"

When he stared at her, Tasha found herself saying apologetically, "Sorry, but there seems to be an open connection between us. As soon as I asked you the question, I saw her face. And her name. Sarah, right? Sarah Mackenzie?"

———

"Any luck?"

Sarah Mackenzie replied to the voice on the phone without hesitation. "Duran wants Tasha Solomon. Badly. And he suspects there's more than one psychic from our side watching out for her and Brodie."

"Since nobody we know can read Duran, should I ask how you obtained that information?"

"Oh . . . just a little out-of-body visit."

The cell was on speaker, so Tucker didn't hesitate to say, "I tried to talk her out of it, but she's convinced Duran will go to bloody extremes to get his hands on Solomon."

"He will," Sarah affirmed. "I'm not sure if it's because she's just plain powerful or whether he has some idea of exactly what she's capable of doing."

"Which is?"

"She has an incredible range, able to read nearly anyone she wants to read. But it's more than that. She doesn't know it yet, but I believe it's just a matter of time before Tasha finds out that she can see them."

"You mean as something other than shadows?"

"Yeah. I think she'll eventually be able to see what they really are. Not the shadows they project, but *them*. The first of us able to do that. Assuming, of course, that we can keep her alive and out of their hands long enough."

"You think Duran will try to kill her or take her?"

It was Tucker who said, "We think he's already shown his hand there. He could have arranged an accident any time in the last few months. When his goons visited her condo, he could have made sure there would have been a gas explosion later that night. A dozen different things Sarah and I have both thought of. Bottom line, if he wanted her dead, she'd be dead. He was on to her before we were, before Brodie could be put in place to help protect her. She was a hell of a lot more vulnerable, even with all the precautions she'd taken instinctively, yet he didn't move against her when the odds of success were very much in his favor."

"So he wants her alive."

Sarah said, "He needs her alive."

"Any idea why? That's one question we've never been able to answer."

"I'm still not sure why, because I can't read Duran, either, and the others are still shadows to me when I try to see past the surface of them. I could only hear what they said, and we all know Duran rarely says much, even to his own people. But I'm convinced that Tasha Solomon, alive and in his hands, is vital to Duran's plans."

"Okay. Not really a surprise there."

"No, but one thing surprised me. We all know Duran doesn't show what he's feeling, assuming he feels anything. Cynical amusement seems to be all he generally allows to escape. That and the cold anger when somebody screws up that definitely scares the shit out of his people."

"Yeah. And so?"

"I caught a glimpse of something just now. Maybe I'm reading more into it than is there, but I get the sense that Duran is feeling pushed, rushed. I think something has happened, something's changed. Just sending Astrid to look for a second psychic here to watch out for Tasha shows he's suspicious, but I think it's more than that."

Tucker asked, "*Has* anything changed recently? Something that might have put Duran off his game?"

There was a brief silence, during which they waited patiently, and then she spoke slowly, "We have a new ally. A very powerful psychic. Inside national law enforcement."

"That," Tucker said, "would certainly give him pause."

"He shouldn't know about it, not this soon. Unless . . ."

"Unless what?"

She was once again silent for a moment, then said, "We

aren't the only ones monitoring psychics, Tucker. And neither are they."

Tucker looked at his wife, brows rising as realization dawned. "I'll be damned. An ally in national law enforcement who monitors psychics. I know who it is. There's nobody else it could be, not with those credentials. He's in federal law enforcement, right? As in FBI?"

"Let's not mention names." The voice was quiet even through the phone's speaker. "Not out loud, anyway."

Sarah was nodding. "I got it when Tucker realized. And, yeah, I'd say Duran would be worried about that ally if he knew. A very powerful psychic, but beyond his reach. Somebody he can't disappear, somebody who won't play for his side, and who commands almost unlimited resources. Somebody who has spent years learning to understand and control psychic abilities, his and those of his team. Somebody who cares about psychics, deeply. And if a psychic or two that ally is or has been monitoring suddenly disappeared . . ."

"That might bring him here even though he's supposed to be a background source for us. And, if we're right about newly abducted psychics being read by Duran's people, they might have given away more than they intended, even calling out in a psychic sense for help."

Sarah said, "So whether he's close or not, Duran could easily know about him by now. And if there's anyone with the kind of connections to make Duran very nervous, it would be him. Law enforcement at the highest levels— *and* a formidable psychic."

Tucker said, "Why do I think this war of ours just moved into an entirely new arena?"

———————

"What do you know about Sarah?" Brodie asked Tasha.

"What you do." She shrugged. "Sorry, but it's . . . sort of automatic with you. I have no idea why."

"Can you turn it off?" He didn't sound especially bothered, but his face was more than usually expressionless.

"I guess I could recite multiplication tables in my head or something, but otherwise—"

"Never mind." He sighed. "Who knows, it might come in handy. I'm thinking I won't have to explain nearly as much whenever we talk."

"There is that."

"Okay, well, then we'll learn to live with it."

"You mean you will."

He eyed her, then slid off the stool and began clearing up in the kitchen and putting away leftovers. "I mean we will. Most people don't filter their thoughts, and I'm usually no exception. I can project a kind of shield if I'm concentrating, but that tends to be short-lived. I tend to have more important things on my mind than the need to guard my own thoughts. You may pick up things that make you . . . uncomfortable. Memories triggered that flash into my mind without my conscious volition. Emotions that flare up before I can tamp them back down."

Tasha was making a concerted effort not to pick up anything at all, but the instant he said that, she saw something she wished she hadn't. "Oh, God. You had a partner, a young woman. She—"

Brodie interrupted her with utter calm to say, "I don't work with partners anymore. What I risk is mine to risk. I came into this war with my eyes wide open, and I can take care of myself. I can also take care of a psychic in my charge."

"As long as you don't have an inexperienced partner to worry about," Tasha murmured.

"Yeah, something like that."

"Cait was fragile. I'm not."

ELEVEN

"Tasha," Brodie said in a warning tone.

"Look, you're thinking about it. Her. Remembering. I'm sorry, but I can't tune that out."

"You can stop talking about it," he said with more than a suggestion of gritted teeth.

Tasha slid off the bar stool and took her iced tea into the living room, settling down at the far end of the couch. She was wondering if putting even a little distance between them would at least dim the awful images and muffle the emotions in him.

It didn't.

She started reciting the multiplication table in her head, having a mental argument with herself about the fact that she should have paid more attention in school, because for the life of her she couldn't remember all the nines—

"Tasha."

She blinked, finding him sitting on the coffee table right in front of her. "Well, that's interesting. If I really occupy my mind, maybe I can block you at least a little. Or for a little while. Because I didn't know you were coming over here."

"I'll do my best to keep my mind and emotions quiet," he told her. "As much as I can, at any rate. But leave that to me, okay? I honestly don't know if it's wise for you to even try to shut down the connection. Even temporarily."

"Why not?" It wasn't a question she found answered in his mind, which was something of a relief.

"Because one of the things we've figured out about all this is that experience—and pressure—tend to cause a psychic's abilities to evolve. Sometimes get stronger. Sometimes change in ways nobody can predict. For whatever reason, what comes of it is almost always a kind of self-defense mechanism, or can be used that way. An extra weapon you might be able to use somehow to save yourself if you're facing a threat."

"And no matter where I go or what I do, I'm bound to face a threat," she said. "Sooner or later."

"It's a war," he said simply. "The other side wants you."

"But you're here."

"I'm here. And I'll *be* here as long as you need me. Unless they manage to take me out. The way they took out Cait."

"They could never take you out that way. Not you."

"Not that way, probably. But I'm a realist, Tasha. I've been in this war long enough to see a lot of our soldiers fall, some taken, some killed or otherwise destroyed. We've saved psychics—and we've lost psychics. Those of us who protect or fight are committed, and most of us are highly trained, some former military or law enforcement, or trained by others on our side once we join up. And we can be well armed when we need to be. But we're not invincible. And not knowing their plans, their endgame, puts us at a disadvantage. All we know, all we can really be sure of, is that they want psychics."

"But *why*? Why are psychics so important to them?"

"If we knew that, we could at the very least fight them more effectively. All we can really do now is try to gather information, locate and protect psychics, and keep growing our organization of . . . soldiers."

Tasha drew a breath and let it out slowly. "You've been in this war . . . almost ten years. Right?"

"Right."

"Then you must have some sense of whether we're winning or losing. Don't you?"

"We're . . . fighting a holding action, most of the time. Or so it seems to me. Win some battles. Lose others. Save some psychics. Lose others. Face off with the other side rarely, in the flesh. And even when they're right in front of us, it doesn't seem to help. We have hardly more information about them than we had ten years ago."

"But your army has grown."

"It has. When I joined up, we had maybe a dozen cells, and all in this country. Now my guess is that we have close to a hundred cells. All over the world."

Tasha knew her shock showed. "All over the world?"

"Psychics are born and created all over the world; the other side hasn't shown a preference, really. Except . . ."

"Except?"

"We have people whose only function in our organization is to collect and assimilate information. From all over the world. To look for patterns that might identify players on the other side. To look for psychics. Computers and social media have made that easier for us—and the other side, unfortunately. But if our estimates are on target, America has a disproportionate number of born psychics. Highly disproportionate, relative to the nonpsychic population."

Tasha frowned at him. "You're visualizing an ocean. And that's working, by the way. But I can feel there's something you've left out. Something you haven't told me. What is it?"

He leaned forward, elbows on his knees, still frowning. "I would say it's something that doesn't really matter with you, but . . . we've learned to our cost not to think in absolutes. So . . . something else we're reasonably sure of is that new psychics, those who have suffered some kind of trauma that triggered their abilities, have about a six-month window."

"What kind of window?"

"Before the other side really pulls out the stops trying to get their hands on the psychics. They follow, they watch, they apparently have some way of determining how strong a psychic is, what abilities exist and how they're used, presumably by using their own psychics to probe—possibly why that window exists, because it takes them a while to be sure. Once they are . . . they act. Most of the time they take a psychic by stealth, sometimes leaving an unidentifiable body behind, or the psychic becomes just another missing person with no family to care very much. A very few, they walk away from. Don't take, stop following, stop watching. We don't know why."

"A matter of strength, maybe?"

"Doesn't seem to be. They've walked away from strong psychics and weak ones. Walked away from psychics with every variety of ability. So we don't know what criteria they use to determine which psychics can be . . . useful to them. But whatever it is, once they make that determination, they move. With utter speed and ruthlessness."

Annabel Blake looked younger than her ten years. But she felt old, far older than ten. It was visible in her eyes to those who could look deeply enough, past the still, placid surface she had learned to show the world. But few in her short life had seen what she hid so carefully and used only when she had to—to stay one jump ahead of her abusive foster parents.

And sometimes that extra sense failed her.

The bruises were easier to hide this time of year, when long sleeves were common. And they were certainly warmer when she chose to huddle outside, as she did tonight, barely a couple of blocks from home and sheltered from the slight breeze by the inset door of an old-fashioned specialty candy store.

It was a quiet night, peaceful. Such a change from her

house, where her foster father was drunk and getting drunker. Ironically, Annabel knew she was less likely to be punished by him for staying out all night *because* he was drunk and would pass out eventually; sober or with only a couple of drinks in him, he usually picked out a target on which to vent his unceasing, blind rage at the world.

Annabel didn't ever want to be that mad. Not at the world. Not at anything or anyone. It seemed a miserable way to get through life. For him and everyone around him.

But at least he would be out cold when morning came, and Annabel knew she could creep back early and get herself ready for school before he woke.

And hopefully before her foster mother woke. She didn't drink, but there were pills and she was . . . mean. Unpredictably mean. Annabel didn't need to be told that her foster mother was mentally unstable, kind one day and explosively angry the next, as likely to backhand the nearest foster child as she was to order them to stand in different corners of the house for hours on end, or lock them in a closet—or buy them a new toy or something pretty to wear.

Annabel actually dreaded the unexpected gifts more, because they usually preceded one of the explosive rages. And that meant punishment. Annabel didn't like being locked in the closet. That was the worst. She had nightmares about that. So she did her best, when she had to be in the house, to be quiet and still and no trouble. To break none of the Rules of the House—even though that was often difficult because they changed on a whim and were more often than not puzzling.

One day she was backhanded for simply asking, while in the process of clearing the table after supper, if her foster mother was ready for her plate to be taken to the sink and washed. The next day her effusive foster mother had lavished praise on her for being "such a good, sweet girl" because she had set the table for supper, carefully laying out the plates and forks and spoons as she'd been taught.

Something she had done every single day for over a year, one of her regular chores. But never before to praise.

Fosters came and went in the house, some running away or getting into trouble that sent them to juvenile facilities, and a very few lucky ones forced to live in the rambling old house only a few weeks before going to new homes where kind people wanted to adopt them.

The younger kids, usually.

Annabel had no such hopes for herself. She'd heard too often that she was skinny and ugly, that her unusually dark eyes were "witchy," and that nobody wanted to adopt a girl like her. Her foster mother seemed to take great delight in reminding her of that daily.

All Annabel wanted to do was survive with as few broken bones and bruises as possible until she was old enough to escape. Because as bad as her situation was, she also didn't need to be told that the foster system was overloaded and underfunded, and that there were worse places she could find herself.

Much worse places.

She had thought she could stick it out at least until she was sixteen, but she knew herself well enough to understand that the deadline was less about age than it was the lack of an escape plan. She had no way of earning money, wasn't brave—or perhaps foolhardy—enough to try stealing from her foster parents or anyone else, and was too bright not to know that she could hardly trust to luck or a cold world to provide for her.

Still, in the last few months, Annabel had felt something shift in her lonely world. While reaching out with her extra sense one day to judge whether she could safely enter the house after the school bus let her out on the corner, Annabel had become aware that someone else nearby had an extra sense as well.

It was only a tendril, she thought that day, a brief probing much as she probed herself. She immediately wanted to seek out that person, because brief though it was, that light touch in her mind had felt warm and kind. But before she could do that, she sensed something else, another probing, and it was dark and cold and very, very dangerous.

Someone, something was . . . hungry. It wanted what it didn't have. It needed what it didn't have.

It wanted what that other person had.

And what Annabel had.

It wanted. And it was meaner than Annabel's foster mother and foster father put together. It didn't put little girls into corners or closets or hit them with an open hand or a fist unexpectedly. It did worse things, much worse things.

Annabel had been very careful after that in using her extra sense. As badly as she still wanted to seek out that first, warm contact, all her instincts warned her to keep to herself, to watch and listen and wait.

It had been hard to do that, but if her young life had taught her nothing else, it had taught her the value of patience. So she watched, and used her extra sense sparingly and briefly, and she waited.

But right now, tonight, she was just really tired. Really, really tired. She needed to sleep. And she was so tired that she did, even in that chilly doorway. She curled herself into the smallest ball she possibly could, and she slept.

———

"That's the . . . disappearances, the bodies burned or mangled beyond recognition. That?" Tasha asked, already knowing the answer.

He nodded. "That. After that point, or if it's a psychic like you, born with abilities, the actions of the other side become less . . . predictable. It becomes more difficult for us to figure out who their real target is and when they're most likely to act, especially if we know they're watching at least a dozen psychics."

"And are they?"

"At least. Virtually all the time. Just in this country."

Tasha felt herself frowning. She wasn't at all sure she wanted to bring this up now, except that she hadn't gotten anything from him to know whether it was something he was aware of.

And she needed to know.

"You know, that's been bugging me. If this thing is as huge as you believe, we have to be talking about an awful lot of psychics. I mean a *lot*, especially over years, decades. Plenty with their abilities triggered by trauma, but even more born with their abilities. And correct me if I'm wrong, but isn't that a fairly recent thing? I mean, fifty or sixty years ago, we didn't have nearly as many psychics, did we?"

"You're quick," he said matter-of-factly. "Most don't seem to pick up on that."

The ocean in his mind was very calm and very blue. Impenetrable.

"So what's the deal? Accidents I get, though I don't see how they could arrange an accident that just happens to trigger psychic ability in someone. A greater danger of killing them, I'd say."

"We don't believe they arrange accidents to trigger psychics. Just that they . . . monitor accident victims searching for psychics."

"Okay. What about those of us born with this stuff? There are more than there used to be, aren't there? I mean, generations ago, a psychic was either incredibly rare or amazingly good at hiding it."

"Information wasn't as readily available fifty years ago," he pointed out. "It traveled much more slowly than today. No Internet. No twenty-four-hour news cycles. The world was still a big place. A place where secrets could be more easily hidden than today."

"Okay. But tell me I'm wrong. There *are* more psychics being born now than there were fifty years ago."

"We believe so."

Tasha could feel herself getting tense and she wasn't

even sure why. Except, maybe, something she felt in Brodie even beneath the calm surface of an ocean he was
holding in his mind, and the memory of what Elizabeth
had told her. She attempted a laugh that didn't quite come
off. "So what is it? Why so many of us now?"

Brodie looked at her steadily, then spoke in the same
calm tone, as if what he was saying weren't absolutely insane.

"Tasha, we have evidence to support the theory that
the other side is breeding psychics. And has been for
decades, at least."

Tasha pushed aside the first thought that entered her
mind, and instead went with the second. "How could
you—we—know that? What kind of evidence?"

"No courtroom would buy it," he admitted wryly.
"But we have bits and pieces of information some of our
psychics have picked up. Not from the other side—the
shadows. But from psychics they've taken, in the early
days, before . . ."

"Before?"

"Before they're taken or put beyond our reach. Physically, maybe. Psychically. We're not sure about that. But
for a little while, some of them are still able to reach out
to us. Are strong enough even through their fear to try to
warn us. Tell us what they can. And from what they've
told us, and a few other sources of information, we're all
but certain one of the goals of the other side is to breed
psychics.

"Maybe it's because we've been more successful than
they expected at protecting psychics or because they

simply need a lot more than are naturally born or triggered; either way, it seems they decided at some point to
embark on a program of . . . eugenics."

"Positive eugenics," Tasha said a bit numbly. "Breeding
to encourage, not eliminate. Breeding for psychic ability.
Which makes a born psychic—"

"Extremely valuable to them," Brodie finished.
"Assuming, of course, that psychic ability is genetic. That
it *can* be passed on from one generation to the next."

"It can," Tasha said. "At least I believe it can. I did a
lot of research years ago when I realized what I was. I
don't know if it's genetic or something else, but psychic
ability does tend to run in families. I didn't find any
evidence of it in mine before me, but that happens too."

She was remembering what Elizabeth Brodie had told
her, that Elizabeth and Eliot Wolfe were supposed to be
together, according to him, because they were a genetic
match. Both born psychics.

Brodie said, "It's because that happens that we aren't
sure if they're choosing psychics based on genetics or something else. We've mapped the human genome, but so far
no scientist we know of has isolated a gene controlling
psychic ability. Probably few if any are even looking. In any
case, there are too many families with only one psychic on
the tree to be able to declare genetics is everything."

"Maybe so. But, to them, to the other side, it must still
seem like a good idea to match up two born psychics and
expect at least some psychic offspring. It's just common
sense . . . breeding."

"True enough," he said.

She drew a breath and let it out. "What do they do with the children?"

"We don't know. Our guess is that the psychic couple lives on the surface a normal life. Probably married, or posing as married. Jobs or careers, a comfortable house or apartment. And they raise their child or children. Whether those children are taught or trained in how to use their abilities, we don't know."

"Our side hasn't located a psychic child?"

Evenly, he said, "Not in time to save them. There have been a few over the years that we learned about, but they vanished before we could get to them. Abducted is usually the police theory. And in every case we know of, the parent or parents seemed genuinely distraught—and nonpsychic. So there's at least a chance some children born of two psychics are placed up for adoption, for reasons unknown. Maybe to ensure they have a normal life. Maybe to help make them a lesser target for a group like ours, looking for psychics."

"Adoptions come with documentation, don't they?"

"Supposed to, yeah."

"But you haven't found any?"

"No. We know they're exceptionally good at altering, even forging, documents. But whether they use that skill in hiding the psychic children they've . . . bred . . . is an open question."

"So we really don't know how their . . . eugenics program works. We're just guessing. Theorizing."

After a moment, Brodie nodded. "It's what makes

sense, as much of any of this makes sense. But, no, unless they've learned to hide them in plain view or else wrapped one of those weird shadow shields around them, to our knowledge we've never come across a child born of their . . . program. Or even one of the couples they've matched, assuming they live normally *as* a couple, and we can't even assume that. Still, the breeding idea has become one of our working theories. They aren't putting all their eggs in one basket, that's certain. They seem to put as much effort into searching for psychics whose abilities are triggered by some kind of trauma. And as much effort into searching for psychics born of nonpsychic parents."

"And they try to make them. Breed them." Tasha drew a breath, wondering when it had become a conscious thing to force herself to breathe. "The Nazis did that, didn't they." It wasn't really a question.

"The Nazis did just about every ungodly thing their evil, twisted imaginations could come up with," Brodie said. "The paranormal was something they were interested in, so they did various . . . experiments throughout the war. But they weren't the first interested in it, and they haven't been the last."

"Now we have these people. These shadows."

"Yes. Now we have them. And maybe the driving force behind them *is* eugenics. It seems at least once or twice in every century, there's a movement or cult or some charismatic leader convinced they know how to make the human race . . . better. Usually by getting rid of whatever subset of humanity they personally believe to be inferior."

"I know. Scary. And so hateful."

Brodie nodded. "At least this group appears to be more interested in adding than eliminating, when it comes to their breeding program. For now, at least. Maybe they believe psychic humans are superior. Maybe they believe they're . . . forcing evolution in that direction. We don't know, Tasha. We don't know what's driving them, assuming they have a philosophy, why psychics are so important to them. We don't know what their ultimate goal is. All we *know* is that they don't hesitate to kill someone who gets in their way."

"Is it the government?" she asked steadily.

"We don't think so, though they wouldn't be covering all their bases if they didn't have ears of one kind or another inside government, state and federal. We know they have cops on the payroll; if law enforcement, then why not government? It gives them access to information, it gives them a certain amount of power, and maybe it gives them leverage when they need it."

"How about our side?"

Brodie nodded. "We also have people inside law enforcement, and at least a few inside government. We have our hidden aces, just as I'm sure they have theirs. Just as closely guarded and protected, unless and until they're needed."

Pendragon glided down the sidewalk, right up next to the buildings, unnoticed. Even unseen.

Who sees a black cat at night?

He turned off the main street and onto a side street, where there were still shops popular with both tourists and locals, a street where people walked often during the day, and hardly ever at night.

Except for the little girl.

Pendragon found her where he expected to find her, huddled up against the locked door of a candy store. She was already asleep, her thin arms in their thin sleeves hugging her thin body. Sort of in an upright fetal position, not lying down but sitting with her knees drawn up and her forehead resting on them.

It was how she always slept, making herself as small as possible, always so exhausted from the many household chores on top of the tense waiting for a slap or a shove or a twisted arm.

People could be so cruel to the fragile spirits among them.

So cruel.

Pendragon lifted his nose to test the air, and decided it was too cold for fragile little spirits to sleep in doorways without even anything to help them stay warm. He glided closer, listening to her breathe, knowing she was deeply asleep.

Then he gently wrapped himself around her, enclosing her in soft, warm fur, slipping between her and all the hard, cold surfaces. He wrapped her in himself, and felt her relax, heard a little sigh of contentment.

He kept her warm, that fragile spirit, and he settled in to keep watch all during the dark night.

Pendragon intended to keep her safe.

She was important, this fragile soul.

———

Tasha lifted her hands slightly in a baffled gesture. "Then, what? Are you telling me those secret societies some people and tabloids are always going on about are actually real? I know there's a novel out every so often about some secret society or other, and movies love the idea, but there are supposed exposé stories and books as well, and TV programs calling themselves documentaries. Some of them trotting out some pretty educated and convincing people."

"Yeah, I've seen a few of those. We don't know, Tasha. I would have said something as huge as this organization seems to be couldn't possibly be secret, not for this long. And maybe they're not. Maybe they're hiding in plain sight, behind the logo of a Fortune 500 company, with offices all over the world."

"Jesus."

"Well, it's as likely as anything else. Maybe more so. For all we know, the vast majority of their . . . employees . . . don't have a clue what's really going on. I can't speak for anyone else watching, but from what I've seen over the last ten years, it looks like their soldiers, the ones who actually commit violent acts, are only a very small part of their operation."

"Their field operation? Led by Duran?"

"From what I've seen, yeah. Very highly trained in any

deadly art you'd care to name, from hand-to-hand to the skillful use of any and every weapon any soldier at war would use. And they kill with the cold and ruthless efficiency of trained assassins, leaving no evidence behind to identify them. I would guess there are similar small groups in other parts of the world conducting the same sort of activities Duran commands."

"But no idea who he answers to."

"None. And we have some very good intelligence sources."

Tasha caught a ripple in the ocean that was hiding his mind from her, and couldn't help but smile. "You know, you're too good at projecting something besides your own thoughts to hide them. You had to be taught how to do that."

"I was," he replied readily. "By a psychic I worked with for years." He paused, then added, "She's gone now. They took her from under our noses while we were watching what we thought was their real target. Duran is very good at that. Sleight of hand. It's why we always have to question our assumptions about him and his goals."

Tasha didn't need to try to look beneath that placid ocean surface to know what dark emotions lay underneath. She merely said, in an abrupt change of subject, "So what's the plan with me? I can't stay here indefinitely. In Charleston, sure, even here in the condo, but I have to go out sometimes. I mean, I can have some semblance of a normal life, can't I?"

"I hope so." Brodie was frowning. "But . . . that maze

thing, if it was a test, is something I've never encountered before, not personally. I don't know what it means, but if you're right in believing something about it, about you, surprised Duran, then we need to figure out what and why. What it is about you or your ability, and why it surprised Duran."

TWELVE

Brodie thought about that, trying at the same time to keep his mind quiet and calm, a placid ocean that wouldn't distract Tasha. Or himself. "How do you *know* it surprised Duran?"

Tasha considered the question, trying to recall the specific feelings. "Astrid was surprised. She knew Duran would be surprised. I knew it too, somehow. That he'd be surprised. That he wouldn't like it."

"Wouldn't like what?"

"Wouldn't like it that I got out of the maze. That I had help, that I connected with you, that Astrid couldn't control me the way they both expected she could. And . . ."

"And?"

Slowly, she said, "And he wouldn't like that I escaped the maze without first being drawn to the center."

"What's at the center?"

"I have no idea. But being drawn to the center, finding whatever was there, I think that was part of the test."

"A part you didn't complete." Brodie's frown deepened. "I wonder if he'll repeat the test."

"No idea." She didn't like the thought that followed. "Unless . . . maybe they decide to try when I'm asleep. I get the feeling they do that sometimes. Test psychics who don't know they're being tested."

"So the psychic thinks it was only a dream," he said slowly.

"More like a nightmare, but, yeah, why not? That's how it looked and felt, really, and being lost, even in a maze, is a fairly common dream. I was awake and very aware of having gone into your mind, but if Astrid and others like her are strong enough, they could be testing other psychics by getting past the minimal shielding most of us have when we sleep."

His lean face took on an even grimmer expression. "We've always known psychics are more vulnerable when they sleep, just as nonpsychics are. We've even had at least one deadly situation when a psychic's companion was more or less hypnotized in his sleep. That was another time Duran surprised us because he didn't go directly after the psychic."

"But the psychic was his goal?"

"Definitely. He made her come to him. Or, at least, that's the way we read it. He surprised us again that time. He surprises us too much, catches us off guard too often. We need a way to . . . nullify that somehow."

"But you said psychics can't read Duran."

"So far, we've never found one who could. And there have been hints from the other side that even their own psychics can't read him."

"Would they admit it if they could?"

"The hints came from psychics newly captured. While they could still communicate with us."

Tasha hated to say it, but she had to. "How sure are you that they're *ever* able to freely communicate with you, even at the very beginning, after they're first abducted? Maybe whatever information you believe has come from them came from Duran instead. Misinformation."

Frankly, Brodie answered, "About as sure as we are of everything else. Which is to say, not very. It isn't something we'd count on when forming any kind of plan but, at the same time, our psychics are convinced Duran has an impenetrable shield so complete it's able even to hide his personality, the unique electromagnetic signature we all possess."

"Maybe he doesn't have one of those," Tasha suggested, not really joking.

"Well, he's real enough," Brodie said. "I've met him face to face enough times to be certain of it. He doesn't come across as a thug or even as a soldier or any kind of crook. He comes across as educated, wealthy, sophisticated. Very smooth, very polished . . . and deadly as a poisonous snake."

"You respect him," Tasha noted.

"I do. He's smart, he's ruthless, and as far as I've been able to tell, he's completely unflappable. I doubt we'll find a weakness in him by catching him off guard."

After a moment, Tasha said, "Then maybe we're look-ing in the wrong place. Maybe the weakness isn't in Duran. Maybe the weakness we can use against him is in his plans."

———————

Murphy moved through the neighborhood surrounding Tasha Solomon's condo, keeping to shadows and manag-ing to avoid alerting watchdogs or tripping any motion-sensor security lights.

She had a second sense about the latter, and always had. Or maybe that would be a seventh or eighth sense . . .

Hey, Murphy.

The inner voice was one she recognized. Murphy quickly rounded a corner and pressed herself back against a building where neither the lights of the occasional pass-ing car nor a pedestrian out for a casual walk on these safe streets would find her.

She shifted her inner focus, making it as narrow as possible.

Hey. What's up?

You knew Duran tested Tasha Solomon?

Yeah. The maze. That was you helping Brodie help her?

He didn't need much help.

Murphy considered that for a moment. *He isn't psychic.*

Not so sure about that. He connected. Reached out instinctively before I could guide him.

Huh. Okay, so what does that mean?

For one thing, Duran got it—and is worried about it.

Duran worried? That's something I'd like to see.

I don't think any of us wants to see that. Or, at least, see what he might do because of it.

Solomon's in even more danger than we thought?

Duran wants her more than we thought. And unless I miss my guess, he wants Brodie out of the way, and as soon as possible.

As usual.

No. Permanently.

Murphy straightened unconsciously. *Sarah, you know that for sure?*

I'm as sure as any of us can be when it comes to Duran. He has some plan for Tasha, an important one, and knowing she connected with Brodie is a threat to that plan.

You still think that's the major reason he didn't go after you, don't you? Because you and Tucker formed a connection.

That plus going public. But I think the connections are the important thing. Maybe what we've been missing all along. Two of us connecting that way somehow puts Duran at a disadvantage, or puts us beyond his reach. Think about it. No psychic with that kind of connection, that kind of bond with another person, has ever been taken, right?

Not as far as we know, though like everything else, we can't be sure. But . . . Okay. How do we use that against them, assuming it is a defense for the psychic? We can't just start linking up psychics, you and I both know it doesn't work that way. It's an organic thing, something that happens naturally, not something we can force. Right?

True enough. The right two people have to click, and it's always male and female—usually one psychic and one latent.

I never knew Brodie was a latent.

I'm not so sure he was. Is. I think Tasha forged that connection, and not because I had already made contact through you.

Have I mentioned, by the way, how lovely it is to channel you? No matter how much you tone down the wattage, that's a lot of energy you funnel through me. Being Murphy, she had to bitch about that.

Headache bad? Sorry. There was nevertheless a tinge of amusement in Sarah's mind. *Your cross to bear that you can channel other psychics. Comes in awfully handy when we want to keep another psychic or the second circle of protection a secret.*

Why are we doing that, by the way?

This time, because Duran's too close for comfort. Because he wants Tasha in the worst way. He sent Astrid out tonight. You knew that, right?

Yeah. Suspicious bastard, isn't he?

Well, he knows at least some of our tricks. And since he always has a backup plan or three, he'd assume we would as well.

So how did you hide yourself from Astrid? I let her sense me, naturally, but what about you?

She didn't even get close, but even so I . . . made her headache quite a bit worse. For which she'll undoubtedly blame contact with you since I timed it that way.

Thanks a lot. You know, for someone I thought of as a pretty frail flower when we first met, you've turned out to be fairly tough and ruthless.

I'll take that as a compliment.

I meant it that way. Murphy was honestly surprised it could have been taken any *other* way.

Sarah's mental laugh was like quicksilver. *Never mind. Just know you won't have to worry about Astrid for the rest of the night. Duran won't be happy, but even he knows better than to push a psychic too far, especially one already in pain.*

I think you're giving him too much credit.

Not this time. He needs Astrid. She's been in Brodie's mind, established that pathway, and whether or not Duran knows something has changed with Brodie, he'll still expect that by now Brodie has put up whatever walls he can—and he's been around psychics for years, long enough to learn some pretty good defenses. One thing I'm certain of is that only a psychic with an established pathway might possibly get through when Brodie puts up his guard, and even that isn't certain. Duran can't afford to push Astrid too far.

Why does he need her? I mean, I get that she touched Brodie's mind and that'll make it easier for her next time, but what's the point of getting inside his mind at all? Intel?

Not exactly. I think Duran learned something from Tucker and me. I think he learned that if he wants to get rid of Brodie, just killing him—assuming he could—would damage, even destroy, Tasha. Because they're connected now. So he'll need to try something else first. He'll need to try to sever the psychic connection between them, soon, before it has a chance to grow strong enough to protect them both. And for that, he'll need another psychic. He'll need Astrid. She's strong enough. And ruthless enough.

Murphy felt decidedly grim. *Any way you can incapacitate her for a few more days? Long enough for us to get the both of them out of here and somewhere not under Duran's eye?*

No, she'd catch on, and I figure the less she knows we know, the better. I'm pretty sure she's out of commission for the rest of tonight and probably most of tomorrow.

So that's all the time we have to come up with a plan?

Well, I think maybe it gets worse.

Christ, how could it get worse? Even as the thought flew from her mind, Murphy reminded herself that things could always get worse. Always.

Maybe not worse. Maybe just more complicated.

More complicated is always worse.

Well, that really depends on who knows what. And considering that Duran sent Astrid out looking for the second psychic despite the fact that she was pretty much walking wounded, I'd say he's a hell of a lot more than suspicious. I think he needed confirmation of a worrying suspicion.

That we had a second circle of protection and it's you?

No. You know about our new ally?

Murphy could feel herself stiffen, but years of practice enabled her to keep her thoughts calm. *You think Duran knows about him?*

Just after I put Astrid out of commission, I caught something. Murphy, it was the mental scream of a psychic. A psychic being . . . turned inside out. Something beyond torture. Changed in some fundamental way she'll never recover from.

Murphy could feel herself frowning, even though she struggled to keep her mind calm. *Taken? Who? Someone we were protecting?*

Sarah was grim now herself, and her mental voice reflected that. *No, a psychic we weren't even aware of. But someone else was aware of her, because in that mental scream, she was trying her best to contact him.*

You think he's nearby? In Charleston?

Somewhere close. And I think that's who Duran more than half expected Astrid to find.

But if you caught it after Astrid was out of commission— Wait. There was another?

At least two others, earlier. Psychics who went missing, psychics he was keeping track of, for whatever reason. The one who cried out is clairvoyant, and she knows there were two others very recently. Two she expected our new ally—oh, hell. Two she expected Bishop to know. He must have made contact with all three of them at some point. And I'm betting one or both of the first two taken also tried to call out to him when they realized they were in trouble. I think they tried to reach Bishop because they knew he could help them. That he was the only one who could.

I think that is what has Duran worried. There are people fighting against you, that's bad enough. And then there are people you really, really don't want in that fight. People who could seriously hurt your operation. People like Bishop.

———

"No," Brodie said with a tone of finality.

Tasha wasn't a woman to accept that sort of thing, even from him and even about this. "Look, I'm not going to hide in this condo for the duration," she told him.

"Nobody has said that's the plan," he reminded her. "Just for now. While we try to figure *out* a plan."

"We can't figure out a plan if we don't completely understand what's going on around us. Would it be better to stay here? Go somewhere else? What does Duran expect us to do?"

"And how do you propose we figure out that last one?"

"Test the boundaries," Tasha said.

"By dangling you out on a hook like bait? I don't think so."

"I didn't suggest I go alone. In fact, he'd be suspicious if I did. But we've been inside all day and well into the evening; nobody would be surprised if we took a stroll along a very well-lit sidewalk a couple of blocks to a pleasant restaurant."

"We ordered takeout."

"They have bands every night, sometimes really good ones. And they have desserts people come from miles around to try out. We walk down there for dessert and music. Makes perfect sense."

"I don't like it, Tasha."

"I didn't expect you would. It's easier to guard something you can keep inside and . . . unexposed."

He opened his mouth to respond, but whatever he'd been about to say never got said when a buzzing sound from his jacket drew his quick attention. His jacket had been hanging over the back of the bar stool where he'd sat earlier.

Brodie rose from the coffee table and went to his jacket, then came about halfway back to Tasha and remained on his feet as he opened the cell phone.

Not, Tasha noted, an expensive phone, but a very simple, almost stripped-down version. Was it what she'd heard characters on TV call a "burner" phone? One meant to be used once and then tossed?

"Yeah?" Brodie answered. He listened for several moments, frowning, his gaze on Tasha.

"That's a dangerous way to test a theory," he said finally. "Yeah, I know, but— Okay, if you're that convinced. But it has to be her choice." His frown deepened as he stared at Tasha. "Yeah, reasonably sure. There's a restaurant a couple blocks down she wants to walk to. No, I couldn't bring a gun into this building, the security's too good. Okay. Yeah, I know where that is." He looked at his watch. "Fifteen minutes. Tell her not to be late."

He closed the phone, and then immediately popped the battery out, then turned and went down the hall to the condo's powder room. Tasha heard the toilet flush. When Brodie came back, he dropped the now-useless phone into her kitchen trash can.

"You flushed the battery? Why?"

"We usually just toss them and keep walking," he answered readily. "But this is where you live, and I don't want to take the chance that Duran's side hasn't figured out a way to track a specific battery. Power sources emit signatures, so who knows?"

Tasha was curious about several things. "Can't cell phone calls be picked up by someone with the right kind of equipment? I saw that on a TV show."

"Not our cell phones. We've modified them extensively. No Internet access, no GPS, no emergency button, and they transmit and receive on rare, virtually unused frequencies. Otherwise, they're just plain old cell phones intended to be used for one call and only one call."

"They call that a burner, right? Without all the modifications, I mean."

Brodie nodded, then said briskly, "Okay, you get your wish, if you still want to go out. I don't know if you want to change or just put on shoes, but we're about to leave here and head for that restaurant with the music and desserts."

"I want to change," Tasha said, getting up from the couch. Then she paused, looking at him. "What is it we're really doing?"

Brodie's face was even more impassive than usual, and in his mind that ocean she could see so quickly and easily was very calm and very deep. "If I told you, it could affect . . . the outcome. Just get changed, Tasha, okay?"

She still had questions but went into her bedroom to get changed into something less casual. It wasn't a dressy kind of restaurant, so she settled on keeping the jeans but switching to a pretty, lightweight sweater—winter in Charleston really wasn't cold, even the nights—and exchanging the dorm socks for warm socks and running shoes.

Because you never knew. Given what was going on in her life right now, *and* the fact that Brodie and whoever had called him obviously had something other than a casual stroll in mind, it wasn't all that farfetched to consider the possibility of having to run for her life.

She brushed her hair quickly, then came back out in the living room to find Brodie shrugging into his jacket.

"Directional microphones," she said. "I saw that on TV too. Couldn't someone be outside listening?"

"All your windows have blinds," he said, almost as if he'd expected her to ask the question. "They help prevent the glass from vibrating. No vibration, no way to listen in from outside. Aside from that, it's also security glass."

She blinked. "It is?"

"Yeah. Not bulletproof, but thicker than normal. Helps with soundproofing with traffic so close outside. That's probably why the condo designers chose it."

"So even harder for anyone outside to hear us."

Brodie nodded. "You really picked an excellent building. If Duran and his goons were garden-variety thugs, they'd never get in here. Unfortunately for us all, they're considerably better than that, and so far we haven't found a security system they haven't been able to bypass."

"A guard with an Uzi outside my door?" she suggested, not really serious.

"Remember what I said about the nonpsychic they were somehow able to hypnotize? We believe they've been experimenting with mind control, using the psychics working for them. And they've clearly had some success at it. So we're fairly careful who we arm and when."

Tasha suddenly wished she'd chosen a thicker sweater. "Great. That's just great."

"Your extra senses and your instincts are your best protections," Brodie told her seriously. "Always listen to them. If your instincts are telling you to run, *do* it." He glanced down at her shoes approvingly, then offered his arm. "Shall we?"

She took his arm a bit gingerly, muttering half under her breath, "I have a feeling I'm not going to enjoy the music nearly as much as I thought I would."

"Sorry about that. Don't take your purse unless you want to, but you'll need your keycard for the building."

"Travel light?" she said, snagging the keycard from the table in the hallway where she always dropped it and her purse and sliding the card into her back pocket.

"Usually not a bad idea." He paused at her door and looked down at her seriously. "There may come a moment when you'll have to decide to leave everything behind except what you can easily carry. And it's not a bad idea to have that figured out in advance. Just in case."

"Right," Tasha said somewhat hollowly. "Just in case."

"Aren't we taking a big chance, being here just now?" Miranda Bishop said to her husband. They were sitting in a cozy booth in a dim back corner of the restaurant, and since a new band was busy setting up, it was fairly quiet in the spacious room.

Well, except for bangs and thumps and the occasional discordant note of some instrument.

"A slight chance," Bishop admitted. His veiled gaze was on a couple who had just come in and were being shown to an equally semisecluded booth in the corner opposite them. The man was tall and dark and powerfully built; he moved in a way Miranda had come to recognize in men of action, with every muscle fine-tuned and under his complete control, ready to react to any sort of threat instantly.

The woman was tall and lovely, with a figure most any other woman would envy and dark hair that showed a red glint here and there under the low lighting of the restaurant. She didn't move with quite the ease of her companion, but neither did she appear to be jumpy or nervous.

"Is it my imagination," Miranda murmured after sipping her drink, "or is she handling all this pretty well?"

"I'd say pretty well. But even having watched those goons break into her condo, so far the only real threat she's faced has been in her mind. Or, rather, in his. I don't think it's quite real to her yet. And won't be, until she faces real physical danger."

"Is that why we're here?"

Bishop looked at his wife and smiled. "No. In just a minute, you and I are going to slip out that side door over there and leave. Before Brodie has the chance to spot me. He would not be happy to see me."

"Then why are we here at all?"

"We can't use our extra senses or even amplify the normal five, but we can still use those senses. I wanted to see those two together. Try to . . . get the measure of them."

"You've already met Brodie."

"Yeah. But my bet is that something's changed since he became Tasha Solomon's Guardian."

"And you want to know whether that'll prove to be a strength or a weakness."

"I can't know for sure without using senses I can't use, at least for the moment."

"But there's that profiler training and experience," she said.

"Coming in handy," Bishop admitted, still watching the couple intently and yet obliquely, making sure his gaze wasn't fixed on them for too long.

Long enough for one or both of them to feel it.

"So what do you see?" Miranda was also a profiler, but Bishop had been at this game quite a bit longer than she had. Besides, she always found it fascinating to watch him work.

"A man born to be a guardian, a caretaker—and the armed watchman at the door. And a strong woman who has felt fear, but isn't entirely convinced she can't take care of herself no matter what comes at her."

"I'd agree with that assessment. And so?"

"I'm wondering what kind of team they'll make. Unfortunately, without seeing them work together *and* without use of our abilities for the time being, there's really no way to be sure. I'd hoped I'd see something that might tell me how Brodie, at least, is going to react when he finds out we're still in Charleston and a *lot* more involved in this than he planned for us to be at this early stage."

"Something we're not alerting him to just yet."

"I think we need to bring along some hard information to that meeting."

"Peace offering?"

"Well, something to convince him he can not only trust us, but that we can help a lot more by getting into the war now. I really don't think this is the time to hold back any of the assets."

"The endgame is a lot closer than they realize?"

"Yeah. A lot closer."

"As if we didn't have enough trouble with serial killers," Miranda said, but she slid from the booth, her hand
in her husband's, and followed him out a side door, waving cheerily to the waiter they had already paid and tipped
for their meal.

Just a couple of steps out the door, Bishop paused and
looked at his wife. "Maybe it's knowing damned well I've
lost psychics who could have tried to reach out to me
when they were being abducted. Maybe it's being a profiler and knowing only too well that there are monsters
in this, deadly ones, and they won't stop until somebody
stops them. Either way, we have to put the pieces together
and figure out what's going on. And fast."

Realizing, Miranda said, "You believe there's still a
chance to save at least some of the abducted psychics,
don't you?"

"I have to believe that."

She nodded back toward the table no longer in their
line of sight. "Even though their experience, maybe
decades of it, tells them lost psychics stay lost?"

"Even though."

"So we check out the place Henry McCord was restoring. And we check out the house waiting patiently for
Grace Seymore to return. And if we're very lucky or very
good, we'll find something useful."

"Exactly."

"Well," Miranda said, "I've learned never to bet
against you, especially when it comes to getting into the
minds of the bad guys. But we *have* been up for nearly

forty-eight hours. I think we need a good night's sleep if we expect to be any good at all, to anyone."

Bishop looked at her with a smile very few people ever saw. "One more stop to make. She's going to be mad as hell about it—but she won't betray us, to Brodie or anyone else."

"Because?"

A low laugh escaped him. "Because she's keeping secrets on top of secrets on top of secrets. And I'd back her against Duran any day. Probably the most valuable operative this side has. I only hope their leader realizes it."

"Now this one I've *got* to meet," Miranda said.

THIRTEEN

Tasha said, "I gather that quick stop you made two steps into an alley just before we got here was to get a weapon?" She kept her voice low.

"I'll get rid of it before we go back to your condo," he said. "But I was advised to be armed just in case."

"Obviously by someone you trust."

He nodded, but didn't offer an explanation. Not that she had really expected him to.

"Okay," Tasha said. "We're here. Nice drinks and desserts. Nice band playing soothing stuff instead of rock. A lot of my neighbors appear to have decided to while away an hour or two here."

It was true; quite a few people had greeted Tasha when they had come in, though Brodie had made sure they hadn't lingered long enough for introductions.

"Is that usual?" Brodie asked, casually sipping his drink.

"It's not unusual. As far as I know. I mean, I'm not usually here on a Sunday evening." She felt an odd little shock then as she realized she had met Brodie only that morning.

It felt like a lifetime ago.

She braced herself mentally. "I know we didn't come here for the drinks or desserts or the music. So . . . what's the dangerous way to test somebody's theory?"

"You don't have to do this, Tasha."

"Tell me what it is." She kept her voice light. "Then I'll tell you if I want to do it."

He looked at her for a long, steady moment, then nodded. "Okay. I noticed this morning that when you use your abilities, you close your eyes."

"I always have," she said. "At least, I learned to pretty young. It's hard enough to sort through all the voices without having . . . visual clutter too."

"What happens if you don't close your eyes?"

"That depends on where I am. And who's around me. A place like this, I'd probably see what you see. The people around us. I'd just be hearing their thoughts in my head. It's confusing, and sometimes I get dizzy and *have* to close my eyes."

Brodie was frowning.

"That's what you want me to do? Use my abilities but keep my eyes open? Why? What's the theory we're testing?"

"I still don't want to influence you," he said finally.

"But if you're willing, open up all your senses. Without closing your eyes. It might help to start out looking at something very specific. Not a person." He looked around briefly. "Maybe that tapestry on the wall over there. It's just color and pattern, not really any shapes."

"Never tried that before. Okay." Tasha had to brace herself even more, but that was more experience than anything else. The dizziness she had suffered in the past had made her physically ill, far worse than just a headache or weariness.

She had to turn her head only a little to focus her gaze on the tapestry, and Brodie was right, it was a sort of wash of colors, soft rather than bright, with no discernible shapes. So she fixed on that, just sort of let her eyes relax in a way she couldn't explain—and then opened up that other sense.

A cacophony of voices at first, then whispers as she gained some control, and then she began to sort through them so that she was actually getting words, phrases, bits of sentences.

. . . I still don't know why she wanted to go out tonight . . .

. . . hate Mondays, just hate them, and tomorrow's gonna be even worse than usual . . .

. . . man, this band sucks . . .

. . . people would think I'm crazy if I said anything . . .

. . . I deserve another dessert, don't I, even if it'll mean longer on the treadmill tomorrow . . .

. . . it's just the nightmares, I could handle the rest, but . . .

. . . I know he's cheating on me, I just know he is . . .

. . . just don't get this hide-in-plain-sight shit . . .

Tasha.

She sucked in a breath and let it out slowly, staring at the tapestry but recognizing his thoughts among the others.

You know it's me?

"Yes," she said softly out loud. "People's voices sound the same in my head. I'll always recognize yours."

I'm glad. Tasha, can you turn down the voices in your head? Like turning down the volume on a TV?

That was a new thought.

"I have no idea," she murmured.

Try, he said in her mind.

Because she couldn't think of another way, she visualized a knob, visualized turning it slowly to the left.

The voices softened to whispers.

"It worked," she said to Brodie, her gaze still fixed on the tapestry. "I just hear whispers now. Almost like background noise. I have a feeling that's going to come in handy."

"All right." This time, he spoke out loud, but quietly. "Now, if you think you can do it without making a sound, slowly begin to look around the room. Look at the people."

She wondered why he thought she would make a sound, but as soon as her gaze slid over one older couple sitting at their table smiling at the music and then to the next table—Tasha heard her breath catch.

Brodie reached out and covered one of her hands with his. "Tell me what you see," he said, still quiet.

"It's . . . two women from my condo building," she whispered. "But . . . they aren't alone."

"What else do you see?"

"Shadows." She was still whispering. "Behind them. Looming over them. Not their shadows. Not normal shadows. Distorted. Creepy. I have to warn—"

"No." His hand tightened on hers. "Listen to me, Tasha. Keep looking around the room. Look at other people. Don't look at anyone too long, just a few seconds. But try to see everyone."

She did as he told her, forcing herself to look from table to table, to see the people who looked normal.

And the ones who had shadows behind them or beside them or seemingly . . . moving in and out of them, a sight that made her skin crawl. She kept looking around the room. All the way around. Until she reached Brodie.

Thank God, he didn't have a shadow anywhere near him, just a frown of concern on his face.

Tasha knew her hand was cold. She felt cold to her marrow.

"Okay," she whispered. "Okay. Can I—"

"Close your eyes," Brodie said immediately. "Raise your shields."

She'd never been so happy to obey an order in her life. Still, even with her shields up, the voices gone, it took her several seconds to work up the courage to open her eyes again.

She didn't look around the restaurant, she just looked at Brodie.

"What the hell," she said, "does that mean?"

"You didn't see shadows near everyone?"

"No. No, but . . . almost everyone with a shadow is someone . . . near me. In the neighborhood. In my condo building, or one of the other buildings close by. Where I volunteer. Or they work in the neighborhood. Some are . . . people I talk to almost every day, even if it's just to say hi to. That couple at the table near the band. The girl works at the coffee shop across from my condo. She gets my order almost every morning. But . . . the young man she's with doesn't have a shadow."

"Just a casual date, probably. They'd have to keep up appearances." Brodie's voice was grim.

"John, what are you talking about?"

"The women from your condo; how long ago did they move in?"

"The same week as me," she said numbly. "The super said he'd been lucky, that almost as soon as a condo was ready, there was someone interested in moving in. Every condo is occupied now. Do you think—"

"No." Brodie shook his head. "Not all of them. Not everyone. Just like not everyone here tonight. But . . ."

"But all around me. They've been all around me from the beginning, haven't they? Watching me? I didn't escape them when I left Atlanta. I'm exactly where they wanted me to be."

Murphy had completed three slow patrols around the neighborhood, the last one when she'd known Brodie and Tasha Solomon were in the restaurant, and she did *not* like how unsettled she felt. She had tapped in to Tasha just far enough and long enough to get more than the gist of what was going on.

And even though she was no longer in mental or emotional contact with Tasha, she knew she felt nearly as shaken as the other woman did. Because this was something new, something different, and Murphy didn't understand the tactic.

Feeling that way, rare as it was, usually drove her to ground until she could figure out what was going on. But this time, she had a source.

At least, she hoped so.

She checked her watch, scowled briefly, and then slipped into an alleyway that provided a shortcut. Hardly ten minutes later, she was slipping into the unlocked back door of one of the rare industrial buildings in the area. Hulking machinery loomed silent in the mostly dark building, but she quickly found her way to a security spotlight that wouldn't be visible to anyone who wasn't actually in the building.

She stepped to the edge, just far enough into the light to let herself be seen, and said, "That's a dandy shield you two have."

"It does come in handy," Bishop admitted as he and Miranda stepped into the light a few feet away.

"It's you," Miranda said, more in understanding than surprise. "Noah said we'd crossed paths with some of the operatives in your organization, but I didn't expect to see you."

"That's sort of the point," Murphy said, but more in amusement than sarcasm.

"True enough."

Murphy looked between them, then settled her gaze on Bishop. "Behind that dandy shield, want to tell me how you knew about this place before we did?"

"I was right?"

"In spades. I suggested that Brodie utilize Tasha's talents in a little test of a theory. And it worked; she saw them. Way too many of her nice, friendly neighbors with unnatural, distorted, and usually invisible shadows attached to them. So *she's* totally freaked out."

"Can't say that I blame her."

Murphy nodded. "So answer the question. How did you know?"

"Didn't know for sure," Bishop admitted. "Some of us have developed something we informally call spider senses, because they let us know if something is wrong, off—even behind our shields, though what we get in that case tends to be muffled. When we can use the spider senses, our normal senses are enhanced, even though we still don't read as psychics."

"Okay. And so?"

"The whole neighborhood just felt wrong, from the moment we were even close to the area. Off-kilter. I took a guess, given how badly you say Duran wants Tasha Solomon, and given that he knows about your standard security practices—right?"

"Yeah, he knows. Like we know his." Murphy nodded. "Which is why he might try something different when his target is especially important to him."

"It's pretty damned elaborate," Bishop noted. "And

uses up a lot of manpower. Either he's put a disproportionate number of his assets here around Tasha, or else
their organization really *is* huge."

"Either way is not good for our side." Murphy frowned
at the two of them. "Appreciate the theory and the intel,
but you shouldn't be here. If Brodie found out, he'd put
you on his very long list of people he doesn't trust. And
that's not what we want."

"I know. But I also know something I didn't when I
first met with Brodie."

"Let me guess." Murphy's voice was still grim. "One
or more of the psychics you've been monitoring has
disappeared."

"That's a very good guess."

Murphy made a sound that was half amused and half
angry. "It just figures. You wouldn't be this close to the
action after you were told we needed another ace more
than we needed another soldier unless the stakes were
very high. Very high for you, personally. How many?"

"Four in the last few weeks, two of them very recent."

"Shit. And from here, in Charleston?"

"Both the recent abductees lived in the area."

"Strong psychics?"

"In different ways. Two born, two triggered in their
late twenties. A clairvoyant, a medium, a seer—and a
telekinetic."

"Rare birds, telekinetics."

"Yeah. She's one of those triggered by physical trauma,
a head injury. Her control tends to slip when her emotions
run high, but she was working on that."

Murphy hunched her shoulders, then sighed. "Bishop, I know your reputation for success in your work, but this . . . We don't get them back. If the other side has them, they're gone."

"I can't accept that. Not without doing everything I possibly can to find them."

"I was afraid you were going to say something like that."

"I think Duran knows anyway, Murphy."

"About you?"

"Yeah. All my senses are muffled and I can still feel the tension, especially around Tasha Solomon. All around her. I don't know what his plans for her were, but between us all, we've managed to somehow upset them. I don't think it's just me, but I'm betting I'm the last person he wanted to get involved in this."

"On our side, at least," Murphy said with a sigh.

"Look, I'll do my best not to get in anyone's way. But I can't just accept that four gifted people have been abducted and I can't do a damned thing about it."

"Yeah, yeah."

Bishop smiled faintly. "Who gets to tell Brodie?"

"Oh, Christ. I may just let our base do that. And I don't want to be in the area when he's told."

Miranda said, "I don't know him, but my bet is he's too concerned about Tasha Solomon, especially now, to worry too much about us as long as we aren't a threat to her."

"You don't know him," Murphy repeated darkly.

"We have a couple of places to check out first thing

tomorrow," Bishop told her. "Outside Charleston. If we find anything useful, I'll be in touch."

"I hope you find something," Murphy told him honestly. "I really do. Something that'll lead you to them. But . . ."

"But?"

She drew a breath and let it out slowly. "We don't get many happy endings, Bishop. And the one thing we *are* reasonably sure of in all this is that the psychics are never taken for some . . . benign reason. And whatever they go through happens pretty much right away. Even if you find them, even if you find them alive, they won't be the people you knew. They'll never again be the people you knew."

It was Miranda who said quietly, "We have quite a lot of experience in helping . . . damaged psychics. Maybe whatever was done or is being done to them can be healed."

"Know a good healer, do you?"

"We know a remarkable one," Bishop told her. "But the first thing we have to do is find them and get them back."

"I know better than to try to stop you. But if you do find them, don't try to go after them alone. Call me."

"Understood." Bishop took his wife's hand. "Watch your back, Murphy. You and Brodie both. And the Mackenzies."

She sighed again. "Why am I not surprised you know about them?"

Taking that as a rhetorical question, Bishop said, "I know they're outside the perimeter of this . . . web Duran has surrounding Tasha and Brodie. I don't think he knows they're here. Not what or who he's focused on. I'm guessing Sarah is even more powerful than she was when I—crossed their path. And I'm fairly certain she's going to be able to help you more than you know."

Murphy lifted her eyebrows in a silent question.

"Call it a hunch," he told her.

Miranda lifted her free hand in a parting wave, and then she and her husband melted back into the shadows.

Murphy remained where she was for several minutes, frowning in thought.

Outside the perimeter, he'd said. Murphy hoped he was right.

Sarah?

Yeah? came back instantly.

Don't do your out-of-body thing, but can you sense the area close around Tasha?

Astrid is gone, so the extra-strength headache worked. I don't think they've replaced her, at least for tonight. What do you need me to sense?

Any other psychics.

There was a long pause, and then: *You—barely. Good shield. Tasha, mostly because she's shaken up; she's shielding, but not nearly as strongly as normal. And . . . Brodie.*

Brodie isn't psychic.

Well, he's reading as one now. I caught the glimmer of an ocean, maybe a mental projection he uses to visualize his shield, but that's down now. He's worried about her. They're headed back to her condo. He's armed.

I know. I made sure he would be.

He needs to lose the gun, Murphy. Before he gets back to the condo.

Oh, Christ, don't tell me.

Something odd about one of the security guards. Doesn't read as psychic, but something off about him. Best I can tell you without getting closer.

No, don't do that. You and Tucker stay where you are for now. And stay away from Duran, Sarah. Promise me.

Okay. I promise. Just get that gun away from Brodie. I have the awful feeling that security guard is just looking for an excuse to use his own gun, and I'm betting he's trained to spot a weapon, especially when he's looking for one.

Got it.

Murphy was already moving, away from the light, out of the building, with a silence beyond stealth. She could cover a lot of ground very fast, especially when she trusted the information that no psychics from the other side were lurking to get in her way.

Of course, that didn't mean the other side wasn't represented. But Murphy had been certain earlier today that Duran had pulled back his "visible" watchdogs. She had no idea why he'd done it, unless it had been to offer Brodie and Tasha a false sense of security so that his web of "unthreatening" neighbors and friends could get even closer to Tasha before either she or Brodie was aware of the threat.

And it could still work, despite Tasha and Brodie's awareness of just how close the shadows had been lurking. Because they'd only been watching Tasha, creepy as that was, just watching her, so where was the real threat?

Why? Why like this? He could have grabbed her and didn't. He could have killed her and didn't. He planted bugs and cameras in her condo, and what was the point of that? What the hell is Duran up to?

What is he waiting for?

She caught up to them half a block from Tasha's condo, just out of reach of the very good security cameras, emerging rather suddenly from an alley—and it was only because she softly called Brodie's name that she didn't find herself looking at the business end of the automatic she'd slipped to him hardly more than an hour before.

"Jesus, you know better," Brodie snapped, but low. One hand was in his jacket pocket, and the other held Tasha's hand. "Coming at me like that out of the dark."

"No choice. You need to give me back the gun."

He didn't move. "I know the building security is good, but—"

"It's not just good. It's been infiltrated." She looked at Tasha. "The way some of your neighbors aren't really neighbors."

"Oh, God," Tasha said numbly.

"How do you know?" Brodie demanded, his voice still low. "Tasha can see them, but you can't, can you?"

"Through her." Murphy offered Tasha a slightly apologetic gesture with her hands. "Sorry. I tapped in, but only for a few seconds."

Tasha merely nodded.

"That doesn't explain what you know about building security here," Brodie said. "We were two blocks away."

Murphy's inner debate was brief, because she'd known he would ask. "Sarah and Tucker are a mile away," she told him. "She didn't see shadows in the condo, but one of the security people felt off to her. The way this whole neighborhood feels off. And that's good enough for me."

Brodie handed over the automatic in his pocket immediately, but said, "What the hell are they doing in this?"

"Orders, just like us," Murphy said without really explaining. "Ask me, it's a good thing we've got them nearby. Because for the life of me, I can't figure out what Duran is up to this time."

"It's like a web," Tasha murmured. "All around me."

Brodie looked at her for a moment, her strained expression clearly visible in the street light, then looked back at Murphy. "What's Duran waiting for?"

"Yeah, that's my question. Look, you two get back to Tasha's condo. I want to do some recon around the neighborhood, and tonight is as good a time as any."

"Murphy—"

"You know it's the right thing to do. Unless and until we have some idea of what Duran is planning with all this, making any move could be playing right into his hands. Let's take a little time and try to figure out what's going on. Astrid's out of commission, probably well into tomorrow. It's too late for Duran to bring in another of his psychics. Look, I'll have Sarah on alert. She can reach farther than any of us."

"Check in every four hours," Brodie told her.

"Don't worry. For once, I'm really not crazy about

being out here alone." And before Brodie could say a word, Murphy had faded back into the darkness of the alley and vanished.

"Will she be all right?" Tasha asked.

"If anybody can take care of herself, it's Murphy." He frowned suddenly. "Sorry there were no introductions."

"She's on our side, I got that. It's enough. For now, at least."

"Come on." Brodie's hand tightened on hers, and he led her toward the entrance of her building. "Your hand's like ice."

Looking at the attractive building looming above them in a way she never had before, Tasha murmured, "I wish it was just that."

FOURTEEN

"Sorry," Astrid said rather thickly, through the folded handkerchief pressed to her sluggishly bleeding nose with one hand, while her other hand adjusted the ice pack on the back of her neck. She was more or less just leaning back on that, using the chair's high back to hold the ice pack in place. She hadn't been conscious very long, and she felt like holy hell.

Duran was watching her, his pale eyes narrowed slightly. "Murphy did this to you?"

"Well, she was the only one I sensed, the one circling the neighborhood on guard against any kind of psychic probing of Solomon. And I was focusing on her when it felt like a truck hit me." She squinted a bit as she returned his stare. "Can you turn down the lights a bit in here?"

He didn't move. "You're sure it wasn't Solomon?"

Astrid didn't move her head because she was certain it would have fallen off if she did. "Absolutely certain. I've been in her mind, I'd recognize the touch of it. Brodie's too."

A slight frown drew Duran's brows together. "Brodie isn't psychic."

"Yeah, we've had this conversation before. I'm telling you, the more I think about it, the more certain I am that he's some kind of psychic now. Not sure what kind, but whatever it was, it was triggered by your little maze test. She needed help getting out, and he helped her. Solomon may be the only one he can connect with, like Tucker Mackenzie and Sarah Gallagher." She blinked. "I mean Sarah Mackenzie. But he can damn sure connect to Solomon."

"But it wasn't either of them who put you down."

"Nope. It was Murphy's mind I was touching—and I was only able to do that because she was probing the area for other psychics. So I guess they've caught on to that little habit of yours."

Calm, he said, "They caught on to that some time ago."

Astrid hurt too much to waste a glare. "And you sent me out without even warning me. Knowing it was nothing more than an exercise in futility and an invitation to the worst headache of my life? Wonderful. Then this is on you. Whether I go to one of the healers or not, I'm useless as a psychic for at least the next couple of days, and maybe longer than that. So if you think you're going to need one of us, better call somebody else in."

"Do you think Murphy knows she put you down?"

"I wish you'd stop calling it that. It makes me sound like an animal being put out of its misery. But, yes, I'm reasonably sure she knew exactly what she was doing. I got the sense just before the train hit me that she was even a little gleeful about it."

"And she knew who you were?"

"Yeah."

As he continued to frown at her, Astrid said, "You know, this is my room. I asked them to help me in here so I wouldn't have to get up again. So unless you happen to have something stronger than aspirin on you, please do us both a favor and either call for a strong painkiller or a healer. Seriously, Duran, if something isn't done soon, you may be short a psychic entirely."

She was in too much pain to feel much else but was aware of a flicker of surprise when he turned and left her room. Then she heard him tell someone outside the door to send for a healer, and a chill was added to her agony.

A healer would take away the pain; that was pretty much a certainty. But how she would feel after having . . . that . . . in her mind was already causing her skin to crawl.

The agonizing headache was almost better.

Almost.

———

Jeffrey Bell had lost all track of time. If there even *was* time wherever they were holding him.

It didn't look like anything. It looked like everything.

The bright, hard glare was constantly in his eyes, in the space around him he supposed, and that made it impossible to really see anything. In fact, he had closed his eyes what felt like forever ago.

He was cold. He was naked. He was strapped down to something that felt metallic.

When *they* touched him, it felt cold and slimy. It felt like if he didn't keep his eyes and mouth squeezed shut, something horrible would ooze into the orifices. Into him.

At first, it had seemed almost more comical than threatening. He was a seer and the future was beyond his reach, so all he had were his normal five senses. Waking up naked and catching, before the glare forced him to close his eyes, weirdly shaped blobs of darkness coming closer and then retreating. He felt embarrassed. Uneasy. Baffled.

He tried to ask them what the hell was going on, but for some reason he found himself unable to speak.

Then they began hurting him. And there was nothing comical about that.

He knew he was writhing on the table, but the scream he desperately needed to let out was trapped inside him, crawling around, echoing inside his head as if there were absolutely nothing else in there, just a keening, primitive wail of agony.

What were they doing to him?

He didn't know.

It felt like they were burning him. And tearing at his flesh. Ripping him open to see what his insides looked like.

Pulling his insides outside.

And because he couldn't scream, he could hear them. Even through the horrific pain, he could hear them.

Whispering. Rustling. Talking to each other in no language he had ever heard in his life, something filled with clicks and whirs and a crackling sound like stiff paper crumpling.

And they smelled like dead earth, like the dirt scraped from a deep, deep hole, so deep nothing had ever lived in it or grown in it, something that had never seen light.

Maybe that was why they liked it so bright here and now.

Wherever and whenever it was.

They stopped hurting him for a while, and still the scream he couldn't release crawled around inside his skull, his throat, behind his teeth, until it faded to a whimper, and even that found no escape.

He knew grunts and strangled sounds did escape, knew frantic breaths blew snot from his nose, or maybe it was blood, and he knew he was crying. That he had been crying for a long time.

Then they went back to hurting him, searing his flesh, stabbing him, probing as if they had lost something terribly valuable inside his body and needed to find it. They did things to him he didn't even have words to describe, even to himself, things that were slowly, inexorably, driving him insane.

And when he could, finally, at last, scream, the sound that erupted from his tortured throat sounded more like the agonized shriek of some dying primitive beast, skewered alive on a spit for roasting.

It was only when he was sobbing for breath in the aftermath of that scream that they began to talk to him.

Jeffrey Bell had believed he had known fear in his life.

He hadn't.

Not until then.

————

Tasha had not expected to sleep at all that night. It had taken all the calm she'd been able to muster to walk into the condo building with Brodie, to smile at the security guard at the desk and comment on what a pleasant walk they'd had, plus delicious dessert and wonderful music to enjoy.

This was the usual weekend evening guard, Nelson, so Tasha assumed that Stewart had ended his extended shift. But she had no idea when that was, or which of the guards might be—apparently was—an operative for the other side.

One of the shadows.

By the time they got up to her condo, Tasha was shaking, mostly from an inner chill, but Brodie nevertheless calmly suggested that she take a hot shower and get ready for bed, and he'd fix her a cup of soothing tea.

Tasha really wanted to object to being coddled, to point out that she'd slept most of the day already, and she wasn't sure if it was a mutinous expression on her face or Brodie's new and rather unsettling ability to read her that caused him to stop her at the doorway of her bedroom, his hands on her shoulders.

"Listen to me," he said quietly. "Whatever Duran has planned is more elaborate than anything I've known him to do, and that means it's been in the works for a long, long time. That means he's committed. It means that taking Astrid out of play, even if it's for a week instead of a day, isn't going to stop him. He's a chess player half a dozen moves ahead, so he considered this possibility, planned for it. He may have to take a detour, we may buy a few more hours or an extra day, but sooner or later, he'll be ready for his next move."

"Me?"

"You're part of it. At least his endgame. Vital to it, I'd guess."

"But you don't know how."

"Even more than usual," Brodie confessed a bit wryly. "This is more than just a desire to add to his psychic collection. He could have grabbed you before I ever got here. And we know now that he had people in place that could have done just that, probably without even raising an alarm. But he didn't, and we don't know why he didn't."

"No," Tasha said, "he just encircled me with a web of enemies pretending to be my neighbors and friends."

"As far as I know, he's never done that before."

Tasha felt incredibly tired all of a sudden, whether because she had used her abilities in a new way or simply because all the questions and puzzles and dangers were simply overwhelming.

"You're safe here," Brodie told her. "I automatically activate the jammer every time we come in, just in case they slipped somebody in to plant more bugs, even though Duran usually doesn't repeat himself. Listen, go take that shower to get warm again; I'll have the tea ready when you are. After that, you need to sleep, and I mean all night. You have to conserve your energy, Tasha, rest whenever you can."

"Because we may have to move. In a hurry."

"We may. Or you may have to use your abilities unexpectedly, and that's always going to take energy. No matter which way you look at it, you need to rest when you can."

Tasha hadn't thought it possible, and later she hazily suspected that Brodie had put something in the hot and soothing tea he had ready for her, but she really didn't care. She needed sleep, and falling into that curiously safe and warm unconsciousness was too blissful to fight.

Brodie stood in the doorway of her bedroom for a few moments just listening to her even breathing, then slowly retreated, drawing the door almost closed behind him. She would sleep, he knew, for at least eight hours and probably more. He wasn't at all sure he should have slipped an herbal sleep aid into her tea, but his instincts told him she needed to rest, deeply, and the combination of herbs they had discovered some time ago seemed to help psychics, especially, rest when they needed to. And so it was something he always carried in an inner jacket pocket whenever he was working.

Brodie debated with himself briefly but finally dug in the other inside jacket pocket for another burner phone, a little surprised to find that it still held a charge, and called base.

"How's Tasha?" she asked by way of a greeting.

He kept his voice quiet. "Asleep. And badly shaken. Do you have any idea what the hell is going on? This is not Duran's usual MO, and I'm baffled as to why he'd change tactics at this stage."

"Maybe to throw us off."

"I don't know. I get the sense this has more to do with a specific plan concerning Tasha than a general change in his tactics."

She sighed. "I get the same sense. But I don't know what it means, John. None of our psychics are getting anything—and I mean even more so than usual."

Brodie frowned. "Can you explain that?"

"No. We have a theory about it, but no way to really test that theory, not without opening up too many of our psychics to attack. Duran has—for want of a better term—thrown up a net of his people surrounding Tasha, whether to keep her in a single area and under observation, or to keep something or someone away from her. Either way, they're taking no steps to harm or interfere with her. Just watching, and even that seems casual and unthreatening."

"Except that now Tasha feels threatened."

"Because she saw them. The shadows. Even more, now she knows she can see them. And as frightened as that makes her, it may be your only way to get her out of there."

"You believe we should leave?"

"Not tonight. Maybe not tomorrow. We have a safe house ready, but . . . I'm not at all sure hiding Tasha away is the answer, not for her."

"Because we don't know why Duran wants her?"

"Yeah. We need to know that, John. We can't really gauge the threat against her until we have that information."

"How do you propose we get it?"

"Sarah believes she can find out."

Brodie knew he was frowning now. "I really wish we had another way. We don't know for sure that going public and being so visible is the protection we hope it is."

"True enough. But she has Tucker, and he has almost unlimited resources—besides being her husband and being connected to her on a psychic level. He's probably better than anyone we have in place to make sure nobody gets to her."

"I know, I know. I just . . . don't like it."

Shrewdly, she said, "Because you aren't their Guardian?"

"I have trust issues; we both know that." He drew a breath and let it out in a short sigh. "But my focus now is and has to be Tasha, so whatever Sarah is up to, the rest of you will have to keep an eye on."

"We will. John, we have more than one operative out there gathering intelligence. Even though the security in Tasha's building has been infiltrated, so far they've shown no intentions of harming Tasha or even going after her. I hate assumptions as much as you do, but for now we need to assume that the two of you are safe locked in her condo. I know she's sleeping; you need to get some rest as well."

"I can't rest not knowing what's happening."

"Get comfortable on her couch and take a few of those catnaps of yours tonight. Look, put something against her door, a rough and ready but highly effective alarm. Use a table with a shaky vase on the edge, something that would wake you instantly if it was disturbed; Duran's people can't walk through walls any more than we can. But get some rest. We both know everything could change in a heartbeat, and you'll be no good to Tasha or us if you're not at your best."

"Okay, okay. Just try to get me some answers, please. I really don't like fumbling around in the dark. And I like even less being at the center of this web of Duran's, especially when I don't know if this is a new tactic he's trying out—or something designed just for Tasha."

"Get some rest, and we'll try to find out."

"Copy that. Let me know if and when you do."

"Of course. Take care of Tasha."

Brodie turned off the cell, then repeated his actions of earlier and flushed the battery before dropping the useless phone into the trash can in the kitchen. Then he did as suggested, rigging a makeshift early-warning system by placing Tasha's small hall table against the inside of the condo's door and carefully balancing a vase he found on the edge.

Any pressure on the door from the outside and, alarm or no alarm, the vase would hit the marble entryway floor, and if Brodie happened to be napping the crash would wake him instantly.

He checked on Tasha again, finding her sleeping deeply, seemingly peacefully, then made himself comfortable on her couch in the living room, the TV on low to a documentary channel.

And despite everything on his mind, with a soldier's long practice he was almost instantly asleep.

———

"There are," Murphy said, "just some things you can't plan for. Not even a chess whiz like you."

"You're the one leaping to conclusions."

"What, because I can recognize sparks between two people?"

"No, because you're assuming they'll do something about it."

"Most people do," she told him dryly. "You can call it chemistry, biology, or just plain emotions, but the truth is that we know instinctively how rare it is. And we're pretty much driven from that point on."

"She's in danger. That's going to be the driving force behind any action Brodie takes. He's on guard for her, not for himself."

Murphy's eyes narrowed. "I really hope you're not planning to try to get to her through him. I told you, I can't afford to lose Brodie."

"What makes you think you would?"

Bluntly, she said, "Because he'll die a bloody death before he does anything at all to help you, Duran, and that goes double for being used to hurt a psychic. There's hate, and then there's *hate*. We've lost too many in this war, and Brodie blames himself for more than one of them. He also blames you."

"And maybe I don't need an enemy with a hatred that personal."

"What, and I'm supposed to believe that's suddenly bothering you after years?" She tilted her head suddenly like a sharply inquisitive bird. "Something's changed. You didn't count on him connecting with Tasha Solomon, did you?"

"He isn't psychic."

"You mean he wasn't. But neither was Tucker Mackenzie. It's not as if it's unprecedented. You had to know
it was possible. And I'm betting Astrid confirmed it."

Duran moved slightly, a rare betrayal of tension. Murphy couldn't see him very well, because as usual they were
meeting in a dim and out-of-the-way place, this time a
deserted section of an underground parking garage. And
she didn't flatter herself into believing she could read him
even after all this time. But sometimes body language
didn't require knowledge.

Watching him intently, Murphy said, "So that really is
the rub. Not so much that he connected with Tasha, but
that it turns out he has some psychic ability of his own.
You really didn't expect that. And it's somehow a threat
to one of your plans."

Instead of responding to that, Duran said, "Astrid said
you were the one who took her out tonight."

That was a topic Murphy had been prepared for.
"Something I've been practicing."

"I didn't know your abilities worked that way."

"Abilities evolve, Duran. Or didn't you know that?"

"They don't evolve in quantum leaps."

"No? Well, if you say so. I'm sure you've tested your
psychics and know all about our limitations."

"Don't assume too much," Duran warned her. "You
know what they say about that."

"Yeah, yeah. We both know I'm assuming nothing; I
may not know why, specifically, you need psychics, but
I'm damned positive your group has been studying the
hell out of the ones you have. Look, I'll work with the

devil if I have to, but only because I'm convinced there's something a lot worse threatening both of us—and there are a few goals we have in common, at least for the time being."

"That was the understanding," he agreed.

"It wasn't open-ended, Duran."

"I know that."

"Then you also know that the moment this . . . understanding . . . between us becomes untenable, it's over. And there won't be another."

Evenly, he said, "You know I do what I can."

"Achieve the goal but minimize the fallout? I know your bosses would approve a lot more violence. I know the line you're walking is as fine as the one I'm walking. And I know if your loyalty is questioned, I'll have a far worse devil to deal with."

"Then deal with me."

"By handing over Tasha Solomon? It's not going to happen, Duran. It was never going to happen, I told you that. Your side beats us to a psychic, I can barely stomach that. Casualties of war. But we have Tasha. Brodie has Tasha." She paused, then added softly, "And we know about your web."

"My web?"

"Don't play innocent, Duran, it's not your best face. Neighbors in her building. People who work in the area. People she thought were friends, or at least nonthreatening acquaintances. People you put in position to surround her. To watch her. You had plenty of time to grab Tasha or arrange some kind of *accident* to explain her disappearance, and you didn't make a move. That might prove to be a costly mistake. We know who they are now. Maybe it's your turn to lose a few soldiers."

"That wouldn't be a good idea."

"No? Why not?"

"Because they aren't there just for her. They weren't put in place only for her benefit. They are . . . an experiment."

"I don't like the sound of that."

After a moment, he said, "We trade in information, you and I."

"So far," she agreed. "Though if you pull another stunt like you did months ago, telling Brodie to look for a traitor in his own camp, I promise to make you very sorry you did."

"Took me seriously, did he?"

"I suppose I should feel grateful you weren't more specific. He doesn't trust you as far as he could throw a Buick, but that warning bothered him. And everybody's background and whereabouts at critical moments had to be gone over and accounted for. Weeks wasted while everybody was checked and checked again."

"Luckily, you're very good at what you do," Duran told her.

"I mean it, Duran. Do *not* play games with me. Trust me when I tell you that for you, I'm irreplaceable."

"Point taken," he said at last.

"I hope so. Information?"

"Tasha Solomon can . . . confirm something for you."

"What?"

"A suspicion. Speculation. Check her parentage."

"What good will it do me to know about whatever this is?" Murphy demanded.

"I don't know," he returned pleasantly. "Add to your understanding, perhaps. Provide you with another piece of the puzzle." He started to turn away, then paused to say, "You realize, of course, that I can't just stand by and allow you to spirit Solomon away without making any effort to stop you."

"Because she's important to your side. To your bosses."

"A habit of failure can't be tolerated," he said. "Which is why it won't be me personally. You understand."

"Yeah. Yeah, I understand."

He half bowed, an urbane, oddly natural gesture, and within moments Murphy knew she was alone in the garage. She stood there for a few moments longer, frowning, then checked one of the burner phones she'd recharged before this meeting.

Four A.M.

Sarah?

I'm here. Quiet night. Nobody's been—you should forgive the expression—shadowing you. No activity around Tasha. I think a security guard from their side works this part of the night shift, but I'm not sensing any threat from him. Not like before. Either he's a different guard or else his orders—or his feelings—changed.

Feelings?

Whoever I was picking up before had definite feelings about Brodie. Didn't like him. At all.

Jealous?

Could be. Tasha is a beautiful woman, and single.

They're generally so cold and ruthless, I guess I never considered one of them having those sorts of feelings.

Hey, you and I have both faced off against them in the flesh, so we know they get mad. Stands to reason they'd have other feelings as well. Maybe surprising to feel something positive for one of us, but then I don't know that it was positive. Jealousy isn't, really.

No, it isn't. You can want something without having warm, fuzzy feelings about it. Could be dangerous, that's for sure. Listen, is Tucker still up?

I'm up, he's up. What do you need?

Research. And nobody does it better.

It was around six when Tasha woke. Early for her, but not really by much. She smelled bacon frying, and it surprised her since she rarely ate breakfast here and so seldom bought or kept breakfast foods.

But then she remembered that among her take-out/delivery menus was one from a little grocery store half a block down from the coffee shop. Having groceries delivered was becoming more and more common in these busy days, especially in upscale neighborhoods where very busy professionals led very busy lives. Brodie must have found the menu and called in an order; she seriously doubted he had left the condo for a moment since last night.

She tried to keep her mind mostly blank as she went through her usual morning routine of washing her face, brushing her teeth, getting dressed. She pulled her hair back with a clip at the nape of her neck, but didn't bother with makeup. She usually didn't.

She came out of her bedroom just as Brodie was pouring coffee, and she found herself wondering how his timing was always so on target. But she pushed that vaguely curious question aside, because she didn't want to think about anything that mattered.

Not yet.

There was juice, and two plates with bacon, eggs, and toast on the counter.

"I usually don't eat this much in the morning," she said.

"Yeah, I figured. But eating meals is the same as getting rest; in a situation when you might have to move at any moment, you eat and sleep when you can."

"I get that. I'm just not hungry." She slid onto a stool and glanced over to the living room, where her TV was tuned to a news channel, the volume down low. "Anything happening in the world outside our little bubble?"

"Usual. Crime, war, economics, human interest stories. And politics, of course. Lots of politics in an election year."

"I suppose I should get more involved in that," she said, taking a bite of bacon and discovering her appetite.

"Politics? Why?"

"I suppose so I can vote and then bitch about it later. You can't really not vote and then bitch about what's happening. At least as a voter you try to make your voice and opinions heard."

Brodie sipped his coffee and eyed her. "Why do I get the feeling you're trying to be terribly normal today?"

"Maybe because I am." Tasha pushed her eggs around on the plate, then set her fork down with a sigh and reached for her coffee. "All this time I've been living here, believing I was safe, when the . . . the enemy was all around me. Wearing smiling faces. Pretending to be my neighbors. What am I supposed to *do* with that?"

"Accept it. And move on."

"Figuratively? Or literally?"

"I don't know yet," he said frankly. "We have a safe house prepared for you, but no one is entirely certain yet if that's the way you should go."

"The hide or go public question, you mean?"

He looked at her thoughtfully.

"What's your preference?"

Tasha felt herself frowning. "I don't like the idea of hiding. Of never being able to live anything like a normal life."

"Do you think going public would give you that? There is a cost, Tasha. Plenty of people would be afraid of you, but there would also be the ones who believe you can help them. The ones with lost children, lost loves, the ones looking for lottery numbers and the cures for diseases and a glimpse into the future to give them answers— or an edge."

"So I become a recluse or a sideshow freak. Great. That's just great." She slid off the stool and carried her coffee a few steps toward the living room.

That was when she saw a political ad on TV. She couldn't hear the sound, but it hardly mattered. A candidate for the office of lieutenant governor in South Carolina. A handsome, smiling face. A spotless record in lesser offices in his climb toward the office he now aspired to. A rare bachelor candidate, but young enough to make that a plus.

Eliot Wolfe.

Tasha's coffee cup fell from nerveless fingers and shattered on the marble floor.

FIFTEEN

Bishop rejoined his wife in the spacious foyer of what had once been and perhaps would be again a splendid old home; right now it was partially restored, filled with the clutter of work suddenly stopped. Paint-spattered dust-cloths were draped over pieces of antique furniture, saw-horses and ladders waited to be used again, and leaning against walls beside their too-modern replacements were original windows and doors in various stages of returning to their former glory.

"Nothing out of the ordinary I could find," Miranda reported, frowning slightly. "It's an old house in the middle of being restored. Did Henry's client say she was going to finish the work?"

"If she can find someone as good as Henry. Or if Henry comes back. She said that with real hope."

"Because of the house or Henry? You said he was a bit of a loner, right?"

"Yeah, not at all a ladies' man. But from what I could tell, women were drawn to him. Maybe the sad eyes."

Miranda lifted an eyebrow at him.

"When I was checking into his background, a woman who had gone to school with him made that comment. It stuck in my mind."

"Was he a strong medium?"

"About a five on our scale. He probably would have ranked higher if he had wanted to consciously use his abilities. But he never did. Said the spirits came to him, silent and smiling, and led him to wherever various owners had stashed or packed away original fittings and fixtures. He really didn't want to know how to control it or how to make it work for him. Just wanted to keep doing the work he loved and be left alone."

She shook her head. "That's the hellish part of all this, isn't it? These psychics, at least the ones you kept track of, just wanted to live the most normal lives they could. They struggled to either suppress their abilities or work them into daily living with as little drama as possible. And then one day, somebody just . . . takes them away. And does God only knows what with them."

"I'm guessing that at the very least, they're being forced to explore their abilities whether they want to or not."

"Psychic abilities don't exactly come to heel when called. We know this."

"Better than most, yeah. But I'm also guessing various forms of persuasion are being used."

"Torture?"

It was Bishop's turn to frown. "Murphy was very certain and very clear in what she said about the abducted psychics never being the same again. Since she also said no abducted psychics they know of ever returned to their former lives, I'm guessing she knows what she does because she or members of their group have encountered abducted psychics in the field—working for the other side."

"Persuaded, bribed, tortured, converted. Pick your poison."

He nodded. "Sounds like. Forever altered. But what's *behind* it all? If they were only taking precogs, I'd guess they were in it for profit, looking for someone who could reliably predict the winning team or the next card in the deck or whatever foreknowledge would net the most money. But they're taking people with every psychic ability we know of, pretty much. Where's the rhyme or reason in that?"

"It's coming clearer to me how so many people could have looked for answers for years, even decades, without finding them," Miranda confessed.

"Yeah, a tougher goal than one might imagine. If not for profit, they must have some use for the different abilities. And . . . psychic abilities are *so* different, one from the other, as well as having aspects unique to that individual.

"So no pattern to hold to there. Not, at least, one I can see yet."

"Well, since Henry's ability is as a medium, and neither of us shares that, I somehow doubt we're going to find any useful information here. Just like at Katie's place. You want to go for door number three and try Grace Seymore's house?"

"You don't sound terribly enthusiastic," he noted.

"I just don't think we're going to find anything useful looking at another empty house."

Before Bishop could respond to that, a buzzing sound came from the leather satchel-type briefcase he had left on a dustcloth-draped low table in the foyer. He went to it and pulled out his cell phone. "Might even last till noon," he murmured, noting before taking the call the only-slightly-diminished battery he had unplugged from its charger barely two hours previously.

"Bishop." He listened, his eyes on his wife, frowning a little for a moment before his brows lifted in surprise. "I see. Thank you, Detective, for the call. I won't forget it."

"What is it?" Miranda asked as soon as he ended the call.

"Something remarkable, if we're to believe all we've been told," Bishop said to her. "That was the detective who looked into the disappearance of Grace Seymore. It appears she's come home."

It took only two steps for Brodie to reach Tasha, but when he followed her fixed stare, all he saw on TV was a chirpy blonde offering financial market information.

"Tasha?"

"You aren't going to like this," she said slowly. "But I need you to trust me."

"I trust you," he said, already not liking the sense of foreboding that made him want to stop her from saying whatever it was.

"Good. I need to see Murphy. Alone."

"Why?"

"I said you'd have to trust me. I need to talk to her about something."

"Something I can't hear?"

She hesitated. "Something you can't hear . . . yet. John, please. It's very important."

He hesitated, staring at her. She was pale but composed. Even more, the odd link they had shared since her trip to the "maze" somewhere in his mind had apparently been shut down on her end.

Very, very tightly.

He had absolutely no idea what she was thinking or feeling.

"Tasha—"

"Please. As soon as possible, John."

"Tasha, you're being watched. Very closely."

"She can meet us at the coffee shop. And you can . . . sit a few tables away. Still watching out for me. Still being a Guardian."

"Murphy doesn't have a connection to you yet, not a visible one obvious to the other side. We don't like to expose all our soldiers. It's bad strategy. And her part in all this usually keeps her on the periphery of things and in the dark."

"John." Tasha's voice was very steady, and she still refused to look at him. "I realize there are risks. But I have a feeling Murphy will agree with me that I have a good reason for her to come out of the shadows." She almost but not quite laughed. "That phrase is never going to mean the same thing, is it? At least to some of us. Out of the shadows."

To say that Brodie was curious by then was to grossly understate the matter. He brushed aside phrases corrupted by this war. "You don't believe I can keep secrets?" he demanded. "Now, after all this?"

"It's not your secret to keep." She looked at him finally, her eyes dark and still. "It's mine. For now, at least. John, I need to talk to Murphy. I need to talk to her as soon as possible." She was reasonably sure Brodie had never known the name of the man who had killed his wife, but what she wasn't sure of was whether he had caught a glimpse, or had later—in what must have been an obsessive search—uncovered information that might now identify Eliot Wolfe to him.

Eliot Wolfe, who was a born psychic. Eliot Wolfe, whose campaign schedule, shown on TV, included a fundraiser here in Charleston less than two weeks away.

Eliot Wolfe, who had once been part of the eugenics program of the other side—and probably, certainly, still was. Just waiting for his genetic match to be identified, his mate seduced or compelled to join with him.

As Elizabeth Brodie had refused to do.

Once Brodie knew that . . . Tasha wouldn't have bet a dime on Wolfe's survival. What she wasn't at all sure of was what was best to do, both for Brodie's sake and for their side of this war. Because identifying a player on the other side, especially one who seemed destined to take his place in a high position of state government—quite possibly as a stepping-stone to a national position—could be useful . . . later on.

Unless Brodie killed Wolfe.

"I don't like it, Tasha."

"I didn't expect you to. Get in touch with Murphy, John. Please. I need to see her as soon as possible."

It was patently clear Brodie wasn't happy about it, but he did call Murphy, and twenty minutes later Tasha was sitting across from her at Tasha's regular table at the coffee shop—with Brodie about four tables away and not happy about that, either. Especially since Murphy had her back to him, and she prevented him from being able to see Tasha.

Tasha waited until the waitress she had thought of as innocuous brought them coffee and muffins, taking the time to get a good look at Murphy, since they had met only once and in the dark.

She was a tall woman with short and rather spiky blond hair—a curious and youthful, almost punk style that suited her narrow face and sharp green eyes. She also dressed in a youthful, slightly rebellious sort of style, from the thermal shirt underneath her worn black leather jacket to the khaki pants sporting several belts, and lace-up combat boots that didn't seem at all incongruous on her fairly small feet.

She carried a worn leather bag more satchel than purse, slung across from shoulder to opposite hip, and Tasha had the feeling that if she'd had to leave everything behind her at a moment's notice, Murphy would have everything she needed in that bag.

When the waitress delivered their order and then left with a smile, Murphy said calmly, "She's one of them, I take it."

"I was trying not to let anything show," Tasha managed.

"Yeah, that's when most people do." Murphy smiled briefly, her vivid green eyes watchful. "Don't worry, I doubt she saw it. I did. Brodie did, even four tables away. Why is he, by the way?"

"You're psychic, right?" Tasha kept her voice low, casual. She sipped her latte.

"Yeah. Sort of a telepath."

"*Sort of* a telepath?"

"I pick up things sometimes, once I'm tapped in. But what I'm really good at is serving as a conduit so one telepath who's . . . out of range . . . can communicate with another."

Tasha stared at her. "That voice in my head."

"Another one of our people. She needed to try to communicate with you. To . . . make you aware of what was going on so that when Brodie approached you, it wouldn't be a total shock."

"I haven't met her yet."

It wasn't a question, but Murphy answered anyway. "No, she's outside the perimeter Duran has set up around you. Safer that way."

"Does Duran know about her?"

"About her, yes; she was a target not so long ago. But

I doubt he knows she's nearby. She has a hell of a shield and, unlike most of us, can use her abilities even with it up. Duran has psychics of his own to sense us, but as far as we know he's had only one here."

"Astrid. I sort of met her."

"In the maze, yeah. You gave her a pretty bad headache with that. Our other psychic made it considerably worse so she'll be no good to Duran for another day or two."

"Sarah Mackenzie."

Murphy's brows rose.

"I . . . picked that up from Brodie."

"So it's true, you two are connected."

"I'm not sure exactly how that works." Tasha realized she was picking at her muffin and frowned down at the crumbs. "I think it happened in the maze, but I don't know why. It seems . . . intermittent, that contact. Sometimes I know what he's thinking without really knowing the words. Sometimes I pick up emotions. Other times, I—I have the feeling I could see as deeply into him as I wanted to. If I wanted to."

"You don't?"

"It's an intrusion. An unwelcome one. He hasn't said, but I know it makes him uneasy to know we're connected at all. He doesn't want to be connected. To anyone."

"Yeah, that's Brodie." Murphy straightened her shoulders and said, briskly but still quietly, "I think you wanted to see me for something besides small talk."

Tasha hesitated, then said, "How much do you know about Brodie's wife?" This time, her voice was low.

Murphy's eyes narrowed. "The bare facts, like most

everyone else. She was a psychic. He loved her. They were married. She was murdered. Not one of the fake murders we all know about; she literally died in his arms. About ten years ago. And Brodie never found her killer. That's why he's in this war of ours. At least until you came along and you two connected however it is you connected, the stake Brodie had in this war was emotional. The need to protect psychics. The drive for answers. For justice."

"For revenge?"

"Maybe. Maybe he's entitled."

Tasha looked up, straight into the steady gaze of her companion. "The question is, if someone could tell him why she was murdered, and by who, should they? Even if the man who murdered Elizabeth Brodie, who is also psychic and quite definitely on the other side, may one day be governor of this state?"

———

Katie Swan said, "I can't." She said it, by now, like a litany. Like a plea. *Please stop. Please let me go home. I won't tell anyone. I promise, I'll never tell anyone.*

Jesus, who would believe me anyway?

"Try again." The voice was cold, implacable, remorseless. It might have been a machine, repeating the command again and again with no sign of frustration or impatience.

Before Katie on the stainless steel table lay a dagger, turned so that it was aimed, roughly, at a man-shaped stuffed target across the room. It was, perhaps, ten feet away from her.

It might as well have been ten miles.

Katie had passed exhaustion a long time ago. They had broken her down first with the pain, using some technique she couldn't begin to understand; it had felt like they were tearing her body apart, ripping it to shreds, and yet she hadn't, afterward, been able to find a single mark anywhere on her.

They had allowed her to sleep, or maybe they had drugged her, because however long she slept, she had awakened still exhausted, aching all over. Then they had put her in this room, and one by one a succession of objects had been placed before her, and she had been ordered to move them with her mind.

Easy things at first. A feather. A pencil. A little book.

Then harder things. Heavier things. Larger things.

She had tried for countless minutes to move a cinder block placed on the table. It hadn't budged until something in Katie had snapped, and she had cried out in frustration.

The heavy piece of masonry not only lifted, it literally flew across the room and crashed into the glass protecting her tormentor, safe in her little watcher's booth.

The glass—or whatever it was—had not shown even a scratch. The cinder block was in pieces on the floor. And the face behind the window had never changed expression.

"Again," she had ordered.

They weren't stupid. Between every "test" Katie was ordered to blindfold herself, ordered to place her hands flat on the table, and ordered to remain motionless while someone entered and placed the next object on the table.

Then she was to remove her blindfold—the chains fastened at either end to the table and the heavy metal bands around her wrists just long enough to allow that movement—place her hands flat on the table again, and use her telekinetic ability on whatever they had given her to move.

She had simply refused at first, only to find that the cuffs were yet another instrument of torture, jolting her with intensely painful shocks that increased in intensity every time she refused.

So she stopped refusing.

But she was so *tired*.

"Try again," the emotionless woman behind the glass ordered, her voice perfectly clear even though Katie couldn't see a sign of a speaker anywhere in her stainless steel box of a room.

A faint warning tingle around her wrists made Katie focus on the target across the room. On the red circle drawn just where a human heart would be located. She stared at the target, then at the dagger on the table. It twitched, perhaps an inch or two.

"Try again."

"I couldn't kill a person," she whispered.

"It's a stuffed target. Try again."

"I need to rest. I'll do better after I've rested."

"Try again."

"Something to eat—"

A stronger shock.

Katie whimpered and tried to focus on the dagger. This was not close to the heaviest thing she had moved, or the largest. But this time she had been ordered to aim, to be precise. To hit a target.

Something she had never done before, with the single exception of mentally pulling something toward herself and reaching out to catch it in her hand. A pen. A book she'd been reading. The TV remote.

This was so, so different.

Frightened and wary of the shock, she tried to bargain. "If I do it, if I hit the target, then you'll let me rest."

"Of course," her tormentor said with suspicious promptness.

Desperate to rest, to be out of this horrible room if only for an hour or two, Katie concentrated, and with all the strength and focus she could muster, she made the dagger lift—and then shoot across the room and hit the stuffed target.

"You missed the heart. Do it again."

———————

Grace Seymore lived in a nice little house in a nice little neighborhood where, apparently, most of her neighbors had been certain she had simply gone to visit family and would return.

Which she had. And according to the cop who was Bishop's source, she had returned with as little fanfare as when she had left.

"I really don't know why you worried about me," Grace said to Bishop and his wife as she poured tea for them. In little flowered cups. "I was just visiting family."

"So you said." It was easy for Bishop to keep his voice

even and casual because he'd had a lot of practice, but even he had a difficult time keeping his gaze off what was without question a quite substantial baby bump. "Did you go home to share the good news?" he added.

"About the baby? Oh, no, not really. It was only an aunt and cousin, all I have left of family, so really just a visit. We'd been out of touch."

"But they were happy for you," Miranda probed carefully.

"I suppose." Grace appeared thoughtful, both hands caressing her rounded belly. "I didn't really care. Don't care. The baby and I will be just fine." She smiled.

Bishop tossed tact out the window. "What about the father?" he asked bluntly.

"Oh, he won't be involved. We met on a cruise, you see. He didn't want a baby. But I want her. And I can raise her just fine on my own." Her smile widened. "We'll be fine."

"Your ex-husband—"

"He's not part of this. He didn't want me, we both know that. He didn't understand me, didn't understand the things I can do. But my baby will understand, because she'll be able to do those things too."

Miranda exchanged a glance with her husband, then said, "Grace, you know that Noah looks out for people like you. For psychics. When you disappeared, we did some checking. You didn't go on a cruise."

"Of course I did. Months ago." She was still smiling. "Listen, I really appreciate the concern, but I'm fine, as you can see. We're both fine. So there's nothing to worry about." Her oddly blank gaze shifted to Bishop. "And no reason to look out for me. I am grateful, Bishop, you know that, but I really don't need anyone looking out for me. I can take care of myself. And the baby, of course."

Miranda tried again. "Grace—"

"Really, Miranda, we'll both be fine. I'll let you know when the baby's born, and you can come visit. See for yourselves that we're just fine."

Once again, Miranda exchanged a glance with her husband, both of them certain that as soon as they stepped out the front door, Grace would forget all about them. The only thing in her mind was the child she would deliver, probably within only a few weeks.

They finally said their good-byes and left, a last image of a smiling Grace waving good-bye from her front door a haunting one for them both.

Miranda said, "She doesn't have any family, does she? Not even an aunt or cousin."

"No, and Murphy was right." Bishop's tone was grim. "The woman in that house is not Grace Seymore, not anymore."

"They did that, didn't they? They got her pregnant, and before that they made her somebody else." Miranda shivered visibly. "You know what I kept thinking?"

Even with their easy telepathic link closed down, Bishop knew. "The same things I was thinking. Stepford wives, and pod people."

"I think it's time we talked to Brodie and Murphy. They need to know."

"You won't get an argument," Bishop replied, and put the car in gear.

———

Tucker Mackenzie frowned down at his laptop. "Okay, this is unexpected but not all that unusual."

"What is?" his wife asked.

"Tasha Solomon was adopted. As an infant."

"Do you think she knows?"

Tucker's frown deepened. "I sort of doubt it. I had to dig for information, and dig deeply. If she was aware of the adoption, I doubt there would have been so many layers."

Sarah came and joined him at the dining table in their hotel suite, coffee in hand and wearing a frown of her own. It was early morning, and both had been up most of the night. "Well . . . as you say, not so unusual. So why did Murphy want her parentage checked out? To find out if she was a born psychic? We already know that."

"Maybe . . . to find out if her real parents were born psychics."

After a moment, Sarah said, "Can you find out?"

"Maybe. Adoption records are sealed, but I long ago found a crowbar to unseal official documents."

"You're very bad," Sarah said, but absently, adding almost immediately, "If Tasha's real parents were psychics, do we assume they're connected to the other side?"

Typing briskly on his keyboard, Tucker said, "Not sure. Duran likes tools, so they could have been that, just tools, a means to an end."

"Psychic babies?"

"We've talked about it being possible. Maybe this is the first evidence we'll find to prove it's more than possible. First, we have to find out if she was in the official adoption system or this was a private adoption. We need to know if her mother was an unwed mother. If she was compensated for giving birth and, if so, how well and by whom. If there's even any record of who the father was. And, if possible, we need to find out where Tasha's birth mother is now."

Sarah frowned. "Because if she was connected or being used by the other side . . ."

"Then unless she died in childbirth, it's doubtful she only had one child. Not if they were using her in this breeding program we've been theorizing. The one I really hope we're wrong about."

Sarah leaned back slowly, her frown gone but replaced by a bleak expression. "Tasha's close to thirty. If we're right about this . . . program . . . she could be among the first generations of psychics deliberately produced by breeding two born psychics."

"Could be why Duran wants her so badly," Tucker noted, still typing.

"But wouldn't he have her? I mean, if she was part of this eugenics program, wouldn't their side have kept track, and closely? If they have a particular use in mind for their—their offspring—then why allow her to grow up in a normal life with normal, nonpsychic parents?"

"Maybe she—and the others—needed to grow up that way. To live normal childhoods, normal lives."

"As psychics? Granted, I came to it late, but from what all the born psychics have said, growing up psychic runs the gamut from incredibly difficult to being locked away in a mental ward. *Especially* if you're born to or raised by non-psychics who can never understand what you are and generally consider you to have some sort of mental illness."

Tucker sat back in his own chair, the humming laptop evidence that he had a program running, and gazed steadily at his wife. "Maybe that had to be part of it. Survival of the fittest. You'd have to learn control, good control. You'd have to be mentally and emotionally tough to grow up with abilities that had to remain secret, shielded. The born psychics we've met have all been that way, to varying degrees. It's the created psychics who struggle that tend to be a lot more fragile, at least at first. And sometimes they remain fragile, if they survive at all."

Slowly, Sarah said, "That might also explain the six-month window for psychics who were created like I was, abilities triggered by trauma. Maybe it takes that long for the other side to be certain that we have . . . whatever it is they need. That we can cope. That we can learn control. That we aren't as fragile as we might seem to be in the beginning."

"Maybe, but we still don't know what it is they're looking for in psychics. It can't just be strength or the ability to cope. They've taken strong psychics and walked away from others. Taken well-adjusted psychics—but also taken some pretty fragile ones."

With a sigh, Sarah said, "You know, it's very frustrating that just when it seems we have a glimmer of understanding into their motives, it turns into just more smoke and mirrors."

"Which could also be another of their defense mechanisms," Tucker pointed out. "This side's always been hamstrung by having too little reliable information, too few answers to too many questions. It's impossible to fight anything but defensively when you don't know what the other side is really after."

"Other than psychics."

He nodded. "Other than psychics." A soft tone drew his attention back to his laptop, which had clearly finished running its program, and Tucker frowned at the screen, scrolling through what was obviously a lot of information before finally speaking.

"So . . . Tasha's birth mother spent the last few months of her pregnancy, and her delivery, at a home for unwed mothers not all that far from Charleston, interestingly enough. From the looks of these records, the Solomons had made all the arrangements to adopt the child at least three months before she was born."

"Money change hands?"

"Not enough. According to these records, the home itself paid all the bills, from food and clothing to medical services. The adoptive parents paid a very reasonable fee that didn't come close to even covering expenses."

"That isn't normal, is it?"

"Beats me. But unless there's some kind of giant non-profit funding this—of which there is no sign—or an altruistic millionaire handy, I don't see how a place like this could keep its doors open. Having babies isn't cheap."

He worked a few more minutes, then swore under his breath. "This could take me years. Ownership of the *business* traces back to a dummy corporation, which traces back to another dummy corporation—and so on. It's like a hall of mirrors. Somebody definitely didn't want anyone to find out who actually owned and ran this place."

"Was Tasha's birth mother paid when she left?"

Tucker worked for several more moments, frowning, then looked up at his wife. "According to this, she lived at the home. For years, before and after Tasha was born. There are about a dozen names of young women here, and every one of them stays long enough to have at least three babies, who were already adopted even before they were born, mostly to prominent or upper-middle-class couples. Then those names vanish and new names appear."

"Different girls?"

"Or just an attempt to keep out nosy authorities. Turn a blonde into a brunette, give her a different name, and who would really notice? Although there is a remarkable lack of inspection records I'd expect any place with medical facilities to keep. I'm guessing some pretty hefty bribes were paid to all the right people."

"What about the biological fathers?"

Tucker scrolled a bit further, then looked up at his wife wryly. "John Smith."

"Seriously?"

"Says here. Variations of very ordinary names listed as the biological fathers to numerous babies. Smith. Jones. Johnson. Anderson. Same with the girls, really. Very common, ordinary names—and none of the men appear to be at all involved in the lives of the young women or at all interested in the children. The women are just noted as pregnant, no explanation of just how that happened in a home for unwed mothers even though a name is noted as biological father. It's a safe bet that digging to find these supposed fathers will net me exactly zero info."

"Any way to tell if the girls were psychic?"

He rubbed the back of his neck, frowning. "There's absolutely nothing official about the emotional or psychological traits or health of the mothers. Brief medical notes of normal pregnancies, but that's it. No psych evals, no record of counseling, nothing. At least nothing official. I'm guessing if this place did belong to the other side, they made damned sure there were no records kept that might have even hinted that the mothers were psychic. Given enough time and background info on the staff, I might be able to find someone who kept a private record. But if we're looking at thirty years or more of records . . ."

"What?" Sarah asked.

Tucker frowned back down at his computer and went back to work. "I just wonder . . ."

"What?"

"How long they could have . . . Goddammit."

"I'm afraid to ask."

"This particular home for unwed mothers was in operation for six years. Then it closed its doors. Long enough to make progress, but not so long that anyone became suspicious." Tucker drew a breath, and said, "Why do I get the feeling if I keep looking I'll find more of these in other places. A lot more."

SIXTEEN

Murphy was very still for a long time, leaning back in her chair with her hands clasped over her middle. Expression-less. Then, finally, she said, "How would you know that? Any of that? Don't tell me you found it in Brodie's mind, because I don't believe he knew much except that Elizabeth was psychic, she broke with her family, and some-body killed her."

"No, it wasn't in his mind. His . . . grief and rage, yes. The facts he knew. But that's not how I found out. After that connection was made, after the maze, maybe while I was still sleeping or maybe when I was wide awake, I don't know, I had a visitor in my room. Elizabeth Brodie."

Murphy didn't change expression. "Have you ever had any other mediumistic experiences?"

"No, never."

"But you had a visit from a dead woman."

Tasha leaned forward, elbows on the table, her hands cradling her coffee. "She told me her life story. About being born a psychic, about freaking out her parents—and about an abduction, when she was very young."

"An abduction."

"She was taken somewhere and kept for days. And she was heavily drugged, enough so that her psychic abilities were useless. When she woke up, she was in a hospital with her parents bending over her. She had absolutely no memory of the abduction or the days afterward. Her parents told her the bare minimum, on the advice of therapists, just that she'd been taken from them, but she was safe again and they'd make sure she was always safe. And she didn't know for a long time that they'd made a deal with her abductors to get her back."

"I'm guessing you're not talking about ransom money. What kind of deal?" Murphy asked slowly.

"That when the time came, when she was old enough, she'd be married off to a man she was introduced to while she was still a teenager. Eliot Wolfe."

Murphy opened her mouth, then closed it.

Tasha took that as an invitation to continue. "In retrospect, I suppose Wolfe jumped the gun, maybe pushed too hard too soon. He'd been a welcome visitor in her life for years, another psychic there to . . . help her learn to cope with her abilities, or so she believed. She was a teenager, she had a crush on him, so she didn't look very deeply for a long time. But, gradually, she became suspicious. Things over-heard, looks intercepted. She managed to break through the walls they had built around her. And figured out the truth. That she had been matched with Wolfe years before, presumably while they held her hostage. Some kind of tests, but able to measure whatever they needed measured while she was unconscious. Maybe genetic, DNA. Some marker they'd learned to look for. In any case, whatever they were looking for, they found in her. And so she was intended for Wolfe. So they could breed more psychics.

"Once she knew that, she couldn't stay there. I doubt she even asked herself the why of it. She was horrified. So she ran. Changed her name, started a quiet life somewhere in the midwest. And met Brodie. Not the Brodie we know now, of course. Extraordinary in . . . perfectly normal ways. A law student with a bright future ahead of him. They fell in love. Eventually, they got married.

"And perhaps if Elizabeth had kept her gifts hidden, they would have lived a perfectly normal life. But she . . . encountered young psychics, lost and afraid, who needed a teacher. So she became that."

Grim, Murphy said, "And landed back on their radar."

"She was married to Brodie, living a normal life. I suppose she thought they'd forgotten about her. That her normal life, her marriage, protected her. Until Eliot Wolfe sat down across from her at a sidewalk café where she waited to meet Brodie. Until he told her very reasonably that she was meant for him, that they were a genetic match, fated to be together."

Murphy drew a breath and let it out slowly. "I suppose she told him about Brodie and he didn't care."

"Pretty much. He finally left after telling her again that

they would be together, no matter how much she pro-
tested or how far she ran. She was spooked, unsettled.
Finally left the café for a shortcut, hoping to meet Brodie
quicker. And I suppose she must have convinced Wolfe,
earlier, that she'd never belong to him, because when she
saw him, he had a gun. And he shot her."

Murphy nodded slowly. "Shot her—and disappeared
again. I read the reports. There were no witnesses able to
describe the shooter. No one even remembered seeing a
man sitting with her at the café—however he pulled that
off. No evidence. He'd even used a revolver, so there was
no shell casing. Brodie got there just in time to hold his
dying wife for a minute or two. And then she was gone."

Tasha was silent for a moment, then said steadily,
"We'd just eaten breakfast this morning, when I got up—
and saw what was on TV. A campaign ad. For lieutenant
governor of the state. And it was Eliot Wolfe. I wish I
could think it was a different Eliot Wolfe, but as soon as
I saw him, I knew it *was* him. He's even having a fund-
raiser here in the city in about two weeks."

"Shit," Murphy said. "We definitely have a problem."

"I've managed to shut Brodie out this morning," Tasha
said, still steady. "But he knows something's wrong. And
I don't know how long I can keep the truth from him.
Or even if I should."

"If he knows, he'll kill Wolfe."

"Yes. Kill the murderer of his wife. Kill an enemy from
the other side who has political aspirations. Kill a born
psychic who, if he hasn't already, is certainly going to be
matched again with a female born psychic."

Murphy swore, this time under her breath. "You think it might be you?"

"I think it's a good reason for them to have not grabbed me. To be watching me, but not moving against me. To have this weird and you guys say unusual web of watchers all around me. I am a born psychic, able to control my abilities quite well in public. A trait necessary, I would think, for a political wife. Want to bet I get an invitation to that fund-raiser of his?"

After a moment, Murphy said, "How long do you think you can keep Brodie out?"

"I . . . have no idea. I feel guilty keeping him out now. He has a right to know who murdered his wife. He's spent ten years living with not knowing. Not having any justice for her."

Slowly, Murphy said, "Ordinarily, I'd agree with you. Hell, I even agree with you now. But you tell Brodie, and then what? There's no way to arrest a man for murder with no evidence against him. Brodie goes after a candidate for lieutenant governor, kills him—and goes to prison for murder. Or worse. South Carolina has the death penalty."

Tasha opened her mouth, then closed it.

Murphy was nodding. "There were no witnesses. No evidence. And I'm willing to bet Wolfe will have an alibi that places him far from where Elizabeth was killed. Because Duran doesn't take chances."

"Would he have known?"

"I don't know if he knew ahead of time; at least a few of his soldiers have shown flashes of temper or ambition during which they acted more or less on their own. Those I know of vanished afterward and haven't been seen since." She frowned. "For Wolfe to have killed a born psychic, one their organization had apparently been grooming since childhood . . . I don't know how he does that and lives."

"Maybe Duran doesn't know."

Murphy's smile twisted. "I've learned the hard way to always err on the side of Duran knowing most everything I don't want him to know."

"Brodie said Duran has bosses. That he answers to someone. Maybe it wasn't his decision to make. If he knows, if they know, Wolfe must have more value to them alive than dead, no matter what he's done."

"As a born psychic, that's probably true. None of Duran's soldiers read as psychic, and yet we know he values psychics. Getting a psychic under his control placed high in a state government, his feet on the political path to even greater things, could be a feather in Duran's cap. Whatever happened in the past, he must feel he can control Wolfe now. Maybe *because* of what happened in the past. He's ruthless enough to use knowledge he has to keep that control—and follow Wolfe up the political ladder as far as he can possibly go."

"Then . . . he has to be confident Brodie can never find out who killed his wife. He'd never risk putting Wolfe in such a bright public spotlight if he thought someone, anyone, might be able to place him at the scene of that murder. Even a claim he was there, a suspicion, could completely derail any political career."

"He may have been confident of that when he settled his web all around you. Even when he decided to test you in that maze of his. But when you emerged stronger—and connected to Brodie—he had to know all bets were off."

"But a connection to Brodie would only tell me what Brodie knew; how could that threaten Duran when it never has?"

"I don't know. But what I do know is that Duran and his people have been studying psychics for a long, long time. I believe they know more about psychic abilities than we do. So even though we don't understand how it's possible, maybe Duran knows that a connection between you and Brodie . . . opens other doors."

"That's all I need. Other doors in my mind." She frowned. "Are you saying one of them let Elizabeth in?"

"I'm saying it's possible. Maybe even likely. Especially since the *only* mediumistic experience you've ever had happened right after you made that connection with Brodie."

Tasha wasn't at all sure how to deal with that. "Even if that's true, how could Duran have known I'd have a visit from the spirit of Elizabeth Brodie?"

"I don't know. Are you sure that's what it was?"

"You're the one who talked about more doors." Tasha considered for only a moment. "I'm not a medium, but she was there. She told me their whole story. She also told me . . . not to tell Brodie. Not yet. She said I'd know when it was the right time."

"But you have no idea?"

"No. I just . . . I don't feel this is the right time. As

you said, no evidence against Wolfe, and I'm reasonably certain Brodie wouldn't care."

"Definitely wouldn't care," Murphy murmured. "I mean, even though he trained as a lawyer, not having evidence against Wolfe wouldn't stop him, not if he was convinced the man killed his wife."

"And I could convince him."

"Yeah. Yeah, I'm more than reasonably sure you could."

Murphy, you guys need to come here.

Now? Bad timing.

Can't be helped. Things you need to know.

Tasha's parentage?

Yes. And more. Much, much more.

Only the gist came through, but that was more than enough.

Murphy straightened up in her chair and let out a short breath that was more than a sigh. "Okay. Let's not tell him then. Not now. Not till this is wrapped up and you're safe." She lifted a hand when Tasha would have spoken. "Or until your instincts tell you it's time. I respect instincts, Tasha. Listen to yours. Okay?"

Because there was nothing else she could do, Tasha nodded.

Murphy turned her head and made a slight gesture that Brodie, though out of hearing range, could easily see. He joined them at the small sidewalk table.

"Do I get let in on the secret?" he demanded.

Murphy smiled at him, and Tasha got the sudden sense

that between these two was a prickly, interesting friendship, part siblings and part comrades in arms.

"No," she answered simply. Then she looked at Tasha, and her smile faded. "Though I'm afraid you may be in for a shock. And, honestly, I don't know how to soften the blow."

"I think I'm a bit numb," Tasha confessed. "So, go ahead."

"Did you know you were adopted?"

Tasha blinked. "Maybe not so numb. No. No, I didn't. Are you sure about that?"

"I've had Tucker researching for hours, and he's very, very good at finding information."

Brodie glanced at Tasha's face, then back at Murphy. "What started you down that path?"

"If I say an anonymous tip, will you let it drop?" Murphy being Murphy, she figured the more puzzles he had turning in his mind, the less likely he was to focus on the wrong one.

"No. Dammit, Murphy—"

"In that case, it was just something I've been thinking about. Look, we've been theorizing that the other side might be breeding psychics. Naturally, they'd be most interested in born psychics, whose abilities might be genetic."

"Yeah. So?"

"Well, this web all around Tasha is . . . interesting."

"That's one word for it," Tasha murmured, still looking a bit shell-shocked.

Brodie reached out and covered her hands, which were knotted together on the table. "Murphy never learned any social graces," he told Tasha, clearly trying to lighten the mood.

"Never needed any," Murphy said blithely. "The point is, we aren't sure how long they've been keeping track of her, except here in Charleston. But what if it's been always? A teacher here, a neighbor there. It would have been easy."

"Why make no attempt to take me?" Tasha asked, her gaze fixed on Brodie's hand over hers.

"Maybe because it wasn't yet time." Murphy lifted a hand to stop the question Brodie was about to ask. "Maybe Duran had to keep you safe while he searched for the perfect match for you—using whatever parameters they use for that. I just heard from Sarah. She says we need to visit. Now."

"And bring all Tasha's watchers with us?"

"Not part of my plan." She dug in a pocket and slipped Brodie a set of keys. "Parking garage a block behind Tasha's building. Third level, slot eighteen. It's a Mercedes with tinted windows. The nav computer is already programmed with a destination. They're in apartment 4-D. I'll see you there just a bit later. I'm going to make sure you aren't followed."

Brodie got to his feet, pulling Tasha gently up as well. "Sure about this?" he asked Murphy.

"Positive. Go. See you later."

Murphy waited until they were out of sight. She knew their route from the parking garage would take them in the opposite direction. She gestured for the waitress, handed over the cups she and Tasha had both ordered and barely touched, plus Tasha's crumbled muffin, then said pleasantly, "Two small coffees, please. Black."

"Yes, miss."

Murphy leaned back in her chair and linked her fingers together over her middle, offering the waitress an absent smile when she returned, but not saying anything at all.

Until he sat down across from her.

"Keep your people where they are," she told him flatly. "Tell them to stand down."

"Or?"

She looked at Duran, expressionless. "Keep your people where they are."

He returned the stare for a moment, then said, "I've already given that order."

"I hope so. I really do."

He opened his coffee and took a sip. "I could never quite get used to this," he said almost absently.

"An acquired taste."

"Are you angry about something, Murphy?" His tone was pleasant.

Hers matched it. "Angry? No. It's much stronger than that. I don't like being lied to, Duran."

"Now, when did I ever lie to you, Murphy?"

"You really don't want me keeping score, do you?"

"You really don't want me to believe I have any control over that—do you?"

"Best not." Murphy settled more comfortably in her

chair. "After all this time, I thought you'd learned to hide things better. But a home for unwed mothers, everything paid for and yet the kids adopted out for very reasonable fees?"

He'd gone still, but other than that, there was no reaction.

Murphy was satisfied. "So far, we've found them all over the southeast. I imagine we'll find more. Some still in operation. You notice I'm giving you fair warning."

"I noticed that." His voice was level.

"Our resources are stretched thin. Not sure we're ready to take on pregnant psychics. Carrying psychic babies."

"They do demand . . . considerable expense and manpower."

"But the payoff is worth it, I assume."

"That remains to be seen." He paused, adding dryly, "I doubt we'll get our hands on Tasha Solomon again."

"So she was in the first generation. I'm surprised it took you so long to try that."

"It required . . . extensive planning. Considerable genetic research, far ahead of what was being done at the time. And we had to search for some time before we began finding suitable candidates."

"I can imagine. Most born psychics learn to shield. And the ones who don't . . . Well, let's just say they probably wouldn't be up to the job." She saw a minute change in his expression and added, "Weren't up to the job, I take it. Pregnancy hormones on top of an already unstable mind. How many did you lose?"

"Too many," he said briefly.

"The cost of experimentation. Sometimes it does run higher than expected."

"Yes."

"If I were you," she said pleasantly, "I'd find a different way of . . . achieving that goal. Our researcher is really quite a genius. And now that he knows what to look for, well, he'll find what's there. Everything that's there, no matter where you tried to hide it."

It wasn't often that Murphy got the upper hand with Duran, and she knew she was enjoying it just a little too much.

He inclined his head slightly, expressionless.

Murphy nodded to the cup in front of him and said, "Don't leave without your coffee." She waited until he rose to his feet before adding softly, "Eliot Wolfe killed Brodie's wife. A born psychic, and he killed her. A psychic with a husband who would . . . never . . . give up searching until he found that killer. You do realize that."

"I had my orders," he said finally.

"I see. Well, if I were you, I'd find a way to make sure that Candidate Wolfe meets with a terrible accident, Duran. Soon. And no burned body. No body that can't be absolutely, one-hundred-percent identified as Eliot Wolfe. Proof enough to satisfy me. Proof enough to satisfy Brodie." She waited a beat, then said, "I told you I couldn't afford to lose Brodie, and I meant it."

"What makes you think I can afford to lose Wolfe?"

"What makes you think I give a damn? But just so you know I've considered the matter, your shining political star made a bad mistake using bad judgment. And no matter how certain you feel of being able to control him, I doubt that mistake will be his last. Cut your losses, Duran. Or I'll arrange the accident myself. And you know me. I might leave a mess behind. I don't think either one of us wants that."

Even though he was on his feet, a tall man, and she was slouched in her chair with her head tipped back as she looked up at him, an onlooker would have been hard-pressed to decide which one was dominant in the standoff.

Finally, though, Duran picked up his coffee cup, and said, "Always a pleasure, Murphy. I'm sure we'll see each other again soon."

"But not in Charleston."

"No. No, not here. I have . . . other irons in the fire. I'm sure we both do."

"Yes. And, Duran? Just be sure you take all your toys when you leave Charleston. We can see them now, of course, but I wouldn't want to stumble over any of them in the dark."

"You won't." He turned and strolled away, a man clearly not in a hurry to get anywhere in particular.

Murphy remained where she was for some time, staring into space. Had he guessed, she wondered, that she had realized as soon as she'd learned about Wolfe just what the *real* web was? He wove it expertly, whether alone or under orders, and she had no doubt he had been working on it for a long time. A very long time. But he was also a long way from finished. A long way . . .

And that left them room to maneuver.

And time to get their own webs woven.

She got to her feet and left a few bills underneath the coffee she hadn't touched. He was right; it tasted bitter unless you were used to it.

She hated the stuff.

Then she walked briskly toward a different parking garage, a woman who definitely was in a hurry to get where she needed to be.

State governments. Federal. Foreign. So many people needed to run them all. So many strands of a web needing to be woven.

So much potential for control.

And such a quiet, intelligent way to handle an invasion.

Almost no one would realize until it was too late.

Almost no one.

They'd have to figure out first just how many candidates Duran and his organization already had in place. And how many were up and coming, like Wolfe.

Like Wolfe had been.

Murphy wondered idly how Wolfe would be dispatched, and wondered if Duran would do it with his own hands. Then she dismissed the matter and walked faster.

There was a lot of planning to do.

EPILOGUE

Three days later, Bishop sat with his wife at one of the sidewalk tables of a popular local coffee shop. It was a clear, sunny day, and many people were about, some strolling, some walking briskly.

Some drinking coffee in all its variations.

"You're sure Duran is gone?" Miranda asked rather lazily.

"All of them are. I can feel the difference. So can Sarah. Tasha definitely feels it."

"So can I. Much less tension."

"Yes. Even though Tucker's list of probable shadow homes for unwed mothers is growing, and we also have to search for Stepford moms, I'd say we have a good start in tracking down the kids."

"And a better understanding of some of the things Duran's people have been doing. Even if we still don't have an answer to the central question in all this."

"Why psychics?"

"Why psychics." Miranda shook her head slightly. "Although I think the others are content right now to celebrate the not-so-small victories. Like Tasha being safe. Like that poor little abused orphan girl finding her way to Sarah, the absolutely perfect person—and couple—to raise her and love her and teach her about being psychic."

We'll have one of our own, love. No matter what the doctors say.

Miranda smiled at her husband. *I know. We've beaten the odds too many times to give up easily.*

Out loud, she said, "I do wonder about that cat, though. Annabel swears he led her to Sarah and Tucker. Said he kept her warm at night, and whispered in her ear so she knew things, and she followed him because she knew that was what she was supposed to do. And both Tucker and Sarah said he's turned up in their lives before, very mysteriously but always helpful. And very un-catlike. Seems to get around a hell of a lot for a cat who doesn't appear to belong to anyone but himself."

"Well, cats. They can be very independent. And they're pretty good at taking care of themselves. But I have a hunch Pendragon is going to stick with Sarah, Tucker, and Annabel, at least for now. Most cats are smart enough to know when they've landed in a lucky place. I think Pendragon is a smart cat. A very smart cat."

"I'd say so." Miranda glanced down at the newspaper

folded on their small table, idly noting, with only the distant pang one feels for a stranger, that a promising candidate who had been running for lieutenant governor of the state had been killed in a car accident.

Such a pity.